DADDY ON DUTY

A SMALL TOWN COP ROMANCE

CRESCENT COVE
BOOK 12

TARYN QUINN

RAINBOW rage
PUBLISHING

Daddy on Duty
© 2022 Taryn Quinn
Rainbow Rage Publishing

Cover by LateNite Designs
Photograph by Lindee Robinson Photography
Models: Sam & Kyle Suib

First print edition: September 2022
ISBN Print edition: 978-1-940346-78-6

To the workaholic people pleasers who work themselves into the ground to make people happy. We have been you, and are currently in a never ending recovery program.

Welcome, you are our people.

ONE

 **BRADY**

VALENTINE'S DAY WAS A PISSER UNDER THE BEST OF CIRCUMSTANCES. And my skill at viewing situations as "the glass half full" depended how crappy my day on patrol had gone.

Today wasn't looking awesome, which meant neither was my outlook on the big love shindig.

If you were single, you searched around for a date and then hoped they didn't have excessive expectations. Though the high-quality pickings weren't usually plentiful by then, since a lot of people were so desperate to be coupled up, no matter how dubiously, that they snagged whomever was still available in early February.

If you were seeing someone, then you had to evaluate what level the relationship was at. And God forbid if you realized you were at different levels.

Oh, the horrors.

Then there was always the horniness factor to consider. I was better than a teenage male in the sense I didn't let my pointer dog lead me up all the wrong trees—usually—but I enjoyed sex to a level that had caused unnecessary drama in my youth.

As in before my last birthday. I'd matured since then.

But Valentine's Day fucked with even the most responsible among us. Especially when you were on patrol with your commanding officer who happened to be the chief in our small, sweet, heavily coupled up and baby-infested small town. And *he* was about to split because he was heading home to get some from his Salma-Hayek's-younger-sister-lookalike fiancée.

Bitter? Who me? I was the moron who'd decided to embrace the single life several months ago after the last chick I'd considered dating had decided *casual* meant fifty-five texts per day.

Sixty-five on weekends.

But man, why had I drawn a line in the sand before the holiday that literally celebrated sex?

"I don't foresee you having any issues tonight other than the snow. Christian's headed in with the new recruit and he's well versed in dealing with crowd control for the Fest. But this snow is making things tricky."

"This?" I snorted and gestured out the windshield. A family hurried across the street at the crosswalk, ducking their heads against the slashing white flakes as they tugged along their small child. "This is a day in the park."

Jared slanted me a sidelong glance. "Don't discount it. You've been away for half a dozen years and aren't familiar with recent Cove winters."

"Yeah, but I lived here for over twenty-five years. I think I know central New York winters, Jared. I mean, sir."

It was Jared's turn to snort. "Respect is a rough pill to swallow."

"Not when I have a special Macy's blend in my cup." I grinned and lifted my to-go cup of heavily lightened and sweetened coffee. My little secret since Christian made no bones of the fact he took his black and probably added Pennzoil to the brew to prove the size of his balls.

We were patrolling in twos tonight on account of the Valentine's spectacle—I mean, wholesome holiday event—taking place on Main Street in the Cove. Crowd control wasn't much of a thing for us, especially in the middle of winter, but big annual events like this drew out the townsfolk and tourists alike.

Especially this particular one, because the day of romance had become a week of romance, plus all the attendant festivities. Romance meant getting out to shop and eat broiled meat on sticks and buying candy for your beloved so she'd have sex with you later. Even if, statistically, you were more of a morning wood sort of guy.

I was only a little cynical.

"Rub it in. Besides, I do too. Though I had to cut back and now my special blend is more the green tea matcha variety." He winced and tapped the lid of his own takeout cup. "The terrible twos are killing us right now. Sami's cutting saber teeth instead of the standard baby variety."

I laughed and patted him sympathetically on the shoulder. "Wise move you decided to hire on that part-timer."

Jared's lips twitched. "Wiser than you can even imagine."

I didn't know what that meant, but Jared always thought he was a comedian. "Any line on the other one you wanted to hire?"

"Still interviewing potential candidates. We have another few interviews scheduled for this week and next. One coming in from Turnbull, one a recent city transplant." Jared growled and picked up his megaphone. "Camden Connolly, get that skateboard off the road in this weather!" He shook his head as his blasting voice nearly blew Camden right off the board. "Damn kid's going to kill himself with that thing when it's this icy out. I swear, I'm not ready for teenagers."

I chuckled. "Think you have a while yet."

"True. Thank God. But I still won't be ready."

"Maybe you should go back to the coffee beforehand? Help settle your nerves some."

Jared sent me a sly grin. "Oh, I have other ways to soothe myself, don't worry."

I officially hated the chief with a fiery passion.

"No one likes a braggart."

"Who's bragging?"

"You are. And are you going to hurry up and get married already so you're in misery and having no sex like the rest of us?"

He laughed. "Son, that will never happen, although gotta say, I never expected such woe in that department from you. Didn't you used to have a handful of girlfriends at a time?"

"Not a handful. Just casual dating isn't so casual anymore when you're past thirty. Never mind living in a town where every single woman has an egg timer in sync with the sale season at the baby shops on Main Street." I shuddered as the chief signaled onto a side street and weaved around a cluster of tourists admiring the endless heart decorations and ignoring traffic.

Admittedly, I wasn't much for babies, but in recent months I'd discovered kids weren't so bad. My little sister had hooked me up with a volunteer opportunity at the learning center and now I played basketball a few times a week with little kids, along with helping with some light tutoring here and there. I could handle reading and homework assistance. But these kids were way beyond diapers, unlike the chief's kid. I shuddered again.

Jared heaved out a breath. "Snow's starting to make a mess. Maybe I should tell Bee we'll have a later dinner. She's always my busy bee, she's used to juggling. A delayed meal is nothing."

"You can't put off Gina. She'll skin you alive."

"Nah, it won't be that much longer. I can spend a few more hours on patrol with you, get through the worst of the Valentine rush while the snow's snarling the roads."

"Chief, I'm fine. You honestly think I can't handle this? Do you remember I used to—"

"Work for the FBI. Yes, I remember. But tonight's a busy night, and this ice and snow isn't helping."

"No, but Christian's on patrol too with the new dude. I can always call for backup if I need some help with crowd control or an errant duck."

The errant duck wasn't an idle concern. This wasn't their usual time of year to be around, but our ducks were especially hardy and attached to this area. I wouldn't put it past them to steal a fried brisket out of some unsuspecting toddler's mouth.

They'd done odder things.

Not that I would need Christian's assistance to handle a rogue swarm of ducks, but if it made the chief feel better that I had help, good enough.

"Listen, Bee is making her famous chicken and biscuits on Sunday. She decided it's time we start our own Sunday dinner tradition. You should come over. Bring...a friend."

Did I seem that pathetic? That lacking in feminine company that my boss felt the need to set up a situation where I could invite someone over for home-cooking? And his fiancée Gina—the Bee nickname was solely Jared's for her and probably referred to some weird sex thing I didn't need to know—was one hell of a cook since she worked at the diner, so that would be a pretty thick carrot to tempt someone with.

"Hmm, we'll see. Or maybe she could make me a plate to take home?"

"You're a dyed in the wool bachelor."

I shrugged. "Third wheel isn't my color."

"So, find someone to bring. Bee worries about you."

"Sure she does. Not you though." I shook my head with a smile as Jared swung over to the curb behind my parked cruiser, his radio going off with reports of a power outage in town. Before he could insist he would put off going off duty, I pointed at him. "Go. You're off the clock. You trust your men, don't you?"

Jared's jaw locked. "Low blow, McNeill. Yes, I do. And I'm going."

"Glad to hear it. Have a good night."

He started to issue orders and I shut the door, pointing at the tree beside us listing in the wind with a helpless gesture. Not my fault the gust slammed it shut. He shook his head at me and pulled away as I climbed into my own car and indicated I was available to dispatch.

"McNeill, power on Main Street and in the surrounding area is out. Power company's ETA is thirty minutes. They suspect a weather-related cause."

"What was their first clue?" I frowned at our dispatcher Bonnie, who just happened to be Gina's mom. She also couldn't see me frowning through the radio. Good thing too. My general Valentine's malcontent was getting harder to stifle by the moment.

She ignored me. I supposed when a woman birthed five children she learned to tune out a lot. She also was very particular about doing things her own way. She used standard police codes when she wanted to and skipped them when she did not. Since Crescent Cove wasn't exactly a big city, things were often more informal here than they would've been in a more urban area.

Only partially due to the high rate of duck nuisance calls.

"Two minutes ago, a distress call came in from Sugar Rush, the bakery on the corner of Elm and Main."

Immediately, the long, wavy reddish-blond hair and guileless smile of Sugar Rush's owner Tabitha swam into my mind. And possibly her incredible rack and equally stunning hips. She was curvy in all the right places.

So I'd noticed. Sue me.

I'd been into the bakery a few times picking up donuts for the station and discovered Tabitha made treats for dogs too. Better yet, she catered to a wide range of dog allergies. Apparently, her mom had a dog allergic to wheat flour, which was beneficial for me since my Daisy was allergic to half the foods in existence.

Possibly three-fourths.

Tabitha hadn't said much to me the first few times I'd visited the shop but she'd smiled a lot. After the last time, I'd found a white bag outside my apartment filled with blueberry banana dog cookies—and my dog had nearly mowed me down to get at them. I hated how limited Daisy's food options were and really appreciated Tabitha's sideline business, but when I'd tried to thank her, she'd waved me off and practically shut her apartment door in my face.

Because, oh yeah, we were also neighbors.

Other than chatting at the first rooftop party I'd gone to last summer, saying hi as we passed in the hall was as good as it got. She rarely even made eye contact with me.

But man, her donuts were a wonder. And her eyes were insanely blue. And I was really fond of watching her walk back into her apartment since her rear view was just as stunning as the front.

Might as well make the best of her reluctance to talk to me for more than a moment or two, right?

"What was the call, Bonnie?" I was already signaling into traffic to do a U-turn. Sugar Rush was just a few blocks away in the opposite direction.

"Multiple calls, actually. One about the power outage. And…"

"And?" I prompted.

"She requested someone to help take care of a puppy."

"Help take care of a puppy? Does she think that's the job of the police department?"

"She found the puppy in the trash. It's very young and she requested veterinary assistance."

My known weakness toward dogs made me roll my shoulders. I would not be suckered by a wet nose and a pair of doe eyes—neither the pup's nor Tabitha's. I was in a vulnerable sexless state tonight and had to shore up my boundaries. "From the cops?"

"Brady, she's flustered and she's never dealt with babies before. I suspect not human or canine. Give the girl a break. Eat one of her cookies and chill out."

I narrowed my eyes. Bonnie was using that tone I recognized as a motherly matchmaking voice. My own mother's career in law enforcement had given her a different occupation when it came to her two sons and her daughter—mainly to encourage us to choose any career *but* law enforcement—but I was sure she could rouse that particular tone if needed.

Besides, I had enough trouble picking my own dates. How could someone else do any better?

"Chill out in the dark with her and cookies and a crying dog? Sounds relaxing."

"The power won't be out long. As for the dog, I don't know what to tell you. Tabitha said the two emergency vet clinics near town are full to the seams right now."

I sighed. "Did she call Grant?"

Grant was Daisy's vet and the vet of many of those who lived in the Cove. He was technically located in nearby Kensington Square,

7

but he was close enough and had a good enough reputation to draw clients from all over the area. Not to mention the man would keep his clinic open until all hours if there was an animal in distress. He would help Tabitha's puppy, even on Valentine's Day. The man was a widower and I was pretty sure he hadn't had a night off in ages.

And I did not feel the least bit guilty at throwing him under the bus—also known as shoving my problem off on him. Even if it wasn't my problem anyway because I was a damn cop, not Officer Friendly of the small and furry division.

"I don't know if she called Grant. She indicated the two places she did call were full. I thought you could do community outreach." The next bit she said under her breath. "Not like you have any other plans tonight."

"Hey, Valentine's shaming is a thing."

"Hmm?" Bonnie asked innocently as I swung into Sugar Rush's small corner lot with its attached parking area. Small was an optimistic term for the size, but due to the obvious power outage—I'd never seen Sugar Rush's neon sign with its pair of huge plump lips dark before—no one was here except for the small aging sedan I recognized as Tabitha's.

"You know what I'm referring to. Just because all your children are pairing off and producing grandchildren for you at a rapid fire rate is no reason to be smug."

"I most certainly am not smug. Nor am I shaming you for being single on the holiday designed for love. I just want to help."

I'd just bet she did. She must've had a gap in her baby booty knitting schedule and wanted to get me and my future progeny booked early. "I'd ask why you didn't send Christian to Tabitha, but I know why."

"You're newly on shift. Christian is at the tail end of his and is dealing with the new recruit to boot." She coughed loudly. "He's a handful, like someone else we know."

"Mmm-hmm. And I suppose it has absolutely nothing to do with Tabitha and I living across the hall from each other. Easy access."

"Your access is your business. Though you both have connections to special needs dogs—"

"Daisy isn't special needs. She just can't have rawhide or wheat flour. I hate peas. Does that mean I'm special too?"

"Yes, and not for that reason. Go in there and do your damn job." She clicked off.

Shaking my head, I slammed out of my patrol car and promptly slipped on the ice and had to grab the damn roof to keep from ending up on my ass. Mid-flail, I glanced up at the back door, narrowing my eyes at the woman huddled under the awning and cooing to what I assumed was a dog in a plaid blanket.

My annoyance crackled and melted into a puddle that centered somewhere in my chest. It was warm and spreading and nearly made me forget the sleet pelting me in the damn face as her red hair unfurled in the growing wind and her big damp eyes lifted to mine.

I wasn't one to be fanciful—as shown by my irritation that anyone really believed Valentine's Day was anything but a racket—but maybe Bonnie had put a bug in my ear. Or it could be due to the town's love vibes that seeped into everyone's pores like some kind of happy gas. More likely, my sudden good feelings had a simple cause.

I hadn't gotten laid since last summer. *Officer Horndog, reporting for booty.*

Whatever the reason, as I stared into Tabitha's eyes while she cuddled that sweet homeless dog, a buzz hummed under my skin. My regulation pants shrunk half an inch in the zippered area and the organ in my chest I didn't give much thought to started beating just a little faster.

And then my soul mate opened her mouth.

"About time you showed up. I was about to drive down to Dunkin' Donuts to interrupt your break."

9

TWO

I SUCKED AT FLIRTING.

Not that I had called the chief to practice my nonexistent skills with the opposite sex. If I'd been looking to do that, I would've called the Cove's fire department. Whoa, did they make those particular men fine around here.

And in a bakery, a little grease fire wasn't exactly hard to come by. Not that I would ever risk a dangerous fire just to try to get a fireman naked.

But I had briefly considered it a time or fifty as V-day neared. For the twenty-sixth year in a row, I didn't have a date. Or a sexual conquest.

Better yet, *I'd* happily volunteer to be the conquest.

But forget flirting. I couldn't even talk to men in a way that wasn't embarrassing. If they were hot? I was doubly screwed.

Could be why I hadn't had a date—or worse, sex—in the better part of a year.

Let's just say Brady McNeill had sent me into the triple screwed zone on the morning he'd moved into my building last year. Not that I would've noted it in my diary if his sweet dog Daisy hadn't made a habit of barking for an hour straight from five to six pm every night since but Sundays. I'd deduced that was the night Brady usually had off. Apparently, she didn't like being alone at night.

I understood her plight better than she could've imagined.

Brady's chuckle was strained. "Why would I settle for Dunkin's donuts when I could take a bite of yours?"

I winced at the reminder of my nerves-induced rudeness before the whiskey warmth of his deep voice settled heavily into my breasts. Which was a feat indeed, since the tips were frozen into permanent points.

I'd been out here way too long. After finding the sweet, abandoned puppy, I'd run inside to turn on my emergency lantern and grabbed the old plaid scarf I kept on a hook in the back room to use as a blanket. The puppy was so small and had been shivering so hard. Thankfully, wrapping him multiple times in the scarf seemed to calm him down. As did holding him up near my throat, near my thundering pulse.

Then I'd called the cops. And waited.

And waited some more.

I knew the Valentine Fest was happening in town, which meant tons of people roaming the streets. Add in the holiday and the snow and the snarled traffic and I was sure the cops had plenty to deal with. But I'd been waiting a while when Officer Dickswinger rolled in.

I only called him that in my head, never to anyone else. He was just so confident, handsome, and charming that I imagined a mere cocked brow from him was enough to get panties tossed his way. He probably had a little black book filled with numbers from thirsty buckle bunnies.

Still, I shouldn't assume he'd taken a while to answer my call because he'd been flirting with tourists. This was hardly the weather for that. I also had no right to insult him for indulging in too many donuts, even if mine were far superior to the local chain's. I certainly couldn't identify any potential donut dependency from the snug fit of his trousers.

"You're too stuck on my chicken salad sandwiches to try my donuts. But Christian certainly enjoys them."

Brady growled. Literally growled. Or else my sweet little puppy with his big liquid doe eyes did, which seemed impossible. But no more so than the chance Brady had done his best rabid dog impression before stalking over to me and peeling aside the scarf around the pup, his long fingers skimming dangerously close to the curve of my breast without seeming to even notice.

On one hand, points for being a gentleman. On the other hand, my breasts were one of my best features.

"Hi there, little buddy," he murmured, oblivious to my inner monologue. *Thank God.* "Where did you find him?"

"Dumpster over there." I jutted out my chin in the direction of the other side of the lot. "I heard scratching when I was taking out the garbage and then I heard the most pitiful little whimper from Pancake." He poked his little white and black head out of the scarf and licked my chin, making me laugh. Especially when his tiny tongue nearly touched my lip. "Closest I've been to a French kiss in a year." I laughed harder, all too aware of how Brady's eyes narrowed.

"Pancake? You named him already?"

"He was little and floppy. So...Pancake."

"So, you're keeping him? Why did you need help from the police then?"

"That was more due to the power outage. But I was hoping someone would know what to do."

"Looks like you figured it out just fine." Brady stroked Pancake's head as he nuzzled his small face under my chin. "Did you try calling Grant?" He cleared his throat. "Er, Doctor Thorne. He's open late usually."

"It's Valentine's Day, Romeo."

There I went again.

"I'm aware. But he's committed to his work. As am I." A cold wind blew over us, making me shiver and clutch Pancake that much tighter. Brady gave me a thin smile and held out his arm to nudge me forward. "Let's go in. You're both freezing."

I nodded and bit my lip so I didn't say something rude before I defrosted.

We headed down the long back hallway that led past my office at the rear of the bakery with its adjacent break room. I only had a couple of employees, though I was looking for a full-time counter person. I'd interviewed two people so far, but neither had wanted to work early morning hours and that was kind of necessary for a bakery. I opened early and closed early except during town special events that lasted into the evening.

Like tonight, if the damn block wasn't without power.

"No generator?" Brady asked, walking ahead to enter the main part of the bakery. He checked outlets and flipped switches on the breaker box before turning around and resting his hands on his hips. The streetlight slanting in through the wide front windows added extra highlights to his brown hair and along the granite slab of his jaw. His mouth was sinful, especially the curve of his lower lip. Utterly bitable.

And the only reason I was thinking this way was because he was total eye candy and there was zero potential anything could happen.

"Earth to Tabitha." He snapped his fingers and the puppy yelped, startling so badly I was sure he'd leap free from my arms.

"Sorry." Brady edged forward to murmur softly to the dog. Gently, he patted the pup's head and I kept my hold loose despite his light shudders. "Maybe we should get him to Grant. I can call ahead, make sure he can see us now."

Our heads were so close over the shivering dog between us. "Us?" I asked softly.

No snark detected. It was probably a personal record.

"You called for assistance, so here I am. Assisting." He smiled crookedly. "Even if I'm missing my nightly complement of donuts to do so."

Did I mention he was charming? Yeah. And if this was a normal interaction of mine with an attractive male, I'd say the first thing that popped into my head to drive him away.

Once upon a time, I hadn't been so clueless. But I didn't know how to flirt casually without it becoming a *thing*. Either a whirlwind affair that would take up time I didn't have or the guy wouldn't be interested and I'd pine foolishly, occupying brain space I couldn't spare within the first two years of starting a new business. In a supremely competitive field to boot.

But I could be friendly, if distant. It wasn't good to make enemies of law enforcement. Especially just because I was clumsy and nervous and lacking all social dating graces.

"I'm sure you have lots of other…calls to handle tonight. You know how people get squirrelly when the power goes out." I forced myself to smile as I took a step back. No need to stand quite so close in the dark. "As for a generator, I was told there was a generator backup, and I believe it's necessary according to code. But nothing kicked on and I'm not getting my heating and cooling certificate until next year."

So much for my snark gene taking a rest for the evening.

"A spatula in one hand, a puppy in an apron pocket, and a wrench in the other?" He cocked his head, assessing. "I can see it," he decided. "You seem fearlessly competent every time I come in here."

Which was just often enough to make me flail about and act like a fool while I was making his lunch sandwich and bagging his chocolate croissant.

"I do?" Asking that probably just crossed out the compliment he'd just given me. "Well, thank you. I appreciate that, but I'm far from it. I didn't even know what to do with an orphaned puppy."

Who was still shivering, despite me bundling him tighter into the scarf. Without thinking, I opened the cardigan sweater I'd swapped for my apron when the power went off and tucked him under that too, right against my cleavage.

And this time when I glanced up, Brady wasn't avoiding looking at my breasts clearly outlined in the thin V-neck shirt I wore under my cardigan. Just the opposite.

Brady's radio went off for probably the tenth time since he'd been here. This time, I recognized the dispatcher's voice asking for an update. Then a minute later, I heard another voice I pegged as Christian Masterson's rattling off some codes and mentioning a motor vehicle accident off Croly Street.

I motioned toward the squawking radio. "Do you need to go?"

"Not yet. Listen, I'm on shift late tonight so I can call Grant and drop the pup off at the clinic if he's okay with it. Then I can pick him up when I get off shift. I assume you're late to bed." He took off his hat and brushed back his thick hair before setting the hat into place again. "I mean, I know Sugar Rush is open really early, and don't you have to get up even earlier to make bread or something?"

When I laughed, Pancake cocked one floppy ear as if the sound was foreign to him. I gave him a quick kiss on the nose and he stiffened before my soft crooning settled him once again. "Mama gets up long before dawn but she doesn't want to leave you alone at the scary vet." He pressed his face into my cleavage as I chuckled. "Oh, I know it's no fun."

"Says you. I think he's pretty happy where he is right now." My gaze darted to Brady's, and he gave me an innocent smile. "All warm and cozy."

"Uh huh." I grinned. Guess he wasn't so indifferent after all. "Are you sure it wouldn't be too much trouble to drop him off at the vet?" I bit my lip, glancing at the sign in my front window. "I'm looking to hire some more help, but right now, it's me and a couple part-timers." I glanced at Pancake. "But you're mama's strong, brave boy, aren't you? The officer will make sure you're in good hands."

"I promise. Grant's a great guy, Tabitha. The best." Brady's mouth curled thoughtfully as he studied the dog. "Since you keep referring to yourself as his mama, I'm guessing you don't want me to see if Grant knows of anyone missing a puppy."

"No!" I cleared my throat as Pancake jolted. "Sorry, sweetie. I didn't intend to keep him. I'm not even sure how I can, to be honest. I work long hours and I live alone, as you probably know."

Not that he seemed to spend much time at home himself, what with his job and probably his extracurricular activities, if the rumor mill was to be believed. I'd never noticed him bringing anyone home, but we worked different schedules so I most likely wouldn't notice even if he did.

"No boyfriend?"

Quickly, I shook my head. "No." I sighed and cuddled the puppy until he relaxed again. "I probably should have Grant find someone more suitable for him. Not that he has an owner worth their salt if he was in that awful dumpster. Probably scrounging for something to eat." I shuddered. "Or worse."

Brady nodded grimly. "Or worse, I'm afraid."

"Yeah." I tipped my cheek to the puppy's soft face, hating that he was still shivering. "I'm calling Macy tomorrow."

"Macy?" He hiked a brow.

"She owns this building. What's up with the generator not working in the middle of winter? No wonder Pancake's shaking. It's so cold in here."

Brady quickly whipped off his jacket and draped it around my shoulders. My mouth worked too fast as usual. "I'm a bit bigger than your size, Officer."

"You seem to fit me just fine."

I swallowed hard. He definitely was well built in all ways, especially in the shoulders area. His were broad and strong. But I wasn't some waif. I had no problem with my many curves—just the opposite—but I also wasn't oblivious to them.

"Eyeballing a fit isn't the same as testing it out for yourself."

Whoa, holy crap, had I really just said that to an officer of the law? It wasn't only semi-capable flirting, I'd said it off the cuff. No practicing in my head first.

Then again, maybe that was why it was semi-capable. When my brain engaged, bad things tended to happen.

His sinful lips curved. "Just let me know the time and place."

I blinked. There was semi-capable flirting and then there was slam dunk home run sexual innuendoes. Officer Way Friendly had just scored.

Well, not yet technically, but it was looking positive for him if my trembling upper thighs were any indication. If I could speak again sometime this century.

"Do you want me to put up a sign at the vet's?" he asked. "Do some checking around? Or see how things go?"

"See how things go," I said breathlessly, quite certain we weren't just talking about adopting Pancake.

I'd probably rethink this ill-advised Valentine's Day sexual awakening once Brady was gone. But right now, I wasn't capable of saying no to those deep dark eyes, his gaze hot like chocolate as it roamed my face.

Actually, I was the one melting, which should've been technically impossible since it felt as if it was minus fifty in here. An exaggeration, I was sure.

By five degrees or so.

I shivered and Brady rubbed his hand briskly down my arm. "You have a vehicle here, I assume?"

"No, I walked over this morning." My teeth were on the verge of chattering. "Not my wisest move."

"I'll drop you at home—mine, I have a fireplace—and take this little guy to Grant, then pick him up after my shift."

"Okay." Wait, did I just agree to him basically taking over with my dog—maybe mine—and well, me too? He was bringing me to his place to what, hang out in front of the fire while he made sure the dog was taken care of and he finished his shift? Maybe he expected me to be waiting around naked when he got back from work.

And that's a bad idea, why?

Other than the laundry list of reasons even my currently frozen brain could spit out at a moment's notice.

You live across the hall from each other. Could get so messy.

He's a player. You don't have time for games.

He's a cop and he's always around town. You're a proper business owner.

He's hotter than any man you've ever thought of sleeping with.

Or fucking.

I didn't really want to take a nap with him. Though a nap sounded heavenly right now.

"I thought I was the one supposed to be bribing you to try to get my way." Thoughtfully, I stroked the puppy's head. "Here you are, offering to take care of my—Pancake so I can get some sleep and even giving me the use of your fireplace. What's in it for you?"

He licked along the inside of his lower lip, his expression pure molten heat. Snowstorm outside? Freezing inside? Not in my Spanx, no ma'am. "The pleasure of a job well done."

I had to laugh. "Is everything you say an innuendo?"

"Why, Ms. Monaghan, do you think so little of me?"

I took my time looking him up and down. Even in my shadowy bakery, he was long and lean and muscled in all the right places. His handcuffs gleamed silver dangling off his belt and my heart literally jumped.

"Actually, my thoughts are rather...large right now."

And we were back to me sucking at flirting. At least he was grinning and seemed pleased with my lame attempt.

"I'm better with my mouth than it probably seems like right now." At his choked laugh, I held up a hand and closed my eyes. "Maybe I should just stop talking."

"That's up to you, but I like hearing your voice. And I want to be sure you're okay with what I suggested."

"You mean me waiting for you in your place?"

He nodded.

Ah, to hell with it. "Clothes optional?"

He wrapped one of my loose curls around his fingers and playfully tugged. "Very optional."

"Though I gotta say I have no clue how we got here from my insult about donuts, my answer is yes."

"To all of it?"

He didn't spell out what all of it was. He didn't have to. I licked my dry lips, taking an extra beat as he watched every nuance. "All of it."

His grin spread, slow and sure. "This night was complete shit before you called me."

"I didn't call you specifically." I stepped closer, shifting so the puppy was nestled against his firm chest, hugged tightly by his snug uniform shirt. "Though I'm glad you came."

That lethal grin flashed once more in the dim light. "Not quite yet. But give us time."

THREE

 **BRADY**

A SOFT SNORE SOUNDED FROM THE FRONT SEAT WHERE THE PUPPY HAD curled up in the scarf and gone to sleep. Apparently, car rides calmed him right down.

I was too focused on another kind of ride altogether.

What are you doing, man?

I didn't actually know. I'd checked in with the station and told Bonnie I'd need a bit more time before I could be called into rotation again, explaining about the puppy. She'd sounded all too knowing as she asked if Tabitha was accompanying me to the vet's. In fact, she'd seemed downright dubious when I said Tabitha had gone home.

What I *hadn't* shared with her was that Tabitha was actually in *my* home—fireplace lit, cocoa made from her own personal stash she'd retrieved from across the hall, and my dog Daisy curled up at her side. They'd met each other once or twice when I'd been out walking her, but they were fast friends regardless.

And I was reasonably certain my dog wasn't slayed by the long strawberry hair she'd had up under a cap in the bakery but had loosened to fall in loose waves down her soft sweatshirt.

Tab hadn't gone for something sexy when she stopped by her apartment. I wouldn't have minded if she had, but somehow her choice just intrigued me more. She had moments of shyness but then she'd toss a zinger my way and let me know there was more to her than just her occasional verbal fumbles and the way she always averted her gaze when I came into the bakery.

That hadn't been an issue tonight. At least not much. Maybe concern over the puppy had taken her focus elsewhere? Or Valentine's Day had infused her with more boldness.

Whatever. I didn't know the reason, but I was glad. I liked this more confident side of her. I was curious what other sides there were to Tabitha Monaghan. I hoped I'd get to find out.

My radio crackled to life and the puppy jerked awake with a yelp. Murmuring softly, I reached toward the passenger seat and rubbed Pancake's white and black spotted head until he settled. He had the cutest black bullseye over one eye. I kept petting him while Christian relayed his location and a situation with a car in a ditch and possible injuries. We chatted back and forth and he told me the new recruit was still with him so he didn't need backup at this time, since the EMTs and fire were en route.

"I'll be done in just a few minutes," I informed Christian as I pulled into the parking lot of Grant's vet practice, Thorny Paw Clinic. He'd said he would fit in Pancake, that it was no trouble at all, and his calm, reassuring voice had made Tabitha feel better about hanging out at my apartment in the meantime. She'd already been yawning her head off when I left, so I figured she was probably asleep by now.

And if she was still asleep when I brought Pancake home, that was okay too. I didn't have any expectations. It wasn't as if I'd anticipated the night going this way.

My dick, on the other hand, had plenty of them, but little Brady lacked all morals. Not that he had a say. This was Tabatha's show entirely. If she changed her mind or wanted just to sleep, I'd be happy just to just snuggle in front of the fire until the power came back on.

Snuggle. *Me.* What the heck was happening to me? Did the town pump in lovey-dovey vibes through the air filtration system in the cop shop? I wouldn't put it past the town board.

The Valentine Fest wasn't over yet either. Since V-Day wasn't on a weekend this year, the event stretched into the next weekend to maximize the couples' date night chances. There were all kinds of outdoor shindigs that highlighted the supposed joys of winter—a chili cookoff, the wine crawl, an ice sculpture reveal, live demonstrations of activities for snow enthusiasts, endless raffles, and finally, the big dance Saturday night.

Other than an occasional yen to ski when the powder was just right, my preferred winter activity was chilling in front of the fire with my dog—and maybe with a gorgeous baker who'd made my whole fucking month and nothing had even happened yet.

Maybe it wouldn't. That would be okay too. If we just ended up being friends, that wouldn't be a bad thing, especially since we were neighbors.

I parked and turned off the car, turning to study the wary puppy. "Hey, buddy, this won't take long, I promise. Dr. Thorne will check you over and make sure you don't have any nasty mites or anything like that and then you'll get to see your new mama. And *I'll* get to see your new mama, which go me. Okay?" I climbed out and rounded the hood to open the passenger door.

Pancake promptly scampered into the driver's seat and burrowed his face into the gap between the seat and the door.

"C'mon, buddy, nothing to worry about. No one likes the vet, but this one is nice, I swear." I picked up the scarf and leaned forward to grasp the wiggly dude, lifting him into my arms while he struggled and whimpered.

Dammit, he hadn't done this when Tabitha had helped me load him into the car. Did she have a magic touch?

God, I hoped she did. I also hoped I'd get to find out just how magical very soon.

First, I had to fulfill my duties as a good neighbor and honorable public servant with very non-honorable thoughts.

"Here we go, buddy." I cuddled him against my neck just as Tabitha had done, making sure to swaddle him tightly in the scarf. He wasn't really having it and his whimpers were increasing, verging on yelps that caused the couple in the car beside me to look at me with alarm.

"He's not my dog," I said to the woman as she climbed out of her vehicle. "He's a stray. Or he was. My neighbor is adopting him."

The woman exchanged glances with her partner across the roof of their car. "He seems...distressed, poor baby."

At her soft, soothing voice, Pancake leaned out of my arms, nearly making a noose of the scarf in his haste to get out of my hold. He did not succeed. I didn't do one hundred pull-ups every morning in my living room doorway for nothing.

But I wasn't ashamed to say he nearly thwarted me. And since Pancake being delivered home safely was probably a necessary part of sex with my neighbor, this dog was not escaping.

I hoped.

"Aww, poor sweetheart. You're so scared." The woman rubbed Pancake's downy head while his eyes nearly rolled back in his head and his body vibrated with barely suppressed joy.

"My neighbor found him in a dumpster behind her bakery. She's going to take him in, but we want to make sure he's in good shape first. And make an appointment to get him neutered and all that."

Pancake whined and strained toward the woman.

"Hey, pal, I wouldn't like my balls threatened either, but it's the way of the world. Especially in the Cove. Babies everywhere."

The woman laughed and glanced back at her clearly impatient husband. "You believe all that nonsense?"

"Not saying what I believe, but there are lots of babies. It's just a fact."

"Hmm. Well, good luck with your neighbor's sweet little dog," she said as she hitched her bag up higher on her shoulder.

The moment she turned away, Pancake cast a panicked glance at me and whimpered at her retreating back.

"It's not my fault, pal." I hurried after her through the double doors of the clinic, thinking maybe if I stayed close Pancake wouldn't freak out and take a flying leap after her.

Which might have been true if she hadn't arrived at the intake counter and identified herself as "Cher's mom" which then led to a huge gray Persian-looking feline being carted out in a pink sweater with fringe.

Fringe. On a cat.

The cat looked pissed off, and I couldn't guess whether that was because of the sweater indignity or the vet visit humiliation. In any case, she took one look at Pancake and let out a hiss worthy of the forked tongue she revealed.

Fine, it probably wasn't forked, but that didn't mean I didn't expect her head to revolve at any time.

I figured Pancake would dive to the floor and split for God knows where, ending my chances with Tabitha for tonight and probably every night. But nope, like all males, he risked life and limb for one last hurrah before his balls were snipped and lurched toward Cher with his big pink tongue flailing all over.

The cat took one look at the dog trying to lick her from stem to stern and hissed again, this time extending a giant extra-toed paw, claws extended. Which got nowhere near Pancake and took approximately five ounces of flesh out of my right arm.

I wasn't sure who howled louder, Pancake or me. But the hope of sex is man's last bastion apparently, because I hung onto that dog with all my strength even as I bled out on Grant's black and white tiled reception floor and the pretty young night receptionist gawked.

Cher's indignant mother risked certain death by grabbing the cat and trying to insert her into a soft-sided carrier that had appeared from parts unknown. Cher appeared stunned by current events and went into it docilely—until Pancake took her sudden submission as a reason to try again. His head practically detached from his wiggling black and white spotted body as he tried one last time, and Cher pressed her massive paw against the webbing to indicate her opinion of his ardor.

"I can't believe you're carting that little terror around without a carrier." Cher's mom sniffed.

"Guess he's not a poor sweetheart now, huh?" I was tempted to grab her clearly cashmere scarf to mop up my blood but instead I used the scarf Pancake had been wrapped in, belatedly remembering it was Tabitha's.

Fuck, my reasons to be denied a pleasant end to this day were growing by the second.

I hoped the scarf wasn't dry clean only, or I'd be searching online for a replacement. Knowing my luck, it would be an irreplaceable family heirloom or something.

Besides, what said romance like a bloody splotch on your lovely wool scarf?

"A pet is only as well-behaved as it's been taught," Cher's owner said with a sniff.

"Oh, is that why Cher is a holy terror? Also, please tell me there's not a Sonny to match her?"

I could've sworn her heretofore silent husband smothered a chuckle before his wife pinned him in place with a death glare before clutching her cat's carrier to her chest and strolling off to let him handle the bill.

The receptionist checked him out while darting glances my way. They didn't seem to be the kind that indicated concern for my welfare and definitely not for Pancake's. Her gaze kept landing on the big bold word Police on my puffy vest.

My suspicions were confirmed after Cher's dad left with a muttered, "Good luck," in my direction.

The receptionist purred, "Hello Officer. How can I—I mean, we—help you today?"

Silly me, I figured the dejected puppy in my arms should've been a strong clue.

"Oh, I'm sorry. I'm Cori. I'll bandage that arm for you, sir." She bent beneath the counter and came up with a first aid kit. "Looks like the bleeding has slowed, but let me apply pressure on your forearm. If you can just make a fist—"

"Cori, I'll take this from here." Grant appeared, already rolling up the sleeves on his white vet's coat.

She visibly bobbled the first aid kit. "Oh, of course. Of course. He didn't have an appointment," she added accusingly, although how she could be certain of that without knowing my name, I had no idea.

"Actually, he did. He's a friend. C'mon back, Brady." Grant turned to go down a hall and I followed him with a now whimpering again Pancake.

"Bye Brady," Cori called after me before she turned to the next person in line. "Oh, a fireman. Thank you for your service!"

I rolled my eyes. My favorite badge bunnies were the ones who didn't even care which kind they cozied up to. Fire, police, probably mailmen—all were equally good if they had a uniform or badge.

Grant turned into an exam room and we followed him in, Pancake now perking up once again. I'd thought maybe he didn't like men as much as women, but judging from the look of adoration he threw at Grant, I had to assume it was just me that caused him panic.

Another line item for my résumé: *causes sheer terror in small animals.*

"Now tell me more about this little man. You are a man, aren't you? Strong boy that you are." Grant's Irish accent rolled out, charming the pup even more as I set him down on the examining table. "We need to get your paperwork filled out, but that can wait a few. Stray, you said?"

"Or worse. Found in the dumpster behind Sugar Rush."

"Oh, Tabitha's place? She has the best sticky buns in town."

The quick spurt of jealousy was both unwelcome and unnecessary. And I didn't even have to say a damn word for Grant to give me a knowing nod. "It's like that, is it?"

"What, are you hanging out a psychic shingle now to go with your other talents?"

His laughter was rich and long and made Pancake cock his head in curiosity as Grant gave him a quick, careful exam. "No, but I do have eyes. She and her twin are smart, kind women. Any smart man would give them a second glance or more."

"Twin? There's two of them?"

He laughed again. "I wouldn't say that. They're definitely not a matched set, other than having beauty, intelligence, and kindness in common. Though Van is definitely the sharper-tongued one of the two."

"Hmm. How come I haven't seen the twin? I've been in the bakery a few times. And I live across from Tab."

"Oh, forced proximity." Grant's blue eyes twinkled. "Isn't that a Lifetime movie of the week?"

I snorted. "You watch those?"

"Poppy turns them on now and again. They're fairly safe for her. Nothing worse in them than a kiss and the occasional corny line. Oh, my sweet boy, you have a little hot spot right here." Grant smoothed away some of the fur near Pancake's tail and the puppy made a noise that sounded like some of the yelps I'd assumed were from fear. "I don't see evidence of mites or fleas, so could be an allergy or possibly—"

I frowned. "Not some kind of abuse?"

"I wouldn't say so, no. He's in decent shape from what I can tell. He has full mobility, no other obvious signs of trauma, and his fur is in nice condition. He just needs a good bath." He lifted Pancake carefully and the dog's pink nose wiggled adorably in time with his tail. "You're such a handsome boy, aren't you? So, he's going to be yours and Tabitha's?" Grant asked, his lips curling slyly.

Matchmaking ass. Was it an epidemic in this town? Or did Tabitha seem like she was looking for love or something?

Surely *I* did not. After what had happened with Liz just before I'd come to the Cove, that ship had sailed. Sure, at first I'd been offended that she didn't see me as the kind of dude who could ever settle down and be husband and father material. But then I'd started wondering if she was right. I was iffy on the whole family deal anyway. So, she might've seen something in me I just hadn't fully grasped.

If anyone could, it was one of the country's preeminent criminal profilers, right?

Some people weren't meant to be dads or husbands. No big deal. There was room for all kinds of people and relationships. I was fine with being single most of the time and then I'd scratch the itch when need be. Maybe someday I'd find the right woman who didn't want the whole traditional setup. Crescent Cove probably wasn't the wisest place to hope to find that particular woman, but it was always possible.

And to make sure no accidents happened, I'd had a vasectomy late last spring after I'd been in town long enough to be sure I wanted to stay. Couldn't be too careful in baby town.

I smiled at Grant as he cooed softly to Pancake. "He's going to be Tabitha's dog. We aren't like that. No hearts and flowers in my future. Besides, she's not looking for that either. We're on the same page."

Was I trying to convince him of that or myself? It wasn't as if we'd talked about expectations. But I'd just gotten the feeling she was focused on work, maybe even to the detriment of her social life.

We could help each other out there. No stress, no strings, lots of orgasms.

With a gusty sigh, Grant glanced toward the ceiling before he set down Pancake. Then he reached into a nearby drawer to withdraw some cream he carefully applied to the hot spot on the dog's rump. Pancake promptly rolled over and showed him his spotted pink belly.

"What was that look for?" I demanded, pointing to the ceiling.

Almost forlornly, Grant shook his head. "Now you've done it. You've tempted the Crescent Cove fates." He aimed a grin skyward again. "Be gentle on him, he knows not what he's unleashed."

FOUR

BRADY'S LONG, SUPER-WIDE PLUSH LEATHER COUCH WAS MADE FOR sleeping.

Or sex.

Which I couldn't believe I was going to do. Was I?

I flashed back to Brady standing in the falling snow in his shirtsleeves and his Police vest with an absolutely pissed off expression on his gorgeous face. The instant tingle in my belly—and way lower—indicated my morals were currently booking a ticket for Cancun.

Ah, to hell with that. What did morals have to do with spending a few fun hours with a hot guy who probably did not want to date me? I didn't want to date him either. I was happily single and had one focus right now—making my bakery a success.

The first couple years of a brand new small business were the most vital. Most businesses failed before their second birthday. That was not going to be me. No matter what. If I had to work eighteen hour days for the rest of the damn year, I wasn't going to give up.

I could do this. I *was* doing it. Honestly, I didn't even have time to be spending valuable sleeping hours pondering sex with a ridiculously hot cop.

"Daisy, I need your opinion."

The sweetest golden Lab on the planet looked up from where she was sprawled on the big, thick rug in front of the fire across from me. The flat screen TV on the wall above the fireplace was playing an old Golden Girls episode I'd turned on to nudge me into sleep—I did best with voices to lull me into rest—but it hadn't worked. Instead, I'd found myself using lusty Blanche's life choices as encouragement for my own.

So what if I know not one thing about this man? I don't know about his family or his personality or his favorite color or hell, if he's kinky or not.

I really needed to know if he was kinky, and not just for my mental file. My curiosity was wholly personal.

Daisy waited patiently, one soft ear cocked.

"I know you're entirely biased, but should I sleep with your daddy?"

Her liquid brown eyes widened.

I covered my face with my hands. "Never mind. Awkward. You never ask the children. Sorry."

She lumbered to her feet and padded over to the sofa, climbing up beside me and settling down as if we were old friends. Smiling, I rubbed between her silky ears as she rested her head on my outstretched arm and looked up at me.

Almost immediately, I felt calmer. I knew plenty about Brady. He had a sweet, smart dog who clearly adored him. The instant he'd come inside the apartment, she'd trotted over to give him a hug on her hind legs. He'd laughed, sheer joy filling his handsome features. She'd followed him around for a few minutes, and then after he'd explained his friend would be staying for a while—no pressure or hidden meanings—she'd ambled over to sniff me, tail wagging. And that was even before I'd pulled out the hidden bag of her preferred allergy-safe treats I'd secreted for her in my bag.

I also knew he was an honorable public servant. I'd seen him doing crowd control and escorting kids off the bus across the street and also, a few weeks ago, I'd happened by as he was collaring a petty thief from the convenience store down the block. In a community like ours, he was called on to do all kinds of things, including helping a clueless shop owner with the puppy she'd found in a dumpster in a snowstorm.

Speaking of the snowstorm…

I leaned up to look over the back of the sofa toward the wide windows that faced the street. His apartment was at the front of the building and mine faced the back, and I could see just how slowly traffic was moving on the street below. What had started as relatively light snow a few hours ago had briefly changed to freezing rain before going back to all snow. The changeover had clearly happened again, and the pelting ice against the glass would've made me feel cozy on the comfy couch with the crackling fire and the snoring dog—if not for Brady being out in that crap with my sweet Pancake.

"How do you do it, Daisy?" I stroked her flank and she kept right on sleeping. "I know you worry about your daddy, because I hear you barking when you expect him to be home. But his job can be dangerous. Yet you're so calm."

Calm was probably an understatement. Her snores was soft and rhythmic, more relaxing than the voices on the TV.

My heavy lids started to close though I struggled to stay awake. I'd been up since three a.m., part and parcel of running a bakery. I prided myself on fresh baked goods daily and always having the finest quality for my customers, so that meant rising early every day—no excuses. Exactly why I didn't have time for late night booty calls.

Maybe I'd have to beg off. Tell him another night would be better. But I needed to stay and make sure he and Pancake came home safely…

Then I was frolicking in the Caribbean surf while wearing a bikini —I loved my curves, but a bikini was a bit much even for me—and laughing as Brady lifted me in the air and tossed me in the water as if I weighed nothing. And when he leaned down to scoop me up again in those strong, tanned, tattooed arms, there was nothing but naked appreciation in his sexy dark eyes.

"Strawberry, it's time."

"For what?"

He pointed up at the relentless sun, warming my skin. "It's too bright out here. You'll burn. Time for me to rub you down."

I shivered despite the heat. "Yes, Officer."

His laughter was pure carnal sin. "With suntan lotion. Why, did you have something else in mind?"

Shrieking metal and screeching tires had me jerking up in bed. No, not bed. On the couch. Not mine. I pushed a hand through my crazy waves and squinted blearily, trying to remember where I'd put my glasses. I was blind without them or my contacts, and I'd taken out my contacts to sleep.

Sleep. Dammit. At Brady's. Waiting for him to come back with my dog. My new puppy. The one I wasn't sure I had time for. Forget not sure. How could I take care of a dog while I worked all the time? And I hadn't even properly considered that while I was busy considering other pressing matters—like screwing my delicious neighbor.

My gaze swung to the ornate vintage clock on the wall. It was past one and Brady wasn't home. He hadn't said when he'd be off shift, but he definitely hadn't indicated it would be this late. And he had my baby—my dog.

Oh, God, was he okay? Was Pancake? What had that noise been? Had it been in my dream?

I jerked to my feet, wobbling enough I had to steady myself on the wide arm of the couch. Daisy was at the window, her nose pressed to the glass as the telltale red and blue lights of the squad car swept over the glass, illuminating the room.

Oh, no. Someone had crashed. Was it Brady?

My heart lodged in my throat as I ran to the window. On the street below, a squad car was parked across the road, blocking any traffic. A sedan was partially up on the curb, its front end smashed into another car's rear end, probably that had been parked at the time of said ramming. And thank God, there was someone who looked like a cop with dark hair standing on the sidewalk with a couple other people, taking notes on a pad.

Dammit, I couldn't be sure it was Brady. I had to get my contacts out of my purse. And where was Pancake?

I was turning to grab my purse when a phone rang in the apartment. I looked around wildly for the source of the sound, spotting an actual old school landline phone on the table beside the door. I rushed over to it and lifted the receiver with shaking fingers.

"Hello?"

"Strawberry, it's me."

I frowned. *Strawberry?* Like my dream? What the heck? "Brady? Is that you?"

"Who else would it be at this time?"

"You have a landline phone? No one has a landline. Why do—" I waved a hand through the air although he couldn't see me, cutting myself off. "Are you okay? Is Pancake? Is that you downstairs?"

Daisy let out a sharp bark and I looked down to find her at my side, nosing at my hand.

"I call her when I'm late and leave her messages on the answering machine," Brady said sheepishly. "She thinks the call is for her."

Laughing helplessly, I drew her against my shaky legs. "Just tell me you're okay. That Pancake is okay."

"We're both perfectly fine." His warm reassuring voice flowed over me, easing the tight muscles in my belly and back. "Were you worried about me, Strawberry, or just the furry one?" Amusement laced his question.

"Why are you calling me Strawberry?" I demanded. "Where did the nickname come from?"

Make this whole crazy night make sense. Stuff like this does not happen to chicks like me.

He chuckled again, his buoyed mood surprising considering the lateness of the hour and what he was currently dealing with. Then again, this must just be another usual day at work for Brady. "It just popped into my head. Your hair," he explained. "And your complexion. All peaches and roses." His voice dropped. "I can't imagine you with a tan line."

"Me either. More like a burn line."

"Sexy."

"You into lobsters?"

"They're delicious with butter." The sound of a siren cutting off behind him made him groan softly. "I gotta handle this."

"Okay, do you need help?" As soon as the question was out, I slapped myself in the forehead with the heel of my hand. Right, a cop needed help from the town's sweet stuff baker. "I mean, Pancake. I can come get my dog."

"I'm good, babe, but that would be great."

Babe? Was that hookup lingo? He didn't say it in a creepy way, more like it just rolled off his tongue. I kind of liked it.

Man, Valentine's Day wreaked havoc on a single woman's lines in the sand.

"Though if you're...not dressed, I've gotta say he's making friends and influencing people down here. Even Christian appears to like him, and he hates everyone who doesn't share his last name."

"I heard that," a deep voice snapped behind him.

"Aww, because Pancake's so sweet and loves everyone."

"Except me. He led me to get a war wound."

"Oh, baby, do you need wound care?"

Now I was doing the baby/babe stuff. It had to be the lack of decent REM sleep.

"Why is that sexy? That shouldn't be sexy." He lowered his voice. "And thanks for making it very awkward to stand facing front right now."

I giggled and twisted the cord from the landline—still, a major what the heck there, did he get it on eBay or what?—as I gazed down at a very pensive Daisy. I'd stolen her man's phone call.

Shameless hussy. At least I was about to be.

I really hoped.

"I didn't intend for it to be sexy, but I do have a way with a tube of Neosporin and a butterfly bandage."

"Holy shit, warn a guy when you start upping the ante."

"Your dog is mad you're more interested in my tube skills than in reassuring her." It was almost impossible to keep the grin off my face.

"I can come down. On my way with my sentinel. Or I should say your sentinel."

"Doggie introductions on the street. Wise move in case we need intervention. Though we won't. Daze loves babies."

"I like your confidence. Human or dog?"

"All. Even feline. See ya, Strawberry."

Shaking my head, I replaced the receiver and glanced at Daisy. "Where's your leash, pretty girl?"

As if she understood English perfectly well, she pranced across the living room to the galley kitchen. Brady's apartment layout was very similar to my own, so it made it easy to guess where Daisy was headed. She stopped next to the refrigerator where a pegboard was hung on the wall with a couple of hooks, one of which contained a purple leash with daisies on it. I grabbed it and Daisy dropped her rump to the floor, tail wagging frantically.

"Hang on, girl. I gotta pee. Soon as I stand up," I muttered, setting the leash on the counter and heading down the hall to the bathroom in the same spot as in my own place. The familiar layout certainly helped me feel more at ease for my impromptu booty call.

Though I wasn't really nervous at all. Hmm, what did that mean?

I took care of business and washed my hands and then stared at myself in his spotted mirror. Not too much, just enough to show he wasn't overly fussy, which was a good thing. As did the scatter of bottles of shaving cream and aftershave on the counter. No dirty towels, no hair in the sink. The room just looked comfortably lived in.

I narrowed my eyes at myself and fluffed my wilted hair, deciding this was as good as it got on a couple of hours sleep. Might as well make sure he knew what he was getting into. But I did have enough vanity to put on some lip gloss—coincidentally, berry—and mascara. Then I whistled for Daisy, who was willing and ready.

She wasn't the only one.

I clipped on her leash and grabbed the apartment keys and my purse. I didn't have a carrier for Pancake yet, but it was at the top of my shopping list for tomorrow night after work. I'd briefly considered doing an Amazon Prime order until I'd remembered my commitment to buying local. I hadn't been born in the Cove yet I was zealously committed to supporting the town.

After hurrying down the steps to the bottom level, Daisy keeping pace at my side, I opened the side door and did a mental shriek at the pure wall of white streaking from the milky sky.

"You okay? Where's your coat, Tab?"

Guess my shriek hadn't been mental after all.

"Oh, I'm just popping out for a moment. My sweats are warm." I flashed our neighbor Caleb a quick smile, taking in the thick layer of white on his golden brown hair. "You've been out in the thick of it, huh?"

Caleb Beck would be moving out soon with our other neighbor, Luna, who just happened to be his new wife. She was also hugely pregnant and they'd had a house built on the other side of Crescent Lake. Their baby was due in about two months, so they were more than a little relieved the house was almost finished.

As happy as I was for them, I was sad to see them go. Luna, especially. She was our resident tarot goddess, and she'd started a monthly tarot circle held on the rooftop deck in the warmer months. She'd promised to come back monthly after the baby was born to keep it going, but I didn't have high hopes.

Things changed when people paired off and had kids. It was hard to balance friendship and work and a growing family. It was even harder to pick and choose what you wanted to focus on unless you were a freaking laser like me. I was determined to be a success. The first person in my family to graduate with a master's degree. The first one to run their own business.

The first to not let anything get in her way, no matter what, even if that meant she had a closer relationship with her vibrator, the Hulk, than some of her neighbors.

Caleb peered at me curiously. "Isn't that Brady's Daisy?"

At her name, Daisy stuck her head forward and wriggled toward Caleb, who gave her an obligatory round of petting.

I'd just sidestep that question for another moment. Not that it was a big deal. Neighbors walked each other's dogs.

And touched their naked ass and maybe gave it a little nibble, to see if it was really as firm as it seemed in those snug uniform pants.

"So, you were out there?" I nodded toward the street at the other end of the driveway. Police lights were still revolving slowly and I could hear the constant low hum of voices. "What happened?"

"Mr. Jakes had a couple too many at The Spinning Wheel and clipped Bess's BMW. I think the two of them will be dating by the end of this." Caleb grinned. "The Cove is a hotbed."

"You can say that again."

We also would not mention how I'd almost thrown myself at Caleb the previous summer before Luna moved in. After that, he'd only had eyes for her.

True love was sweet—and annoying when it was the last serving bowl at the family dinner and you always arrived after it was empty.

Not that I was looking for love. I just needed Valentine's Day to end, thanks.

"Tab? Walking Daisy for Brady?"

I cleared my throat. "Yes, just doing my part to help with neighborly relations."

The sound of footsteps through the slush made me whip my head around, as did Daisy's sharp barks. My gaze connected with Brady's as he strode toward Caleb and I, looking windswept and snowy and sexy as hell with my puppy cradled in one arm and a rose in tissue paper held in the other. Wordlessly, he extended it to me, sliding a glance toward Caleb.

All I could do was stare at him.

"For you," he said needlessly, handing off the slightly ragged flower and then Pancake who strained toward me excitedly as Brady easily slipped his dog's leash out of my hand.

"Thank you." I sounded way too breathless.

Now that butt-biting desire was back hardcore, and I almost didn't care if Caleb saw the lust probably shooting out of my eyes like fireworks.

After a night spent taking care of my puppy and keeping the peace, somehow Brady had found the time—not to mention a place this late

—to buy me a rose? Even if did have a 2-for-1 sticker on the side of the plastic.

Didn't matter. This boy was getting some. And soon.

Brady lifted his brows at Caleb's quizzical expression, then added a smirk. "It's the neighborly thing to do."

FIVE

 **BRADY**

By nature, I wasn't a jealous sort. Why should I be? I spent the bulk of my life single.

And before this confounding evening, I'd only had a mild curiosity and possibly an occasional dick stretch toward my zipper when it came to Tabitha Monaghan. I'd thought she was beautiful and her shyness and lack of engagement with me had fascinated me, but I hadn't spent hours pining for her or something.

The weird thing was I wasn't sure I wouldn't now, and I hadn't even touched her yet. And as for these unwelcome spurts of jealousy, well, they were only logical. She was a gorgeous siren of a woman, so who wouldn't want to nail her immediately? It was practically a biological need.

Maybe it was just me. I assumed my buddy Caleb had more than enough to occupy his time with his pregnant wife, who was also objectively hot as hell. Even pregnant. Especially pregnant. Her glow was like a heat lamp.

But she still wasn't as magnetic as Tabitha. Especially when she had my dog's leash in her hand and hope in her bluebell eyes and snow dotting her red ribbons of hair.

Oh, look, I'd picked up the convenience store rose, and now I had the bad poetry for Valentine's Day too.

"Neighborly relations worked for me too." Caleb grinned and slapped me on the back before giving Daisy's ears a rub. "I'm headed in. You two naughty kids have a good night. Happy Valentine's Day."

"Hope your wife doesn't shoot out that kid before morning," I called after him just before he flipped me the bird and the heavy door clanged shut behind him.

Tabitha shoved her hands in the front pocket of her sweatshirt. "He thinks we're having sex."

I cocked a brow. "Are you saying the sandwich board I set up on the corner was too much?"

"Funny guy."

"Among my other talents." I stepped forward and slung my arm around her waist, savoring the feel of her giving curves against me for the first time. I wanted to sink into her and relish every second. For now, I contented myself with lowering my face to the curve of her neck to breathe in her seductive lavender scent.

Washing my hands with Bath and Body Works' lavender soap at the store sink when I was on fill-in mall security duty would never be the same again.

"Brady," she said with a hitching laugh as I slipped my cold fingers under the hem of her sweatshirt. Just a teasing hint of her forbidden skin made me stone hard. "We're outdoors."

"Why I'm assuming you're not naked yet." Immediately, I eased back, bending my knees until our eyes were level. She was around average height for a woman, but she was no match for me, especially in sneakers. "Cross that out. I don't expect anything. But certain parts of me are pigs."

"Well, then, oink, oink, because certain parts of me are too." She grinned and looked around to make sure no one had sneaked up on us. At this point, everyone was still occupied with the fender bender. Our only conversational snoop was Daisy, who was pawing at some questionable smell in a frozen patch of grass at the side of the driveway. "I wanted to bite your butt."

"Wanted? Has the bloom faded so fast?" Lightly, I poked her underwhelming rose. "Confession, I actually got it for thirty-eight cents because it's not technically the holiday anymore."

"My panties aren't tied to a calendar."

"No? I wouldn't mind if they were. Though I'm keen to see you in them before they're off and draped over the wall hangings."

Her laughter helped smooth out the jaggedness from the long tedious night. It actually hadn't been that bad, all things considered, but I'd thought about her in my bed—or on my couch, or in my minuscule shower stall—about sixty-nine times. Conservatively. "Think that can be—" She let out an enormous yawn and then looked at me in alarm, popping her eyes wide. "I'm not tired."

"Sure you aren't, honey. I totally believe you." I glanced down at Daisy and decided she'd get a walk around the building to pee while Tabitha took her dog inside for a cuddle. She was shivering and flushed with fatigue and Pancake was now trying to get her top off faster than I'd had a chance to.

In his defense, I was pretty sure he was attempting to burrow inside. I would not be doing that.

"Let's go in."

"What about the accident?"

"Christian has everything under control. I just need to let this one take a load off. C'mon, Daze."

My dog lifted her head and cocked her ear. She glanced at Pancake Velcro'd to Tabitha, then filed the puppy under the heading *not my problem,* unlike her needy bladder.

Little did she know the little stinker was coming in with us. And might be staying a while. Or visiting often. Hell if I knew. I also didn't fully get why I'd inserted myself into this situation when I worked a lot and didn't really have time to run herd on two dogs, especially a tiny, scared one. Even if Pancake was Tab's, she'd need help with him. That was already obvious.

Public servant, right? Right.

"If you're coming up, why did you want me to come down?"

"I hadn't planned on it right away," I admitted. "But Christian has it all handled and you look tired enough that a swift wind could take you down." I tucked one of her windblown curls behind her ear. "I want to spend a little time with you before we get some rest. Even if it's just introducing the dogs."

I didn't miss how her gaze softened. "You'd really be okay with that?"

"Absolutely."

And I was. It was late and she had responsibilities. As did I. To be honest, curling up with her and getting a few Z's sounded damn good.

"Besides," I grinned, "it's not like we don't live across the hall from each other."

She laughed softly and adjusted her hold on Pancake as he craned his head to study Daisy, who was now prancing back and forth in her urge to go to her preferred peeing spots. "Good point, Officer."

"Is Officer going to be my nickname? Gotta say I like when you say it better than Cori at the vet's clinic."

Seeing Tabatha's eyes narrow even in the dim lights beside the building was oddly gratifying. "Hot cop with a puppy, I just bet."

I had to laugh. "At least you think I'm hot, though work on a better nickname, huh?"

"Officer is a title, not a nickname, Hot Cop. Now *that's* a nickname." She gave me a light shove and reached behind her to unlock the door before I could do it for her, then disappeared inside.

The wind-driven snow pelted me in the face with a sleet chaser as I shifted toward my dog. Who gave me a look as if to say if you weren't standing around chatting, we could be done and inside by now.

She had a point.

"Here we go, Daze." She trotted ahead of me down the driveway, making a beeline right for Christian. He was noting down some information from Bess, who stood imperviously in a sleek full-length black coat over her shimmery evening dress. Guess she'd been on a date tonight like everyone else in the Cove.

Not me though. And no post-date nookie either. But I was kind of onboard with snuggling.

I had to be tired and/or almost hypothermic to be having those sorts of thoughts. Next time I was wearing my damn jacket not just a vest.

"There you are." Christian cocked a brow as Daisy blessed the fire hydrant with her offering. "I figured you were off the clock."

"Had to do the dog swap." I shrugged noncommittally. "Besides, you had it all in hand. You still need me?"

"No." His mouth twitched as he flipped the paper on his pad. The rest of took notes digitally but not Mr. Traditionalist. That wasn't good enough for him. "But if you didn't come back out here, I wouldn't have been able to make cracks about your extra-special personal touch to your face. Behind your back just isn't as fun."

"You're a dick." I whipped my head toward Bess, who was laughing openly. "Sorry, Mrs. Wainwright. You know how it is with colleagues."

"I sure do." She leaned toward me and tucked her coiffed silver hair behind her ear, her rings winking in the low light. "Personally, I think he's just jealous. Tabitha is a sweetheart. And gorgeous too."

While Christian coughed, I grinned. My objections died in my throat. "She is both those things, though I don't really know her well."

"Semantics." Bess waved a hand.

"Is everything okay? You're sure nothing hurts? Can I get you a glass of water?"

"I'm perfectly fine. It was just a love tap, and you know I'm as close to home as you are, neighbor." She patted my cheek. "Go on and salvage what's left of your night. I'm just fine with Christian here. He just needs to pull that stick out of his fine behind."

I choked out a laugh at Christian's shocked expression just before my dog decided to yank me up the block. Apparently, she'd saved a deposit for her preferred patch of lawn up the street, even though it was crunchy with ice-laden snow.

And she saved one more for the bush at the edge of our property. Thankfully, none of them were of the more solid variety, because I didn't have any bags with me. Showed where my head was at.

Definitely not on any of my usual tasks.

Daisy shook off the snow now clinging to her glistening golden fur and ran for the side door of our building. I was all too happy to jog with her. My arms were practically numb by now. I was normally hot-blooded, but this weather was even pushing my tolerance.

I unlocked the door and Daisy shot inside like a bullet as she usually did. She booked it up the stairs then ran to our door and whimpered as if she knew we still had company who was more than capable of letting her in. Tabitha opened the door and cooed hello to her, and Daisy gave me a baleful look until I unsnapped her leash from her collar and let her free. But instead of disappearing into the apartment, she stared at the interloper Tabitha was holding. Daisy must've assumed Tab would take her elsewhere, not to *her* apartment.

"Did Pancake get a clean bill of health?" she asked as I tucked away my gun in the safe and my assorted other cop paraphernalia, like my handcuffs.

"Yep. He's fine, except for a little hot spot on his behind. Grant gave me a sample tube of cream to use until we can fill the script." I unzipped my vest and tossed it on the arm of the couch. My hand was on my zipper when I turned to answer her, and her eyes widened.

I shook my head and hiked up my zipper again. "Sorry. I was going through my usual routine without thinking."

"I can go—"

"Strawberry, this has been a very long night and thinking of you making my furniture smell like frosting kept me going. Tonight's lavender was an unexpected bonus. Is the frosting scent an actual perfume or is that just an occupational hazard in your line of work?"

"Definitely not a perfume. Though I do admit to buying a birthday cake scented shower gel from Bath and Body Works one time."

"Give a guy a warning before you put thoughts like that in his head." I dropped onto the couch and she sat beside me with a giggle, placing Pancake on the cushion between us.

The dog stayed true to type and plastered himself to the side of her thigh, staying as far away from me as possible.

"Your dog doesn't like me. Regardless, we'll figure it out."

That was what I did. Solve problems. Come up with alternate plans.

Jerk off at the mental imagery of her naked and coated in birthday cake-slash-lavender-scented bubbles.

Oh, right, that hadn't happened yet. But soon, I hoped.

She reached over to turn on the flameless candles on the side table. Earlier, I'd grabbed some from the cabinet since the power was still out and the fire didn't offer much light. Parts of our building were still in a state of construction, which must be why we had no generator backup.

I'd be making a friendly call to our landlord too just like Tabitha would be with Macy, the owner of the building that housed her bakery. To my mind, having a working generator for paying tenants wasn't optional.

"Figure what out?"

"Well, I've taken several mental leaps, but you're up early and I usually work later in the day. Occasionally, I fill in earlier, but my usual is afternoons on."

"Okay," she prompted, clearly not following me.

I wasn't entirely following myself.

"You didn't plan on finding this puppy, so you didn't make accommodations for him. I can help you."

Her pale eyebrows knitted together. "Um, thanks, but maybe you should wait to see if my rose garden is worth all this effort before you co-adopt my dog?"

I snorted so hard I almost ruptured my sinuses.

"Rose garden is said ironically, by the way." She scooped up Pancake and smothered his face with kisses without even finding out his vaccination or disease status.

I might've fallen in love with her just a tiny bit.

More.

"Naturally. You can just say pussy if it doesn't offend your delicate sensibilities."

"Offend them? I don't have any. I'm the chick who basically propositioned you without knowing so much as your astrological sign."

"Did you proposition me?" I stretched my arm along the back of

47

the sofa to toy with the ends of her hair. It had absolutely no right to be that soft. "I thought I propositioned you."

"Maybe it was mutual." She turned toward me on the couch, dragging her bent leg toward her body while Pancake viewed me with suspicion from partially behind Tab's curtain of hair. "But if you want to talk about my pussy, we can start there."

This girl. I loved that I had no idea what I was getting into with her. "I'm putting you to sleep in my bed, remember?"

"Something else we forgot to cover." She lifted Pancake's paw and waved it at me. "Hi there, let's start over. I'm Tabitha Eliza Monaghan. I'm twenty-seven, my sign is Virgo, I have an unhealthy obsession with eclairs and British crime dramas, and I have a sticker collection I keep in spiral books with glittery unicorns on the front. I have no problematic exes, no STDs, no children, and precisely one dog of unknown breeding named Pancake. Your turn."

"Unicorns and stickers?" I held up a hand before she could explain. "You forgot the twin sister."

"Oh. You know her?" Her freckled nose wrinkled. "I should've assumed so. Van sucks all the air out of the room. She's always the center of attention. I'm just boring, well-adjusted Tabitha. She's the hippie dippie flower child who has all the fun while I work day and night. But I like working." Then she sighed. "Problem is I like sex too. A lot."

I cocked a brow. "If I'm supposed to see where the problem is with any of that…"

"Working means not a lot of sex. Had to pick my priorities if I want my bakery to succeed, and no orgasm is worth setting me back."

"You haven't had the right ones then."

"Sure I haven't." She smiled down at Daisy as she wandered over from inhaling the contents of her water dish to investigate the newcomer. Tabitha held out the now squealing and wriggling puppy. "Daisy, this is Pancake. He's just a baby. Do you like puppies?"

Daisy did not move other than to wheel her eyes in my direction, as if checking to see if I approved of this hairy stranger being in our home.

I didn't have a problem with it, considering his mistress. And hey, maybe someday Pancake would even like me.

Daisy leaned forward to sniff the puppy's head and the puppy thrust himself so forcefully at Daisy that he propelled his little body right out of Tabitha's grasp.

Tabitha let out a sound of distress and bent to lift him up, but Daisy was faster than she was. I lurched to my feet as Daisy grabbed him around the neck, sure I'd have to break up a battle royale before I'd even gotten nude wound care for my last animal-induced injury, but then Daisy headed over to her bed by the fireplace with Pancake's scruff securely clamped in her mouth.

Tabitha peeked out through her fingers as I rubbed her shoulder. "Look. It's fine."

Daisy was licking Pancake from his neck to his belly and Pancake was writhing in puppy joy. "She lost a baby just before I adopted her from the shelter," I said quietly, watching my dog love all over Pancake. "Since then, I've wondered sometimes if she still missed her baby. He was stillborn."

"Oh, no." Just for an instant, a sheen of tears shone in Tabitha's eyes.

"Yeah. So, I'm not offering to help raise Pancake just to gain access to your rose garden. You'd be helping me and my dog as well."

Tabitha sniffled out a laugh. "Hot Cop, you're going to be dangerous for me, aren't you?"

I took her hand and brought it to my lips. "Same goes, Strawberry."

SIX

I WAS IN A KING-SIZED BED WITH A GORGEOUS MAN I BARELY KNEW WHO carried handcuffs—and not for sensual pleasure. And he was spooning me by his own choice.

"Is this weird?" he asked against my hair, curling his arm more securely around me as he sniffed my shoulder and let out a porn-worthy groan.

"Kind of." I chuckled. "But not bad weird. Just...I've never been in bed with a guy and not been naked or on my way there."

"Well, we can fix that..." His voice was thick with humor. "But then neither of us will get any sleep and you set your alarm for what, two hours?"

"Not even. An hour forty. I've got croquembouche to make for my display window. I couldn't make them ahead because they need to be presentation fresh and the cream puffs can get soggy. Lea will get them started but then I need to make our signature strawberry buttercream to fill them with. And I can't go with a simpler dessert because they're our item for the wine and sweets crawl. You know, customers get their QR codes scanned at each shop—"

"Croquem what?"

"Bouche." I laughed and rolled over onto my back to give him a sidelong look. "Your sheets are so soft."

"So's your sweatshirt." He propped his head on his hand and rubbed the fingers of his other hand along my stomach—but on the gap of my belly revealed beyond the hem.

"You're not touching my sweatshirt, McNeill."

"Oh, no?" His voice was far too innocent. "My hand slipped."

"Uh huh." Giving up on any pretense of sleep, I turned on my hip and lifted my hand into his short wavy hair. "Do you think the dogs are okay out there? They're so quiet."

Brady laid his finger over my lips. "They're snoozing in Daisy's bed and are perfectly fine. But don't tempt fate."

"*This* feels like tempting fate," I said as he moved his fingers. He'd taken a quick shower while I got ready for bed and I couldn't stop fixating on the water droplets blooming on his white T-shirt. "Like this is too natural."

"Is it not supposed to be?"

"Well, I don't know what your past hookups have been like, but usually, for me, if the sexual chemistry is on point, the guy doesn't read actual books or thinks haute cuisine is Hot Pockets." I frowned. Hopefully, I hadn't just insulted him, but with my track record, it was highly likely.

"I read actual books," he assured me quickly. "Well, ebooks on my phone on breaks usually. As for Hot Pockets, I haven't eaten those since the academy. But I'm no fancy pastry chef either."

"That's fine by me. You have other talents."

"You don't know that yet." He toyed with the hem of my sweatshirt while I worked on controlling my flush.

Not of embarrassment. More like pleasure. I was all about finding out what exact talents he had. His fingers were interestingly calloused. And his lips were full and looked soft enough that I wondered if he used chapstick, which made me wonder other things, such as how they'd feel against my skin. Add in his growing-in scruff and I was imagining all sorts of interesting sensations against my flesh.

"You don't look the least bit sleepy."

"No," I admitted. "Think I'm on adrenaline now. You?"

"Same. But I can sleep in. You've got all those croquets to make."

I had to laugh. He was ridiculously cute, which I had a feeling he knew. The damp brown curl that kept dipping into his midnight eyes didn't hurt on that score. "I do have help. Lea will get started as soon as she arrives, and Tiffany will be right behind her."

"That doesn't sound like much help to me."

"I want to hire two more part-timers or ideally, a full-timer, but none of my interviews have worked out yet."

He dipped his head, his gaze lasered in on my mouth. "I know someone who's looking for a job. I can introduce you."

"Oh, that's okay—"

His mouth landed on mine, insistent and persuasive in the best way. He didn't go for the goal right off, just nibbled at my lips as if he was learning my exact shape and texture before he went further. I wove my fingers into his hair and pressed my thighs together in a vague attempt not to rub against him like a horny cat.

Play it cool, Monaghan.

His tongue teased the seam of my mouth and letting him in felt as natural as scraping my nails down the back of his neck. Not worrying if I should rein it in or check my pressure. For some reason, I wasn't concerned about scaring him off or reading him wrong.

In his darkened bedroom, the only light from the flameless candle he'd lit on the nightstand, I was free to be anyone. Or scariest of all, I was free to be *me*.

Somehow I wasn't aware of us switching positions until I was on top of him, straddling his toned thighs. He had on loose sweats with the drawstring, the kind that hid absolutely nothing. Judging from what I could feel during the testing rolls of my hips, this Valentine's Day I'd gotten *very* lucky. And that didn't have a thing to do with the sweet wilted rose Brady had put in a coffee cup of water in the kitchen.

"You okay with this?" Brady asked, leaning up to tug down the collar of my sweatshirt to bare my shoulder and the top of my breast.

"Can't you tell?" I was already panting. There was no helping it.

The guy had incredible suction and right now he was just working on regular skin. When he got to something with more nerve endings...

I shuddered and resisted trying to see the clock on the wall. We needed to make very good use of every available second.

"Always gonna need the words, Strawberry." He lifted his head, and his eyes were already as hazy and unfocused as if we'd been making out for hours not just minutes. "And I need to see your tits."

I didn't waste any time easing back to whip my sweatshirt over my head. I threw it and didn't check where it landed. Didn't know. Didn't care. Brady was sucking me down with his gaze in a carnal way that made all the blood in my body surge below my waist. I couldn't breathe, couldn't think.

If I'd ever been worshipped more thoroughly, I didn't remember it. And he hadn't even touched me yet. Not with his hands or mouth on my breasts. My nipples puckered until they were painful and still, he stared, sinking his teeth into his lower lip as if he'd just been confronted with a sundae and had no clue what part he wanted to savor first.

Then he stretched out his legs and nudged me down until I was tilted backward, spread out before him at an angle that let him feast on my skin. He didn't even go right for my nipples. Instead, he kissed between them, drawing his lips downward toward my quivering belly while his big broad hands framed my breasts, his blunt fingertips just outside the fullest part. Teasing me while he nuzzled my skin and made me shiver from the inside out.

"I need to taste you. Watch me."

I figured he meant my breasts, but nope, he wanted to get intimately acquainted really fast. He shifted, lowering me to the bed and yanking off my sweats and panties in one jerky move. His hands weren't even close to steady. Then he drew my legs up over his shoulders before he parted my embarrassingly sticky thighs to explore me. First, with his fingers, then with his lips and tongue.

Sweet mercy, he didn't need a road map to find my clit. Hell, he found everything and even more I didn't even know I had. He also didn't seem to be any hurry. One finger turned into two inside me as he murmured his approval.

"You were hiding all this, and I almost went to sleep and missed it."

I was breathing so choppily I nearly didn't hear his low, rhythmic voice. But I couldn't drag my gaze away from his face as he licked me, his dark gaze zeroed in on my face. No place to hide. I didn't want to. The naked appreciation in his gaze had me leaning up on my elbows to push out my chest, just enough that his expression glazed and his erotic kisses turned feverish. Now it was a competition which of us was making more noise, especially when he shoved his shorts down with his other hand and fisted his dick, the head ruddy with need and a fat drop of precum glistening like an offering.

I wanted his salt on my tongue. In my throat. I made some noise that was half whimper, half plea. I couldn't come up with actual words.

"Oh, baby, you want this?"

I nodded so fast I nearly strained something. His chuckle was dark and promising, but he made no move to speed up his efforts. If anything, he slowed things down, twisting his fingers inside me slowly like a corkscrew I couldn't decide if I wanted to get more of or to escape from. He knew he had me on the edge, but he clearly enjoyed keeping me there, avoiding my clit that he'd worshipped so thoroughly as if he'd forgotten it was there. His teeth flashed as I growled and arched higher off the bed, nearly dizzy with my need to come. My temples throbbed in concert with my abandoned clit. In a minute, if he didn't get up there and finish the job, I'd just do it myself.

Until I realized that was exactly what he wanted.

I bit my lip to hold back my moan as our gazes locked. "Don't be shy," he said against me, his words muffled, and I almost let out a hysterical laugh.

Shy? My interactions with this dude before tonight had consisted of saying hi in the hallway and helping him pick out wheat-free cookies for his dog. Currently, I was spread-eagled on his bed completely exposed to him. If I got any *less* shy, I'd be on a reality TV show.

Then again, I'd gone this far, right? What was a little more when an orgasm waited at the end of the rainbow?

I swallowed and ran a testing hand over my breasts. The sound he made was barely human. So, I kept going, sucking in oxygen as the tips of my fingers met the wetness he was coaxing onto his tongue. He kissed the backs of my fingers, subtle encouragement, then sat back to watch me openly, still pumping in and out of me while I toyed with my own clit.

"I'm going to jerk off to this memory for the rest of my damn life." The reverence in his tone as he rhythmically squeezed his shaft had me wheezing out a laugh—until he plunged harder inside me and turned up the heat from a simmer to a full-on fire. I had no warning I was about to come. It shot through me like a bullet, making my muscles cramp as I gripped his fingers and writhed before him on the bed. My leg trembled so hard I kicked out, nailing him in the head with my knee.

I tried to apologize but I couldn't make my voice work. He was still unrepentantly finger-fucking me and still working his own length, apparently unconcerned about the possible concussion I'd given him. And then I didn't care either. I was coming again, the force so intense I bowed up, gasping for air.

When the pleasure became too much, I pulled my hand away from the apex of my legs to grasp at the sheets. Desperate to find some anchor in the center of madness.

Who was this guy? For that matter, who was this version of me?

He leaned forward to take my mouth, his hungry kisses flavored with me. The scruff on his chin was too. I couldn't be embarrassed when both of the orgasms he'd given me were still racing through my system. So, I chased his lips, wanting more. His hand drove into my hair, guiding my head as we went at each other.

Then I felt the nudge of his cock against my pussy, and it never occurred to me he shouldn't be there. Hell, I was almost sure I'd die if he didn't fuck me right this instant, even if I wasn't sure I could survive coming again.

He wrenched away from my mouth to suck on my nipple, giving

it a sharp pull that echoed in my core. Then he pulled off a feat of clothing magic and got his shorts off while thoroughly devouring first one breast and then the other. Hot, wet pressure surrounded my nipples in turn and I shook against him, around him as his testing thrusts between my legs turned into one long stroke inside me.

I cried out, biting the side of his neck because it was all I could reach. His growl snapped me back into my body and I reared back, eyes wild. I could tell he wouldn't last long and I wanted it inside me. Wanted to watch him shatter just as I had.

"Condom?" I gasped as he stared at me as if I'd just spoken a foreign language.

Maybe I had. Even as I'd asked the question, the concern seemed far away and not important. His thick shaft filling me held all my attention.

"I'm clean," he said breathlessly. "You said you were too?"

Pressing my lips together, I nodded.

"We should've discussed this before, but we're covered, baby. But if you're not okay with it, I'll stop."

"I'm okay with it." I didn't even know precisely what I was okay with or what "being covered" exactly meant. But I trusted those earnest dark eyes.

Which probably made me a chump. I just hoped my instincts weren't wrong.

His lips curved crookedly as he pulled back and sank inside me again with a feral sound that made me ache down deep. He did it again and again, his thrusts forcing my thighs so wide the muscles screamed with exertion.

His next plunge ripped a cry from my throat. "The only thing you have to do for me right now is come on me."

I reached down to grip his perfectly taut ass to drag him farther inside me, so far we both groaned. Too soon, I teetered on that edge again, so much more dangerous when he was crammed inside me.

"So full. So fast." I was mumbling incoherently as he gripped my chin to meet my gaze, his own wild with need.

"That's it. Grip me, Tab, just like that. Fuck, I'm going to—" He didn't get to finish his sentence.

Tab. My name. As insane as all of this was, he knew exactly who he was inside of at this moment.

The quick punch of my orgasm yanked him right along with me. And though I knew it was probably impossible for me to feel it, the hot spurt of his release pulsed deep while his hips relentlessly pounded against mine and his fists locked in my hair.

Holding me in place to take every forbidden drop.

SEVEN

 BRADY

I DIDN'T KNOW HOW LONG WE LAID THERE, BREATHING HARD AND sweating on each other. The air was so humid it felt like every breath seared my lungs. And her scent was all over me. Inside my pores. Inside my head.

She squeaked as I was one snore from unconsciousness and I realized I was about to crush her. That would be a headline for tomorrow's Cove Gazette.

Local law enforcement officer helps save stray puppy and crushes bakery owner with his penis after the best fucking of his damn life.

Of course I wasn't crushing her with my penis, but if a man flushed from an amazing orgasm couldn't exaggerate a little, when could he?

With my last burst of energy, I rolled off her onto my back and stared at my ceiling. And realized her bra was lazily spinning off the blade of my ceiling fan.

I laughed so hard I had to grip my ribs.

She pried open one eyelid. "Do I want to know why you're laughing?"

I pointed at the ceiling and she snorted, cupping a hand over her mouth as she rolled into my side to rest her head on my chest. After a moment, she frowned, pulling at my T-shirt with distaste. "Why didn't you take this off?"

"Triage," I said succinctly. "Wasn't time so I took off the important things. Though pretty sure I could've fucked you right through my shorts. Dammit, woman, you're a lethal weapon."

Her soft laugh was pure feminine pleasure. "Thanks. I think."

"Definitely a compliment. I've never wanted someone so much." It wasn't a line. It was pure sterling truth.

Pursing her lips, she sat up and slid her hands under my shirt, her nails lightly slicing my skin. "So many muscles. I feel cheated."

And I felt a bit like a preening ass as I sat up and dragged my shirt off from behind my head. But the way her mouth grew slack as she took in all of me was worth it.

"Wow." She moistened her lips, her fingers grazing over my pecs and abs with that hint of nails that had an instant effect on my cock. It jumped to attention as if I hadn't just lost every one of my brain cells inside her snug depths. "You have a lot of tattoos."

That was an understatement. I had a sleeve on my left arm, more down my side and across my pecs and curving onto my back. "Yeah. Got them in college. I got the first one, these right here," I sketched around the vintage style gears on my pecs, "on a lark when I was more drunk than sober. I was a business major, didn't have a clue what I wanted to do with my life, and then suddenly, I wanted to be a tattoo artist and decided if that wasn't a practical idea, I'd just use my body as a canvas for others to experiment on." My lips quirked. "Most of the time, I was even sober."

"They're so random." She smoothed her knuckle over a pair of crossed guns along my hip. "Although I guess this one isn't, considering your profession. How did you end up in the police?"

"It's a long story, but I wanted to help. And my mom had some connections in the FBI so—"

Her bluer than blue eyes widened. "Your mom's in the FBI?"

"She was. Retired a few years ago. Not long before I left, actually."

She waited silently, letting me decide how much I wanted to tell. Probably assuming I had some complicated, painful past.

"Everyone assumes it's some tortured reason I left. It wasn't. More like a mixture of shattered expectations, a need to not ride a desk most of the day and..." I trailed off and scraped a hand over my growing-in beard. Normally, I trimmed a little neater than this, but my scruff was intense today. "I missed my hometown. Missed my family."

She placed a hand on my forearm, rubbing comfortingly. "You're from the Cove?"

"Close. Right outside. Ever been to Turnbull?"

"Drove through it, probably. I'm from Syracuse. But who hasn't been to Happy Acres Orchard? And now they've expanded even more and are practically a tourist destination. They have amazing baked goods, but I was thinking of dropping off my business card there, see if I could get some wider exposure—" She broke off, tilting her head with a smile. "We're talking about you. Sorry. Occupational hazard."

"Don't apologize. I like how committed you are to your career. How passionate." I skimmed my fingers over her cheekbone and she turned her face into my palm. I liked that too. Too freaking much. "Your confidence is sexy, you know that? In all ways."

Her lashes fluttered but it didn't seem like a put on. More like confusion. "You've run into me before. You know I'm not always confident. Far from it."

"Yeah. But you are with your business and your body. Which is fucking hot. The rest doesn't matter." I leaned up on my elbow to softly take her mouth. "Maybe you just need to get warmed up."

"Not a problem now," she murmured between kisses, cupping my cheek. "I like you beardy."

"Do you?"

"Yeah. It felt good when you kissed me."

"I'm kissing you right now." I sucked her lower lip between my teeth. "Or did you mean when I kissed you somewhere else?"

She drew back to kiss my neck. "What do you think?"

"I think you're a very naughty girl and I am so grateful."

She laughed and kept kissing me as she reached up to stroke my neck. "You might say otherwise when you realize I just gave you a hickey to go with the bite mark I gave you before." She eased away to meet my gaze, playfully nibbling her lip. "Oops."

"Good thing I have a turtleneck." I grabbed her around the waist and dragged her on top of me, unwilling to waste the erection that was all her fault.

"No way. Are you serious?" She stroked her hands over my chest on her way down to grip my eager dick. "Speaking of being grateful..."

"Very serious. With my level of tiredness, this recovery time is obviously an act of miraculous intervention. And also almost entirely due to these." I hefted her gorgeous breasts in my hands, devouring them with my gaze like I soon would be doing with my mouth. "You're so damn beautiful, Strawberry."

"And you're so sex drunk." Her laughter flowed over me, warm and sweet, as we tumbled across the bed, hands and lips roaming. "Is that why you decided to roll the dice in Crescent Cove of all places?"

I was too busy tugging her pink nipples and doing my level best to give her a hickey of my own on her shoulder. "Hmm?"

"You came inside me."

"I did. And God, it was everything I dreamed of and more."

She wasn't laughing as we rolled once more, putting her on top again. She sat back, bouncing her full breasts as she steadied herself atop me in a way that did not focus my thoughts. "I'm not on birth control, McNeill. I'll have to take one of those pills."

I frowned. "What pills?"

"Morning-after pills. You know, to prevent pregnancy?" She shook her head at me. "Are you really that much of the gambler?"

I waved a hand. "Oh, no. Don't worry about it. I'm snipped." I reached down to fill my hands with her ass, which was every bit as delicious as her breasts. "So, shut up and let me drain myself inside you again before your alarm goes off."

"Wait a second. You're snipped? Why?"

My lips twitched, although I didn't really feel like smiling. "It's not really safe to enjoy sex in the Cove if you're not either triple covered with birth control or unless you do something drastic."

She didn't look as relieved as I'd expected she would. "So, you're that sure you won't ever want children?"

It wasn't so much a lack of want as maybe it was better if I didn't go there. "Not everyone is right for the whole family deal. And besides, in the Cove, how many people end up stuck when, deep down, they weren't sure if a family was right for them? They just do the honorable thing."

She was studying me entirely too closely. Worst of all, let go of the part of me that always got me in trouble one way or another. "You really think that's why? What if the baby just clued them into what they really wanted?"

I crossed my arms under my head and came to painful terms with the fact that the night's perfect ending might be coming to an abrupt end—without me coming again. "Sure, that probably happened too."

She sighed. "You just popped a pin in the Cove's balloon of love and romance."

Jerking a shoulder, I gripped her hip, feathering my thumb over the soft swell of her belly. Her curves made me crazy. "I'll admit I'm far too logical sometimes. But babies and marriage aren't in my windshield right now, so I figured be responsible and take the option off the table for an accident. Are they in yours?"

She couldn't have shook her head faster if she tried. "God, no, absolutely not. I don't even want a boyfriend right now. The first two years are when most businesses fail, and I'm determined not to be a statistic."

"You won't be." Confidence laced my words. "You're making it, Tab."

Her smile felt like being bathed in sunshine after an unexpected storm. "Thank you." She leaned forward to kiss me gently. "So, I guess I don't need to worry about that pill then."

"Nope." I made my tone as cheerful as possible, as if I hadn't seen the doubts in her eyes. She was overthinking all of this now. And maybe I was too.

This conversation—maybe even this whole night—had put questions in my head. What if I regretted the vasectomy? When I'd done it last year, I'd been so certain I wouldn't change my mind. But what if one day I did? True, I could have the surgery reversed, but that wasn't always a slam dunk. And if someday I had a partner who wanted a baby, if I finally drowned out Liz's voice in my head and decided I did too, perhaps a *maybe* wouldn't be good enough.

Not that I had to think about all of this right now. What I needed was sleep, since more sex was off the table and Tab would have to get to work soon.

Her phone alarm launched into "Pony" by Ginuwine and I shut my eyes, smothering a groan. If I couldn't touch her again, I couldn't bear to look at her magnificent body for one more second.

"I'm sorry, Brady."

It was the first time she'd used my name, and my eyes opened without my conscious help. "Me too."

She stroked her fingers over my short beard. "I had so much fun tonight."

"Me too." Words sprung to my tongue, the kind that were guaranteed to get me in trouble.

Will I see you again?

Can I see you again?

Preferably very soon?

But I didn't say anything. Because I was a coward and if she'd decided she wanted an out, I didn't want to make it harder for her.

Fuck it, yes, I did. We were so good together. She had to know that too.

"Are you going to the dance on Saturday?"

She narrowed her eyes at me. "Are you asking me out?"

"If it violates our previous agreement, then no. If you'd say yes, then yes, I am."

Her mouth curved. "I hadn't planned on it, but I'd like to. But what about—"

A sharp bark from the other room followed by Daisy nosing open the cracked bedroom door cut her off.

"Hey, girl. Looking for breakfast?" My stomach roared in agreement as Daisy leaped on the bed.

"She's not the only one, huh?" Tabitha ruffled Daisy's golden fur. "I'll make you a deal. Lunch on the house if you can watch Pancake until I get off work. Or if you can watch him until you go in for your shift and I'll have Van pitch in. My sister," she explained when my bland stare probably scorched the side of her face. For an instant, I'd been jealous of some faceless man.

Again. Still. For a supposed no strings hookup, I seemed incapable of not being envious of any man with the privilege of being close to her.

Probably lack of sleep. And hunger. And continued horniness.

"Assuming Pancake is still alive," she continued, unaware of my thought process. And thank fuck for that.

As if on cue, the bedroom door nudged farther open and the puppy ran over to the bed just as Daisy had. He also leaned up on his big puppy paws to try to drag himself up the side, letting out a whimper when his stubby legs didn't get him very far.

Letting out a sigh that sounded scarily human, Daisy leaned over the edge of the bed and grabbed the puppy by the scruff to drag him up. As soon as Pancake saw Tabitha and vice versa, they both made noises as if they'd been separated for years not hours.

"There's my baby. There's mama's good boy. Did you have a good nap?" She hauled him up into her arms without concern for her nudity, and Pancake showed his appreciation by burrowing between her breasts.

Being jealous of a dog was probably illogical. Then again, who could blame me?

Daisy leaned forward to lick Pancake's wriggling rump, obviously wanting to remind Tabitha of her recent claim. Tabitha grinned and wrapped her arm around Daisy too, dropping a kiss on her head. "You did such a good job taking care of my boy while mama was..." She darted a glance at me with an impish grin. "Busy."

I swallowed hard. The three of them made an altogether adorable picture. "Am I an asshole if I admit I wish we'd gotten busy one more time?"

"No." She shifted forward to plant a kiss on my sulky mouth. "I'll sneak a cream puff into your lunch."

"Hmph." But I was grinning as I tangled my hand in her hair. All at once, it was as if I'd been sent back to eighth grade to ask the girl I liked if she'd go to the winter formal with me. "You never answered my question about the dance."

"If we're both at the dance, who will take care of this one? He's too little to stay alone, isn't he?" She glanced down at the puppy nestled in an entirely unfair place on her chest.

"He can stay with Daisy." At her pensive expression, I let out a long breath. "Hell, come with me, and I'll wear a damn snuggy."

Not that dogs were allowed into the Town Hall without an emotional support dog license, but I was the damn police. Who would dare to question me?

Probably everyone.

She grinned. "You've got a deal, Hot Cop."

EIGHT

FOR THE FIRST TIME EVER, I WAS LATE TO WORK. LUCKILY, NO ONE would be docking my paycheck.

I wasn't much later than I planned, but taking two rowdy dogs out to pee took longer than I'd expected. Well, correction. One wouldn't pee in a timely fashion and the other one peed everywhere, including in Brady's deck shoes.

To his credit, he didn't yell or growl or do anything but admonish Pancake with an extremely authoritative snout kiss. Pancake seemed properly chastised—until he peed under the dining room table about ten minutes later. I offered to mop it up but he waved me off to take a shower and took care of it himself.

How was this guy single? I wasn't supposed to be asking questions like that, I was pretty sure. But after you've already discussed whether or not you want children, what was off-limits?

Still a heck of a lot, it turned out.

We got ready while the emergency scanner Brady immediately turned on after showering squawked through endless notifications. I'd assumed the Cove was a small enough town that it didn't have a lot going on in the fire, EMS, and police department arenas. I was wrong. Just in the short while we spent on our morning routines--though I did part of mine in my apartment across the hall—a call came through for a woman needing assistance with giving birth in her broken down car, a small barn fire, a motor vehicle theft, and several other things with codes I didn't recognize.

"Your job is more dangerous than I realized."

Brady didn't respond right away as he shook cornflakes into a bowl and doused them with milk. If I'd had more time, I would've offered to make him a real hot breakfast.

Maybe next time. Or maybe never. Too early to tell at this point.

He didn't laugh it off as I expected. "Usually, I spend most of my days on paperwork and on some form of community relations. The occasional cat up a tree, motor vehicle accident, petty theft. But crime is on the rise all across the country, and the Cove isn't exempt, no matter what people think."

I shuddered. "Yeah. The Quikky Mart was robbed recently. You handled that, didn't you? I couldn't believe it."

"Just a couple of kids." He put away the milk. "This time anyway. But you never know."

I took a few bites of his cereal before promising I'd grab a muffin at the bakery. Then I made sure to give Pancake some kisses and promised to get him some toys of his own since Daisy's giant bone was too big for him to handle, though he tried. Daisy seemed content to curl up with him after she ate her breakfast and Pancake ate his puppy kibble sample Brady had gotten from the vet to tide us over until we got to the store.

Not until I got to the store. Until *we* did. Brady really was one in a million.

Before sunrise, he walked me down the street to the bakery even though I could've taken my car. I didn't argue against the offer very hard, since the night's snowstorm had turned into a faint snow that meandered from the murky sky. The flakes glistened under the now working streetlights—yay for the power finally being back on—and shimmered on the various Valentine's decorations hanging from the quaint, old-fashioned lampposts and festooning most of the businesses along the street.

The town had done its best to show their appreciation of love and romance with puffy hearts and pink and red streamers and neon lights, and the whole atmosphere was rather magical. And that wasn't saying anything about the carved ice sculptures seemingly set up on every other block in the Cove.

"I just love all the decorations." A light shiver had him drawing me into his side and I smiled up at him. "My favorites are the ice. I requested that polar bear with the cupcake for this block."

His jaw tightened almost imperceptibly as he followed my gaze to the adorable bear placed right at the end of my walkway. The bear was definitely drawing in more customers. "I thought you were going to say he was holding one of those croquet things."

I laughed. "Croquembouche, and that is definitely a cupcake."

"If you say so." He brushed an absent kiss over my temple as he studied the bear. "I know the artist."

"You do?" I couldn't keep the admiration out of my voice. "They're so talented."

"Yeah," he admitted grudgingly. "He is. He's been doing those since we were kids. Started one night in our garage with my dad's blow torch and a hunk of ice he scraped off the sidewalk." He laughed. "Crazy ass was like ten."

"Your garage?"

"Yeah. Mav's my brother."

"Mav's an interesting name."

Maybe I was imagining things, but I would've sworn his gaze darkened. "He's an interesting guy."

"Like his big brother." Lightly, I jammed my knuckles into his rock hard belly. Not that I'd intentionally jabbed him in the hopes of bumping into his abs. Alas, I'd been thwarted by his puffy vest. "Hey, is this bulletproof?" I stroked the material.

He laughed. "Am I safe in saying no or are you feeling violent?"

"Short me on orgasms next time and maybe." I bit my lower lip as his gaze scorched my face. "Joking. Really bad joke. I don't own a gun. Only thing I can aim well with is a piping bag."

"I'm stuck on 'next time' personally."

"Oh, uh, yeah, so what about those Giants?"

Chuckling, he brushed a kiss over my forehead. "I never know what you'll say next."

"Yay?"

"Definitely a yay." Another yay was my hot cop reaching down to securely hold my hand as we approached Sugar Rush.

"Your shop is really nice." Brady gazed at the big plate glass window with the revolving stand that would soon hold my Valentine's-themed croquembouche display. "You've accomplished a lot so young. You should be so proud."

His approval caused a warm flush along my skin as I squeezed his hand. I was pretty sure my palm was wet from nerves, but he hadn't yanked his away in disgust. Yet. He was probably wondering how a woman could willingly get naked with a stranger, including bonus masturbation, but couldn't walk down the street without sweating while holding hands. Just part of the conundrum of Tabitha Monaghan.

Buy your ride tickets here.

"Thanks. I am. I'm neurotic about keeping everything running smoothly though, so don't praise me too much yet. And if I don't find another employee soon—"

"I'm sure you will. I might know someone."

I slid him a sidelong look. He'd said that before and I didn't know if I should be happy or concerned. "Oh, uh, that would be good, but I have certain requirements."

"Do they need a baking background? How about pizza experience? Does that work?"

"Hmm." I frowned. "Well, I guess it's helpful. And I offer training on the job. But they need to be punctual, eager to learn, friendly, and ideally familiar with running a cash register. Baking experience helps, but if they're creative and curious, that counts for a lot."

"Yeah, I just might know someone," he said again thoughtfully, his long-legged stride so fast that I had to hurry to keep pace. He veered right up the driveway of Sugar Rush, heading around to the back parking lot where we'd met the night before. As we passed by the lit windows—a fact I was still immensely grateful for—I caught a glimpse of Lea tossing something to Tiffany as they both laughed their heads off. It was either a sack of rolls or possibly a potato.

"They're very good employees," I said quickly as Brady grinned.

"I'm sure. Everyone fools around when the boss is away. It's in the company handbook."

"You too?"

"Nah, babe. I'm a duly sworn man of the law. I would never fool around." We stopped next to the back door, and he steadied me when I slipped on a patch of ice. "Well, maybe I would with you."

I gripped his shoulder as I side-stepped toward the door. This ice was no joke. "You, sir, are a sweet talker."

"More a dirty talker, but I'll accept whatever you want to call me." He moved behind me as I unlocked the door to the bakery and flipped aside my loose braid to lay a soft kiss on the back of my neck. "Have a good day, Strawberry. Don't forget my lunch. I can't wait to come get it."

"How do you manage to make even that sound salacious?" I wondered with a laugh as I opened the door.

"It's a gift." He pinched my ass as his phone went off with a text. "Staff meeting. Awesome. Probably about the new mystery part-time cop."

When I turned to playfully admonish him for the pinch, he was gone.

Not that my employees had missed a damn trick.

"Oh, so *this* is why you were late." Tiffany with her rainbow pigtails and tie-dyed apron emerged from the shadows of the back room to tap her Apple watch. "Here I thought we'd have to send out a search party, and instead, she's got a police escort. Ooh la la."

"A yummy police escort," Lea chimed in from behind her, her dark blue apron already liberally splattered with flour, as was her neat brown chignon. She was the baking version of Charlie Brown's friend PigPen, but she baked like a boss.

"Don't you two start." I pointed at each of them in turn and headed to my desk in back to do a quick check of my morning To Do list before I hunkered down and got to work. There was never time to waste.

"Gotta say it's nice to feel so well taken care of by the Cove's finest."

I listened to their snark with half an ear as I skimmed my list until Lea mentioned something about the "second cop today."

I glanced over my shoulder. "What do you mean?"

They exchanged knowing looks. "One just left a little while ago. A call came in about a nuisance duck and he wanted to see what we knew about it."

Since this was the Cove and rogue ducks were as much part of the lore here—even out of season—as the baby juice in the water supply, I barely blinked. "Christian came by before dawn because of a duck? At least I assume it was Christian. Can't see the chief getting out of bed for that."

"I'd like to see the chief get out of bed. Hello, hottie." Tiffany pretended to wipe sweat off her forehead while Lea giggled.

They were both only a few years younger than I was, but since I was running on so little sleep, today I felt much older. Not that I could complain over the reasons I was dragging. Even so, I was already looking forward to my post-shift nap.

"Better yet, I'd like to see him still *in* bed," Lea said with a sigh.

"Don't let Gina hear you say that. She takes out the claws when it comes to Chief Brooks."

"Can you blame her?"

"Hell no. He's so freaking yum. But so is this new cop." Tiffany smacked her lips. "Should've expected it since his last name is McNeill."

I dropped my pencil mid-checkmark. It rolled off the desk and across the floor.

So *this* was what they meant when they said you could hear a pin drop.

I swiveled to look at my employees. "The new duck-wrangling cop is a McNeill?"

"You didn't know?" Tiffany and Lea exchanged glances, and I

almost expected them to rub their hands together at being in the presence of fresh off the presses gossip. "He's new. Last night was his first night."

Lea propped a finger against her chin. "Not all that is new since yesterday, huh? How did you hook up with Officer Delicious?"

"Who says we hooked up?"

Lea grabbed Tiffany's wrist and turned her watch toward me. "That he walked you to work before it was even daylight."

Futilely, I tried to roll the kinks out of my shoulders. I needed a massage almost as much as I needed a long nap. "So, since you two have so much time to speculate, am I to assume twenty-four croquembouche are baking? And enough strawberry buttercream to fill those two dozen cream puffs is in the blast chiller?"

They scattered like gossip-hungry field mice.

With a sigh, I yanked out my desk chair to make a quick call to one of my suppliers. A swift rap at the back door nearly made me drop the phone. *Hello, jumpy.* My heart leaped into my throat as I rose to answer the door. It was too early for anyone to be here. "Brady? Did you forget something?" I called out.

"Not Brady," a deep male voice replied. "Police, ma'am."

I shut my eyes. "Is this about the rogue duck?" *And are you the rogue McNeill cop Brady hadn't seen fit to tell me about?* I didn't ask that part though. Besides, how many brothers did Brady have anyway?

"Yes, along with a followup on your call last night. You are the one who called from this business, correct?"

"Yes." I opened the door and swallowed a sound of...well, not distress exactly. He wasn't Brady's twin, but he looked a hell of a lot like him. His dark hair was slightly longer and fell forward over his forehead and he wore dark aviators against the swiftly rising sun now bouncing off the snow. He had a sharp jaw like Brady's, full lips like Brady's, and a devastating smile like Brady's—which caused me some personal stress considering I could've sworn I could still smell Brady on my skin.

I'd showered at his place this morning, but I hadn't been all that thorough because maybe, possibly I hadn't tried that hard to scrub his fresh citrus scent away. I was used to men smelling like leather or cigar smoke or something woodsy like they'd spent an afternoon chopping down trees. Not zesty like a fresh orange or lemon.

I liked it. A lot.

Brady's brother smelled like soap and shampoo. Just clean. Or maybe that was because the wind was blowing in a healthy dose of drifting snow.

"A followup?" I echoed.

"Yes. The power is back on in town, and you don't appear to have any lingering issues?"

"Oh, no. No, everything seems to be fine. Except I need to call my landlord to inquire about a backup generator."

Brady's brother hauled out a pad and noted something on it. "And you had a situation with a stray puppy? Did you find the owners?"

"Yes." I gripped the edge of the open door. "I'm one of them. The other is your brother, at least temporarily."

He lifted his head and removed his sunglasses, hooking them on his pocket. "Brady with a joint pet? There's a new one. I'm Mav, by the way," he added, extending his hand for a quick shake. "I'm new on the force."

"Hi Mav, I'm Tabitha, owner of Sugar Rush here, nice to meet you." I cocked my head. "Oh. You're the ice sculptor?" Before he could answer, I frowned. "Why didn't Brady know you were joining?"

"It's a surprise." His wide grin didn't make me think the surprise would necessarily be a good one.

"Hmm. What if I tell him?"

Mav laughed. "Right from the jump, taking his side."

"Why would your working with him require a side? You're brothers, right?"

"Right. That's how it should be, but it doesn't always go that way."

I thought of all the bouts of sibling rivalry I'd dealt with when it came to my sister. Some serious, some less so. But throughout, my twin had always been my best friend. I couldn't imagine having a brother and not being close to him. Granted, I didn't know for sure that was the case here, but it seemed like there were issues.

"I won't interfere in your business, but maybe he'll surprise you too." I smiled, remembering how Brady had looked as he admitted he'd missed home. I hoped that meant change was afoot for these two, if their relationship was anything like it seemed from this brief conversation.

"He already is." Mav rocked back on the heels of his boots as the radio clipped to his belt crackled with static. "Pleasure to meet you, Tabitha." He took a moment to look me up and down. "My brother has excellent taste. I hope he realizes it."

"What does that mean?" I asked as he turned away. His footsteps crunched on the snow as he walked off, seemingly not having the same trouble with the ice I'd had.

"Maybe I'll tell you someday," he called, slipping on his aviators. "Have a good day, ma'am."

Somehow I had a feeling that *ma'am* was entirely snarky. It better have been, since I was freaking twenty-seven. I hoped not to be referred to that way for at least another twenty years.

With a shiver, I stepped back inside. I would call my supplier, and then it was time to call my landlord about a freaking generator for the next time the power went out.

Then again, the power outage had led me to Brady. Was that really so bad?

I grinned and pressed my thighs together. *No, indeed.*

Maybe I'd just not ask about the generator after all. No need to question fate.

"Oh, shit, boss, call the hottie firemen!" Tiffany yelled. "Flaming croquembouche!"

Sighing, I hurried in the direction of my employees' shrill voices. Pop-up fires happened fairly often around here. But usually it was something easily handled by our fire extinguisher.

No hottie firemen—or cops—needed.

Dammit.

NINE

**BRADY**

WHAT A CLUSTERFUCK OF A DAY.

The staff meeting was postponed until later in the afternoon due to one Mr. Peter Wray mistaking his heart medication for his back pills and blacking out just as he was entering the parking lot of the Piggly Wiggly. Unfortunately, he hit the gas instead of the brakes and came to just as his Oldsmobile halted inches before demolishing the giant crate of watermelons. Even more unfortunately, he'd already mowed down the tomatoes, the bananas, and the entire floral department, most of which was on discount after Valentine's Day. For good measure, he wiped out a large M&M's display, including the giant cardboard green M&M.

Needless to say, the crowd control, cleanup, and general insanity of making sure no one decided to get sticky fingers while the front window had a car in it ate up hours.

Add in paperwork along with an accident involving one of my brother's ice sculptures and a rowdy bird whose lunch hadn't agreed with him—not a duck for once—and the day was jam-packed until the meeting mid-afternoon. Luckily, I just had enough time to stop into the bakery to pick up my late lunch beforehand, though I wasn't so sure about my luck when I walked into a conversation about none other than myself.

At least I was being described favorably.

Rather than striding past the pair of customers standing outside Sugar Rush, I stopped right beside them to admire the croquet-whatever now in the window, dusted in some kind of shimmering pink stuff. They sure looked like cream puffs with pink filling. The artistry of the display was undeniable, as was apparently my sexual prowess.

"I heard they did it right here. Like in the bakery. While the power was out so they could desecrate all the tables and stuff."

My eyebrow arched as I studied the small café tables Mrs. Gunderson was referring to. What kind of thrusting did they think those spindly legs could hold? Certainly not enough. And who wanted to do that against an ice-cold window in February?

I couldn't say I minded the desecration idea, however.

"No way. I don't believe it. A man of the cloth?"

"The cloth is a priest not a cop, Shirl."

"Oh." Shirley Busbee's high-pitched girlish giggle didn't match her steel gray updo, but then again, neither did her hot pink leather motorcycle jacket. "Well, whatever. Surely they take some oath against things like that."

The devil was sitting on my shoulder, probably partially due to my growling stomach. I normally enjoyed some of the town gossip, especially when it had nothing to do with me, but I was currently riding the grumpy side of a mood. Somedays the whole protecting and serving deal sucked hairy monkey balls.

"Sorry to burst your bubble, ladies," I said smoothly, causing both women to whirl around to stare at me, "but the police don't take an oath against sex. We're human like everyone else."

Mrs. Gunderson elbowed her friend. "See, Shirl, I told you to stop spouting that nonsense."

My brow climbed again. "Funny, I heard you say it first."

She flushed right down her neck to the fur collar of her coat. "You look here, Brady McNeill, you may be a newcomer to the Cove's police department, but we watch out for each other here. If someone sneezes, half the town offers them a tissue. That may be inconvenient for you and your lascivious activities, especially when your ex-girlfriend gets wind of it, but that's the rhythm of—"

"What ex-girlfriend? I haven't dated anyone here in months."

"Better tell Misty Coy that then." She crossed her arms smugly. "She's put the word out she dumped you and that's why you're having revenge relations."

I rubbed my temple as I drew out my phone. Almost time for the meeting so I needed to cut this nonsense short. Aw, darn. "I went out with Misty once more than six months ago. We went bowling." And possibly had sex in the backseat of my sedan, which was neither here nor there. "We parted amicably."

"She thinks otherwise."

Shirl made a tsk tsk noise. "I don't know how it works where you came from in Washington D.C.," she said it as if it was a communicable disease, "but here, we look out for each other."

I didn't bother correcting her that I was born in nearby Turnbull. "If someone sneezes, everyone has a tissue. Right. But trust me, Misty wasn't hurt after we ended."

"No, she said you were hurt."

I rolled my eyes. "Yeah, that's why I haven't thought of her in six months. Pardon me, ladies, I have business to attend to—"

"In the back room?" Shirl giggled behind her pink gloved hand.

Ignoring her, I walked inside the bakery, stopping just inside the doorway at the jingle of bells. It was like Valentine's Day had exploded in here, no doubt due to the continuing celebration. The weekend's dance would be the culmination of Valentine's Fest, and in the meantime, cash registers were ringing merrily all over the Cove. The line for Tabitha's baked goods extended nearly to the door.

Pride swelled in my chest. Good for her. Not only did her desserts look delicious, they tasted that way too. I'd tried far too few of them so far, but I intended to rectify that soon.

"Okay, people, for those who've taken numbers from the little machine over here, come on up when it's your turn. Nice and orderly now. You'll all be served in due time." The counter woman's head of wild blondish-red curls peeked over the top an instant before she squealed, "Make way for the police! Officer of the law in residence."

I looked over my shoulder to make sure there wasn't some much more important cop in the place, but nope, just me. The people in line ahead of me turned toward me with an assortment of expressions. Some boredom, some annoyance, some amusement. A lot of amusement, actually.

Guess that desecration rumor—and God only knew how many permutations of it—was making the rounds.

"What can we do you for, Officer?" the pint-sized woman asked. She was clearly standing on her tiptoes, because if she hadn't been, she would've had to look out through the dessert case to make eye contact. Of course she simply could've moved over a few feet to the cash register, but the line stretched in front of the desserts.

Not surprising, because every damn one of them I could see around the crush of people was mouthwatering. And I wasn't even that much of a sweets guy.

Looked like Tabitha was already changing my ways.

"Hi, I can wait. I'm not in a huge hurry."

Lies. But I'd been speculated about enough today. First, for swinging my dick, and now probably I'd be accused of swinging around my badge to get special favors.

At least the ones I hadn't already secured with my personal nightstick.

"Oh, no, we can't have that. Do you have an order in already or do you know what you want?" Pint-sized produced a pad and wet the tip of her pencil with her tongue.

"Tabitha mentioned having a sandwich ready for me." I cleared my throat. "And a cream puff."

"I thought she already gave him her cream puff?" someone muttered.

"Oh, yes, duh, of course, Tabby told me where she kept your very special lunch." She went to the cooler and returned with a white bakery bag with Sugar Rush's hot pink logo splashed along the side. "Chicken salad on a croissant, dill pickle wedges, and a fresh croquembouche." Pint-sized's voice seemed to grow louder until I was certain people walking by the lake would be privy to the contents of my meal. "Let me just grab a fresh one." She opened the case and carefully wrapped a cream puff in some sort of fancy pink tissue paper.

Tabitha truly thought of every detail.

"Here you go, on the house!" She pushed the bag across the top of the case. "Thank you for your service," she added with a wink of her glittery purple eyelid complete with a dramatic mascara wing. "My sister has been in an exceptionally good mood today, thanks to you. Though really, what was she thinking adopting that puppy? She doesn't even know how to keep a plant alive, never mind an actual dog."

Tabitha's sister, present and accounted for. Holy shit.

Tabitha emerged from the back, her wild hair looped on top of her head and her apron dusted with flour and frosting. She flashed a smile at me before she made a sound at her sister that resembled a snarl.

"Van, what did I tell you?"

Van's expression became angelic in a flash. "Hmm, sis?"

Tabitha shook her head and stepped up to the counter to help the next person in line, who just happened to be Mrs. Gunderson. That was a feat of physics I didn't understand since I'd just been talking to her outside and she'd now skipped most of the line.

I peeked into my bakery bag and smiled at the note on the sandwich wrapper that said have a nice day, Hot Cop with a smiley face. Then I frowned and moved to the side of the counter to motion Tabitha over.

Behind me, a literal hush moved over the crowd, likely so they could hear what they assumed would be a salacious conversation. What the actual hell?

Tabitha didn't seem to notice or care, since she slid her fingers over the inside of my wrist as she smiled up at me. A perfectly innocent gesture that made me rock hard in an instant. She had witchy ways I couldn't even fathom. Better yet, how had it taken me until last night to be bowed over by them?

Not that I hadn't noticed she was a knockout before. But now with flour dusted on her nose and her crazy hair and sexy smile, I couldn't even remember what the hell I'd pulled her aside for.

Except the need to have sex on the counter like monkeys, damn our audience.

"Did you need something?" she asked, pursing her kissably soft lips. "I think I remembered everything for your bag."

"So, you packed it? And wrote the note? Not your sister." I lowered my voice. "Twins, really? You're not even the same height."

"She got some of the extra inches she stole from me in her boobs," Van called, proving I sucked at whispering.

Laughter broke out all around us as Tabitha ignored her. "Yes, she's my twin. Fraternal though. I'm only a couple inches taller than she is."

"I'm the better height for blow—"

"Vanessa Vail Monaghan!"

I blinked at Tabitha's perfect school principal impression. Van, however, just laughed and continued taking orders. Yes, imagine that, people actually were continuing to order during this spectacle. Not that we'd done anything untoward here, but you wouldn't know it from the level of interest in our not-so-private conversation.

I smirked. "There's such a thing as better height for—"

Tabitha lightly shoved my chest. "Don't you start. And yes, I packed your lunch and wrote the note. Why, do lots of people call you Hot Cop?"

I slid a look out of the corner of my eye at Mrs. Gunderson, but shockingly, she was more interested in her order of frosted cupcakes in the shape of flowers than in my love life. And thank God for that. I'd thought I was well-acquainted with small town gossip, but today had gone to the next level.

"No. Of course not. Just she seems like a feisty one."

"Heard that!" Vanessa responded cheerfully.

"With bat hearing," I added without bothering to lower my voice.

"All true." Tabitha sighed. "How about you come in back?" She bit her lip, her shyness appearing without warning. "If you have a minute. I don't want to keep you."

Please keep me.

I cleared my throat. I really didn't have time to spare, but depending on what awaited me in that back room... "I have a minute."

"Follow me."

Someone whistled on their fingers as Tabitha strode into the back with me bringing up the rear. I sent a cross look over my shoulder, but a half dozen appropriately innocent expressions greeted me.

"Is it too late to move to New York City?" I asked once the swinging door to the back room shut behind us.

"Alas, yes, though I did consider moving to the city after getting my degree. But I'd never be able to afford rent there, never mind a storefront or salaries or overhead."

I rubbed her shoulder, kneading the kinks upon kinks in her muscles. "You picked the right place and your business is thriving. I'm sure it was even before we offered bonus entertainment."

She flashed me a grin over her shoulder. "We didn't even have to. They ran with the story all on their own."

"Considering I supposedly banged you right where your beautiful tower of croquets are now, I have to agree."

Her light laughter was musical, somehow rising over the din of voices just on the other side of the door. "Sound it out with me, Hot Cop. Cro-quem-bouche—"

I couldn't smile down into her lively blue eyes without kissing her. Physically, it wasn't possible. Her mouth heated under mine and she reached up to grab my vest, digging in with her nails. The vest was so thickly padded I didn't feel the bite of pain so I nipped her lush lower lip instead, and her soft moan poured into my mouth.

"Do you have any idea how much I want to fuck you right here?"

She pulsed her hips against me and slid her hand up my chest to curl around my neck, the feel of her skin against mine sending an electric jolt down my spine. As her curvy body curled around me, nerve endings I'd never known I had sparked to brutal attention. "By that club in your pants, I'm gonna say yes." Teasingly, she sucked on my lower lip. "Not that I'm against a little friendly exhibitionism, but I'm pretty sure exchanging fluids this close to my flowers is asking for a report from the health department."

I shifted my head just enough to see the trays of flower cupcakes on three of the four stainless steel tables. "No way, Tab. You did all these?"

"Not alone, but yeah." She drew her hand away from my neck and wiggled her short, clear polished fingernails, all of which had smears of brightly colored frosting. "Sorry if I messed you up."

"Oh, baby, you could mess me up every damn day and I'd thank my lucky stars." As much as it pained me to release her, I sidestepped around her to move to the tables of flowers. More bowls of batter sat nearby, in the process of being poured into cupcake trays from the looks of things. "They're all little works of art. Each one is different. They're like a rainbow."

"You really think so?" The pleasure in her voice had me reaching back to pull her hard against my side. "Here I was thinking I hadn't done enough different ones. They're going to be judged after the dance Saturday night." She nibbled the edge of her thumbnail. "I was notified today the Valentine Fest committee needed more to put on display because Tricks and Treats, one of the other event sponsors, had to pull out due to a bad batch of caramel or something."

"Can't they just make more?"

"You'd think, but they're running out of time and there were rumors about sabotage."

I laughed. "Caramel sabotage?"

She wasn't amused. "You'd be surprised how cutthroat the candy and bakery goods business can be behind the scenes."

"I guess so."

She cocked her head. "So, about that person you knew who might need a job? The one with pizza experience?"

"Yeah, my little sister. Sorry, I didn't get a chance to call her yet, but she worked at Varsity Pizza all through high school and she's between jobs."

"If she can start tomorrow, I'll give her a dollar bonus per hour until the end of the month. I've gotten three rush birthday cupcake jobs today. Even if she doesn't have bakery experience, if she's used to working at a pizza joint, she should be able to handle it." Tab blew out a breath and braced her hands on her hips. "I just need someone to help get me through this week. At this rate, I'll need to get my mom and dad in here to make stuff."

"I'll talk to her," I promised. "She's looking for something quick because she wants to go back to school for teaching and needs to start saving since no trust fund babies in this family."

"Thanks. I don't normally consider hiring someone sight unseen, but I'm desperate. And if I end up getting more business because of the caramel sabotage situation..." She trailed off and I moved forward to grip her forearms, rubbing them briskly.

"You'll handle it. And Honey will help."

She blinked. "Honey?"

"My sister. How long will you be here? I'll call her after my meeting."

"Oh, I'll probably be here until—"

A loud quack from the front of the bakery had us exchanging a glance. Then came another and what sounded like a flap of a thousand wings, followed by laughter and shrieks.

"Oh, for Pete's sake, not again."

"Let me handle this." I headed down the hall into the front of the bakery with her right behind me.

"About time, Officer! Ducks are not household pets!" Mrs. Gunderson was still in residence, because of course she was.

Might as well sell tickets.

The crowd had grown exponentially in the five minutes I'd been in the back with Tabitha. That crowd included an agitated duck who was running in circles while a small blond child chased after it in hot pursuit.

"She's a baby." Sage Hamilton, the proprietress of one of the Cove's most popular bed and breakfasts, dodged people to race after the child and the duck. She clutched her stomach with one arm. "She just wants to pet the duck. Star, leave the duck alone, honey. He's scared."

"Duckie!" Star sped up in her pursuit.

"Ma'am, I'm the police." I tried to stop Sage mid-flight, but she would not be deterred.

"Call for backup!" someone called.

Which was protocol technically, but we were minutes from a staff meeting and I'd been in the damn FBI. I could handle a freaking child wanting to pet a duck. So, no, I did not call it in. I did not request backup. And I didn't ask for help containing the crowd because we were in a bakery, for God's sake. This wasn't Madison Square Garden.

Besides, we had a secret weapon—one I didn't even realize.

As the din of voices rose, I futilely tried to box in the duck to get it behind the counter where I could hopefully reroute it out a side door.

Then someone whistled on their fingers like a referee.

"Line up, people! No rubbernecking! You've all seen ducks before, so chill out. Now take a number and get ready to order." Van whistled again for good measure, possibly busting a few eardrums in the process.

The child stopped chasing the fleeing duck and she fell back on her butt on the tiled floor, tears immediately springing into her big blue eyes. Sage lurched forward to pick her up, her own face going pale an instant before she shoved her daughter at me and booked for the nearest large potted fake plant.

Into which she threw up. Violently.

I had a second to glimpse Tabitha's panicked expression before she hurried to minister to a still puking Sage. She fussed over her, rubbing her back and holding back her long blond hair, even putting it in a quick braid with the band from around her wrist. Sage sniffled and Tabitha murmured to her while the child in my arms wrapped her arms around my neck and clung to me.

Not to be outdone, the duck ran in erratic circles until some wise person opened the front door and he finally hot-footed it right out of the shop.

The kid started to bawl. Loudly.

"Hey, what's your name, pretty girl?" At a loss, I jockeyed her in my hold. She was small but all arms and legs and cute as a button, minus the runny nose.

Cute as a button? Man, what was up with me? But she was. Her blond hair hung in her blue eyes as she knuckled away the tears. "Star." She hiccuped. "My daddy says I'm brighter than the ones in the sky."

"I know your daddy."

She frowned, her tears slowing slightly. "You do?"

"I do. Someday I might buy a house from him and your uncle Seth." Where that came from, I had no clue. I was quite happy with my apartment, and I hadn't even lived there a year yet.

Damn this baby-crazy town, giving innocent men like me ideas. Of course adorable kids like Star didn't hurt.

"My uncle Seth wants a new house. He says he needs a padlock on the bathroom door. Cause he can't go potty in peace."

Then again, kids weren't really that cute.

"And my daddy agrees, since we're having another one."

I'd thought this kid was pretty young, but she was heavier than she looked and talked like she was on her way to high school.

"Another one what?"

Sage straightened from the planter and wiped her mouth with the tissue Tabitha had provided. "Another one of these." She cupped her belly.

Suddenly, the planter puking made more sense. I'd thought maybe she'd indulged in too many croquets or something. Someday I'd learn.

In these parts, throwing up rarely had an innocent excuse like excessive sweets consumption. Or drinking yourself unconscious when you realized babies and marriage weren't as off-putting as they'd once been.

"Congratulations," I said weakly as Star picked that moment to kick me in the groin on her way to climbing down.

She ran over to her mother and gripped her thigh, reaching up to pat the very slight swell of her mother's stomach. "My baby," she announced.

Sage stroked her daughter's baby-fine hair and waved off a still hovering Tabitha. "Easier to give her a baby than a duck. Also no code violations to worry about." She laughed faintly. "I'm fine, Tabitha, thanks. Second baby. Old hat at this."

As the hum of conversation keyed up around the bakery with this new nugget of prime gossip, she turned to face the rest of Tabitha's customers. "You heard it here first. My husband knocked me up again. Sorry it's not more salacious. The pool boy's engaged to a Swedish model." She shrugged as if she couldn't help what she couldn't control.

I had to grin. I didn't know Sage well, but I liked her attitude.

"And sorry about your planter." Sage winced as she gazed at Tabitha. "I'll buy you a new one. But hey, bright side, at least the spotlight is off you and your swinger cop." She lifted her brows high as if she'd just realized I was said swinger cop. "He's cute though, gotta give him that. And good with kids," she added, tapping her chin.

Tabitha looked as if she was hoping the floor would swallow her whole. I couldn't say I blamed her.

What was this swinger business? A perfectly single guy couldn't date without getting labeled now?

Clearly, there were aspects to small town life I hadn't fully considered before moving back to the area.

"Don't worry about it," Tabitha said brightly, edging behind the counter to help her sister deal with the hungry horde all but clamoring for iced and frosted baked goods.

I took one look at the state of the planter and prepared to haul it to the dumpster. Luckily, trash day was tomorrow.

"You don't have to do that," Tab protested as I lifted up the planter just as my phone went off with my work ringtone.

"I got it, Strawberry," I said without thinking as I carried it out the back, pretending I hadn't heard an assortment of giggles at the nickname.

Did I really want to go to the dance with Tab and encourage more of this nonsense?

If it meant I'd get to spend more time with her, yeah, I did. Easy answer.

I deposited the planter in the dumpster outside, only nearly slipping on what was left of the ice twice, then dragged out my phone to see a text from the chief. Terrific.

Jared: My office, McNeill. Now.

TEN

 **BRADY**

WHEN I WALKED INTO THE DEPARTMENT A FEW MINUTES LATER, I HAD A good idea what to expect. I'd gone off script by not calling in the situation at Sugar Rush, whether or not the perp was a duck.

Or maybe Sage's kid was the perp. Was attempted duck fondling a crime? Or was the true crime duck invasion?

In any case, I'd gone it alone, but we weren't talking a major issue here. So, I fully expected to get a slap on the wrist and that would be the end of it.

What I didn't expect to see was my younger brother attired in a brand new CCPD uniform seated in the chair in front of Jared's battered desk.

Both men stood when I arrived. Neither said anything, but that was okay as I was not similarly afflicted.

"What the hell is this?" I demanded.

Maverick smiled thinly. "Same old Brady. Nice to see you too, brother."

"I just saw you a week ago. You weren't dressed like this." I gestured to his uniform. "Did you run out of the ones down at the mall?"

"No, I'm the new part time officer. Hoping to be full time by fall. If the fit works out for both me and the department."

I cut my gaze sharply to Jared. "Why?"

"Why what?"

"Why did you tell me like this? This is the 'surprise' new hire?" I shook my head. "I know I don't exactly fit in here, but I thought at least I was respected."

"You fit in just fine. And you are respected. But your brother asked us to let him handle it." Jared cast Mav a sharp look of his own. "Until I found out today he hadn't handled it at all and just expected me to break the news at the staff meeting."

"That you didn't bother to show up for," Mav interjected sourly.

"I was dealing with a situation." I cleared my throat. "At Sugar Rush."

"Oh, I just bet." Mav's chuckle rolled out smoothly. "Gotta say, I can see why you're spending so much time on those particular sweets."

I narrowed my eyes. "Listening to gossip? You've got one up on me, because I haven't heard a damn thing about what you're up to. Other than with your blowtorch."

Mav jerked a shoulder. "I considered joining the fire department, but it seemed like a conflict of interest."

"You're a funny guy."

Chief Brooks rose to his feet. "We'll discuss your situation at Sugar Rush in a few minutes, Brady. For now, I'm going to leave you two alone to talk. I have a brother too," he said as I frowned. "I don't want your personal situation to affect your work, but I don't like what I'm seeing here. If working together is going to be a problem, I will have to make other arrangements, Maverick." His tone brooked no argument. "Your brother has seniority. So, think about whether you two can work together and you let me know." He strode out and let the door shut heavily behind him.

Maverick rose, shaking his head. "That's rich. You start pouting over me stepping on your toes and I lose my new job. Thanks, bro."

"Why didn't you tell me? Why let me walk in here and find out?"

"Maybe because I thought if you were in a work environment you wouldn't act as if I was a pesky kid instead of a man who has worked security for years, as you damn well know."

I took a deep breath. He had a point. "You could've come to me and explained you wanted to work with me."

"I didn't want to work with you, I wanted to do the job I've been trained to do and help this town. The town I never left."

The dig hit where it was intended. "You didn't leave Turnbull, not Crescent Cove."

"Yeah, but now I live here. They're miles apart. Not all of us are meant for the FBI like you and mom, but that doesn't mean we can't do good work and help." He held up a hand. "And no, you don't have to tell me I took a while to come to this career. I did. But it makes it easier to know what's a good fit when you've tried other things that aren't." He braced his hands behind him on the chief's desk. "Look, I don't want to step on your toes."

I snorted. "Since when?"

"Since we aren't in high school anymore, tussling after the same chick. Not that I don't think Tabitha is smoking hot."

"She is," I said evenly.

"But I also don't have a death wish and I don't poach."

"We're brand new. Just burning off some steam." Was I convincing him of that or myself?

"Oh, so you're saying I should shoot my shot?"

"You fucking wish."

His laughter was almost easy. Much more like the old Mav I knew. The practical joker, sarcastic guy who didn't take anything too seriously—unless it was trying to one-up his older brother. "Nah, I know when someone isn't for me. Her sister is pretty cute though, I've been told."

I lifted my brows as I slid my thumbs into my pockets. "You live on the edge, my man."

He chuckled. "Sometimes."

"Tab really loves your sculptures though." Saying the words only stung a little. "The one you did outside her place? She adores it."

"Aww, yeah? I'm glad." The flush of pleasure that heated Mav's cheeks with color surprised me and made me wonder if I'd wrongly pegged him as a cocky dick all these years. Could be his bravado covered up the insecurities all artists seemed to have—and there was no doubting he was an artist, just one who worked with fire.

"Yeah. Though a crow or raven was pecking the hell out of your mini ice castle on the corner of Elm. You might have to whip out the old blowtorch again to fix that one or however you do what you do."

He grinned. "I'll take a look. Thanks for the heads up." He cocked his head before extending his fist. "I really am glad you came back to town, man. Maybe I haven't made that clear."

"Maybe you haven't. But maybe I haven't given you much reason to yet either." I blew out a breath and held out my fist, lightly tapping his. "New era for the McNeill badass brothers?"

He laughed, shaking his head. "Mom would certainly be happy. She's been dying to have us both under her roof again for a meal. Honey just thinks we're both morons."

"Well, she's not wrong." I rocked back on my heels. "Speaking of Honey, she hasn't gotten a job yet, has she?"

Mav and Honey were far tighter than I was with my little sister. I wasn't that close with any of my family other than our mother, and I'd realized that when I was in D.C. and felt completely cut off from everyone else. And worse, that it wasn't that different from normal life, because somehow I'd annexed myself from them.

My mom called it lone wolf syndrome. One more reason I wasn't fit to be a family man.

I didn't want to be isolated like that anymore. I also didn't want to live on past memories as excuses of why I didn't try to bridge the gap. Mav seemed like he could extend an olive branch, so I could too.

"Nope, and she's freaking out. She needs something with more hours soon. She has the learning center gig and loves her kids, but anytime she's home, Mom has her cleaning literally everything. She's chomping at the bit to get a place of her own. Truthfully, I don't know how she lasted this long living there, but she was at loose ends for a while."

"Yeah. I get how that is. I'll call her on my break. Tab needs someone in the bakery, so I'm hoping they could be a fit."

"That'd be nice and cozy, wouldn't it?"

"We're new," I reminded him. "Not a relationship. Just friends."

His lips curled. "With a bit more on top. Gotcha."

"But even if there wasn't, I want to help her out. She's really trying to make her business a success and with the Valentine Fest, she has more work than she has hands. And if Honey needs work too—"

"Yeah. I hope it works out for both their sakes. Honey's a hard worker. And she hasn't killed Mom yet, so she's patient too."

"Has to be if she wants to be a teacher. She's so good with the kids at the learning center."

"She told me you are too. Asked if I wanted to pick up some hours volunteering." He didn't shudder, but it was a close thing. "I told her I didn't want to get in your space everywhere."

I grinned. "Right. I bet that's exactly why you aren't chomping at the bit."

He straightened his shoulders. "I'm not afraid of a bunch of five and six-year-olds."

"Sure. I believe you. We play basketball a couple hours a week. Trust me, it's more fun than work. Some of the kids don't have dads, so now and then, I fill in if one of them has a school event. They really appreciate it."

It also made me feel like a chump talking about it, so that was enough of that.

"Wow, you really have changed." He tucked his fists under his arms. "Am I even still talking to Brady 'I never need a wingman' McNeill?"

I rolled my eyes. "Rumors of my prowess are greatly exaggerated."

"Since when?"

I rolled on without elaborating. Last thing I was going to share with my younger brother was my recent crisis of confidence when it came to the dating scene. "Listen, the chief has his heart set on reaming me for not calling in for backup, so I'm not going to deny him that joy. But maybe we can catch dinner later? Depending on when you can take a meal." The pure shock on my brother's face—so like my own, other than his current lack of winter scruff—told me I was right in doing this. Overdue, actually. "Your choice. Just no damn sushi."

He laughed. "You have a deal, brother." He stepped forward and dragged me into a one-armed hug, clapping my back hard enough to dislodge something. "I've missed you."

The sudden rock in my throat made me swallow hard. "Me too." I motioned for him to head out ahead of me.

But as soon as we stepped out, voices from the lobby carried to us. We exchanged a glance. I recognized those voices.

And I had a feeling my craptastic day wasn't over yet.

"Listen, dickless, I can't possibly park in the wrong spot every day. It's not physically possible. Besides, if there's space to park, why can't I park there?"

I shook my head. "Still think Van is cute?"

Mav jerked a shoulder. "Cute and crazy often goes together. Why men drink."

The low modulated tones of Christian rumbled out for approximately thirty seconds before Van started yelling again. "I have a job to do. I know you do too and that it's mid-month so you're probably in the ticket quota bonus round, but guess what? My job actually helps people. I put smiles on people's faces. I don't give them a bad day and make them cry when I show up."

She didn't sound as if she was on the verge of tears. More like Christian might need to get a restraining order against her if he didn't rip up those tickets he'd given her.

And really, multiple tickets? How much of a parking scofflaw could she be? Also, would her negative association with the police influence her hot as heck sister to reconsider future sex with me? If that was a possibility, it was in my best interest—I mean, in the community's best interest—to make sure that no one went away mad.

Or possibly violent.

"You think we should intervene?" Mav wondered.

"Considering tossing Christian to the wolves?"

"Hey, I know to avoid angry women, not run toward them with admonitions to calm down."

I held up a hand. "Watch and learn, son." I strode into the lobby and took a moment to enjoy the view of pint-sized Vanessa leaning over Christian's desk. Though I did not check out her rack, it wasn't hard to notice that Christian was almost nestled there.

That was probably why he seemed remarkably calm. He probably wasn't even listening to her rant. If she was built anything like Tab, I couldn't say I blamed him.

Okay, diverting away from that topic.

"Is there something we can help with?" I asked in my most even tone.

Van spun around, dislodging a chunk of her hair from its updo. "You," she said, pointing.

I cocked a brow. "Me?"

"Yes, you. Did you properly relocate that duck before you ran off after doing a piss poor job of crowd control? No, you did not. So, my legal parking space was taken by that duck and his girlfriend or his duckie ho or whatever, so I made do by—"

"Duckie ho?" Mav repeated under his breath. "I didn't know ducks had laws of fidelity."

I ignored him. "The duck was not visible any longer when I left. I was summoned by my commanding officer and had to respond."

"You made do by parking your traveling eyesore in a space clearly marked for no parking." Christian's voice was level. "You blocked a business's driveway, thereby creating a traffic jam and causing irate customers who couldn't patronize that business."

"Oh, I'm so sorry. I was doing a rush job, picking up an order of tea cakes for the Chamber of Commerce."

"Tea cakes?"

She turned her glare on Mav as I inwardly winced. "You know, Lea and Tiffany said I should've called you to come handle the duck instead of your brother, who seems more focused on my sister's tits than on doing his job. They're a nice pair, granted. But the brother doesn't fall too far from the broken tree, if you ask me." She whirled back on Christian and slammed a literal sheaf of papers on his blotter. "I demand you burn these up. Or vacate them. Or something, because I'm just trying to make people happy, dammit, and you are a royal pain in the ass."

Christian rose to his feet and picked up the pile of tickets. For an instant, I thought he would bow to crazy redhead pressure and rip them up. But I should've known better. This was Christian Masterson we were talking about. He would not succumb in the face of female fury.

Even if she was extremely hot.

"Think of it this way. Fees from tickets help support the police department and to provide vital infrastructure for the Cove. I'm sure the sister of a business owner in the Cove would be happy to contribute. And if you're not?" He slapped the pile of tickets against the palm of his other hand, his smile grim. "Stop parking in illegal spots, Miss Monaghan."

Van sputtered, fisting her small hands at her side. I braced, prepared to dodge forward to restrain her if she decided to bodily attack Christian.

But she did not. She didn't even yell. She just gave him an enthusiastic middle finger and turned on her heel to slam her way out of the police department just as Jared was strolling back in with his arms full of his baby girl, Samantha.

"What was that about?" he demanded, staring after Van while his daughter occupied herself with the zipper on his vest. She was firmly in toddlerhood, with all the sass that came with it.

All three of us remained silent.

The chief cocked a brow. "Is that how it is?"

"Miss Monaghan has an issue with her van being ticketed for improper parking. She has collected numerous unpaid tickets and figured she could get me to revoke them with brute force."

"She's barely five feet tall." Jared set down Samantha, who immediately charged across the lobby straight to my brother.

She grabbed him around the lower legs and looked up at him, her tiny brown ponytail bobbing precariously. "Pretty," she decided, making me snort.

And I snorted even harder when I glimpsed Mav's tormented expression.

"She doesn't bite," Jared informed him.

Mav didn't move. I wasn't sure he was even breathing. Was child-induced shock a thing? If not, it should be in the Cove.

Christian wasn't moved by my brother's plight. He spoke to Jared as if Mav and Sami weren't even in the room. "Miss Monaghan is small, but she's scrappy. I was prepared to give her a citation if necessary. Female or not, we can't tolerate abuse."

I snorted again. "Okay, she was pissed, yes, but abuse? How long has it been since you've dated, man? What she just did was basically a bad Saturday night."

The chief shook his head and went to scoop up Samantha, notching her on his hip. "Sami, this is Maverick. Maverick, this is Sami."

She tried to sound out the name then mumbled something and shoved her gummy fist at him. The fist that had just been in her mouth.

My brother was a fierce defender if someone was in trouble. I'd have no hesitation putting my back to his in a dangerous situation. But he also was fastidious enough that I could not see him enjoying taking the spit-covered hand of a baby. In the old days, he'd even carried a comb in his pocket. Hell, he probably still did.

But he gripped her tiny fist and only grimaced slightly. "Aren't you pretty, Sami?"

"Not as pretty as you apparently," I said out of the corner of my mouth, following it up with a cough.

Sami made grabby hands toward Mav, and her father tried to dissuade her. But must be Mav was trying to impress his new boss, because he picked up Sami with only a modicum of bobbling before he settled her on his hip as Jared had done. "There's a girl. You're a sturdy little thing, aren't you?"

"Even I know not to say that to a woman," Christian said stiffly, narrowing his eyes at me. "By the way, Brady, you may think the rules are for bending, and that certain people shouldn't be subject to them, but I do not. The law is the law. If you break it, you do the punishment. Period."

"I agree, but not everything is black and white. There are shades of gray, even in law enforcement."

"Is that why you didn't see fit to call for backup in a crowd control situation, McNeill?" Jared's brows rose. "Those shades of gray aren't for you to discern. Let me handle those if necessary. Mrs. Gunderson is squawking about going to the paper because you didn't take the situation seriously enough to call it in. Her cupcakes got trampled by the duck as a result."

I laughed. I simply couldn't help it. "Are you serious right now?"

Jared's expression proved without a doubt that he was.

"My mistake." I sighed and held up a hand. "I apologize. Next time, I'll be sure to request backup whether the foe is human or fowl. Or cupcakes that won't stay in their box."

"Uh, Chief? I think your girl needs a change." Mav's face was tinged the slightest shade of green as he shifted Sami on his hip.

This time, even Christian laughed.

ELEVEN

Tabitha

EVIDENTLY, WORK 'TIL I DROP WAS MY NEW MOTTO.

I'd been working like a fiend all week, putting in late nights and even earlier mornings than usual. Orders were coming in fast and furious, and Tiffany, Lea, and even my sister—who normally just helped with deliveries and some counter work—were stressed to the max. Van had put in more than a full-time schedule this week, and even so, we still needed more help or else I would have to start turning down orders.

An idea that made my businesswoman's heart shriek.

Enter Honey McNeill, whom I would be interviewing before I hurried home to get dressed for the dance.

If not for Honey's older brother, I wouldn't have been able to work all those hours without offloading Pancake on my parents. He'd been there just as promised to care for Pancake, and we'd resorted to quick texts to coordinate schedules. A huge sack of toys, puppy food, and even a plush green dog bed had been waiting for me on my doormat a few nights ago, with a note that he missed me and was looking forward to our date.

I may or may not have clutched that note to my chest like a high school girl.

I felt guilty he'd gotten saddled with my puppy, though he couldn't have been more understanding about the whole thing. At least Pancake and Daisy were tight already. I was so relieved about that, but somehow it also made me sad, as if they were becoming a family unit and there would be no place for me with the puppy.

Maybe he was meant to be Brady's, after all.

And maybe Brady and I would just be friends in the end. He certainly hadn't said anything flirty since the back room the other day. He hadn't even sent a sexy text. He claimed to miss me, but when I stopped in to check on my puppy late at night, he hadn't even tried to kiss me.

Then again, I'd barely been coherent enough to talk, never mind make out with my hot cop.

Okay, he wasn't my hot cop. Even if I couldn't stop thinking about getting him naked again. Or him getting me naked and taking control, as he'd done last time. I'd really liked how he'd taken charge and pushed me outside of my comfort zone.

Maybe tonight, we'd test that comfort zone yet again. Depending on how the evening went. I hadn't been on a real old-fashioned date since...

God, I didn't even remember.

On top of that, we were going to have this date in front of half the town, which meant reinvigorating the gossip machine. Not that it had stopped since earlier in the week. Within a few days, the tenor had changed, however. By yesterday, the kind of talk that had reached by ears had been of the 'oh, poor girl, he's probably already moved on' variety.

I wished I could say I hadn't had thoughts like that too. It was hard not to when work took up all of my life and I'd heard so often how Brady had the attention span of a horny gnat.

But I wasn't going to borrow trouble. This whole thing between us was supposed to be fun. No strings or stress. So far, everything was going just fine.

Now I just had to hope his sister would work out as my new employee.

Somehow we'd finished all the flower cupcakes for the display at the dance tonight. Having them available on a complimentary basis for tonight's dancers would most likely increase my orders two-fold. I hoped Honey was prepared to hit the ground running.

And if she didn't work out, I hoped I could have sex with her brother once more before he found out I hadn't hired his sister.

Hey, I could be mercenary where amazing orgasms were concerned, especially after the exhausting week I'd had. I wasn't even sure I could summon the energy to ride him like a pony, but I was going to give it my all.

Hello, coffee shots and Skittles. The energy boosters of champions.

The bells over the door jangled. A beautiful brunette dressed in chic leather thigh-high boots my wide calves couldn't even sneeze at stepped inside the bakery. "Hello?"

I moved away from the prep table and came around the counter. "Hi. I'm Tabitha Monaghan. Are you Honey?"

Though I already knew she was. The one thing Brady, Maverick, and Honey had in common was large, long-lashed brown eyes.

And the quick, crooked smile.

"I am." She made fast work of looking me up and down. "You're hot."

I glanced down at myself. My apron was half untied and splattered with flour, egg batter, and an unknown substance that might've been frosting or fondant. I probably should've cleaned up before this interview, but it was just as well Honey understood fashionable boots were better off not worn to work here. "Excuse me?"

"Sorry, is that not professional talk? But you are, you know."

Was there just something about me that appealed to the McNeill family? I didn't have this effect on most people, especially when I looked like a hot mess at the end of a long workday.

Heck, a long work week. The longest, busiest ever.

"Um, thanks?"

She laughed and hitched her enormous bag higher on her shoulder. Also leather, but the color of red wine. "I'm not hitting on you, don't worry. Strictly dickly here. Besides, my brother would bite me if I so much as looked at you sideways."

"He would?" I cleared my throat and attempted to look virginal—or at least professional. "What do you mean?"

She laughed and shook her head. "Your secret's safe with me."

"What secret?" That I have the serious hots for your brother and pretty much think of him all day and night, even though I promised myself I wouldn't?

"You know. I mean, it's not really a secret. Everyone in town was talking about it this week." She narrowed her eyes as she studied the café tables in front of the windows. "Are those really sturdy enough for that?"

I rubbed the sudden pounding in my temple. I really needed to lay off the coffee shots. "They work just fine for a snack or a light lunch—" As she started to laugh, I frowned. "What's so funny?"

"You haven't heard what they're saying about you and Brady?"

"I've heard some but what?"

"That he nailed you on one of those tables. By the way, this ranks up there as the weirdest job interview I've ever been on. If I wasn't so utterly desperate for a job and if this wasn't the cutest bakery I've ever seen, I totally would've told him forget it. My boss shagging my brother is not a recipe for a good work environment."

"We didn't shag here." My face was so hot I was on the verge of getting a cold washcloth. "Really? They're saying that? Then again, why am I surprised?" I turned around and cupped my face in my hands just for a moment to get my bearings. The backs of my eyes were burning to match my cheeks, and I wasn't sure if it was from exhaustion or humiliation. Or both.

Some kind of professional businesswoman I was, after all, huh?

I took a deep breath and waited until I was sure my voice would be steady. "I'm sorry. We don't have to go through with this interview. I apologize for Brady putting you in an awkward position. I should've thought this through more thoroughly."

She touched my shoulder and I startled, whirling to face her. And was shocked right down to the ground as she drew me in for a hug.

"Hey, you don't have to apologize for anything. I'm the one who should be apologizing. I practically sounded like I was hitting on you. More like I was just applauding my older bro's good taste for once. It hasn't always been the case." She eased back and wrinkled her nose. "Let's pretend I didn't say that. Anyway, I have experience with dough."

I laughed weakly and rubbed under my eyes. "I know his reputation."

"So do I, and you're giving it a serious upgrade. Baker hottie. So, you know, maybe give him another chance if he screws this up. Consider it a favor to his glorious baby sister." She smiled and set her hands on my shoulders. Since she was a good half a foot taller than I was, I had to crane my neck a little to look up at her. "When do you want me to start?"

I laughed again. "Yeah, I see the McNeill resemblance. But I'm desperate for help and I've been leaning into my instincts this week, so let's just give it a go and see where we end up. We should discuss hours and pay scale."

She didn't appear to be listening, since she'd pulled out her cell phone from her suitcase-sized bag. "Mick? You busy? No? Okay, get your behind down to Sugar Rush on Main in the Cove. Hurry. Bye, bish." She clicked off and threw her phone back in her bag. "I just scored you more help. She's on her way."

I swallowed. Swallowed again when little dots swarmed at the edges of my vision. Exhaustion had just encountered mild panic and extreme overwhelm. Either that or a sugar crash was imminent, thanks to my Skittles and coffee shot overload.

"She's a college student, graduating in May with a degree in business. I think. She changed majors a couple of times, but she's super smart." Honey smiled. "But her course-load this semester is light because she doubled and tripled up for the last couple of years. So she'll work her butt off for you, just as I will. Especially if it will get me out of my mother's house." She shuddered. "If I have to polish that mantel one more time…"

The door blasted open with a flurry of bells. "I'm here. Now what?" A curvy brunette with gold streaks in her hair and an Army-style jacket heavily dusted with snow came to a halt just inside the door. "I'm Michaela," she added when no one spoke. "I guess there's a job? Sign me up. Wicked cute place."

The tension in my shoulders just melted away. It shouldn't have. I didn't know these girls. Honey being Brady's sister didn't mean much. Besides, I barely knew Brady. But something about Honey put me at ease. And if I was trusting my instincts about Brady, well, I might as well do that here too.

What choice did I have? I needed these girls. Maybe they needed me too.

And hey, if it didn't work out, I wouldn't be any further behind than I was before Honey McNeill walked through my door.

I smiled brightly. "Hi Michaela, I'm Tabitha Monaghan." I stepped forward and held out a hand. "Your new boss."

Forty-five minutes later, I'd set up a tentative schedule for the girls and they had filled out all preliminary paperwork. Both were coming in bright and early tomorrow and Van had promised to help train them on the basics to get them up and running as fast as possible.

I was jumping in with both feet, operating on gut instinct. Maybe I was making a wrong decision, but at least I was chasing my dreams. It might not be smart to hire two unproven women with no baking experience, or it could end up being the best move ever.

The same with getting to know Brady.

He texted as I was digging through the bottom of my closet, trying to find my favorite sweater dress. I'd put it aside earlier in the week for the dance but now I couldn't find it. And I couldn't even blame a thieving puppy, because Pancake had spent the bulk of the week with Brady.

Brady: If this is the first time I'm being stood up, at least it's by the hottest woman I've ever known.

I frowned and looked at the time. Dammit, I was officially late. I'd told Brady I'd meet him at the Town Hall at nine and it was almost nine-twenty.

Then I smiled.

Tabitha: Really?

Brady: Is it really the first time I've been stood up? Yes. Are you really that hot? Also yes.

Tabitha: You're too charming. I'm so sorry. I'm coming, I swear.

Brady: Starting without me? I see how it is.

I let out a giggle and sank to the floor of my closet to sit amidst the piles of my clothes. I seriously needed to shovel it out when I got some time. Probably not anytime soon.

Tabitha: Maybe we could skip the whole dance thing? I want to spend time with you but I'm sitting in my closet in my underwear right now. Tho guess what? I hired your sis & her bestie.

Brady: Mickey too? Wow. That's awesome tho I'm stuck on you in your undies. But I want credit for wearing a snuggy to the dance. And actually talking to people in it. Tbh, Pancake is far more popular than I am.

I grinned as I leaned back against the wall. Just imagining sexy Brady toting around my puppy in a snuggy had my ovaries doing a happy dance.

Tabitha: Did you happen to see my cupcake display there?

Brady: Oh, babe, everyone has. It's an enormous setup, right near the door. Every time I hear a moan, I expect to have to bust someone for

lewd behavior, but nope, someone else is trying one of my girl's flowers.

Warmth spread through me at his text. Almost immediately, my brain threw up a protest.

Hello, casual hookup?

He shouldn't be thinking of you as his girl.

You shouldn't be liking that he is either.

Or wanting to be his girl.

I blew out a sigh and kicked aside a pair of heels. I was officially a hot mess, and so was my closet.

I glanced around. And my whole bedroom. I needed to get a maid. Or hire a demolition crew and start over.

Brady: do you want to go out or stay in? I'm cool with whatever. Or if you just want to get some sleep, that's fine too. I'll grab some takeout bc you probably haven't eaten and we'll Netflix and chill w the dogs.

I blinked, trying valiantly not to cry. Which was not like me at all. I was chalking it up to extreme exhaustion after the past week. As nice as he was being, it wasn't worthy of tears. I wasn't that sappy normally.

Tabitha: Really? Thanks for being so cool. I could go for some shrimp lo mein if you're good with Chinese.

Brady: Oh yeah, I'm always down with Chinese. I'll be there in a bit. Don't get dressed on my account.

I laughed and dragged myself up to put on a pair of sleep pants and a sweatshirt. I didn't know if we'd be hanging out here or at his place, but after our first night together, I felt surprisingly comfortable with him. I probably should be freaking out and primping too much and making sure my damp hair wasn't a mess, not just piling it on top of my head and skipping makeup other than lip gloss.

But I didn't. I just cleaned off my coffee table of the assorted junk that had accumulated during the busy work week and unlocked the door to sit back to wait.

A soft knock on the door almost an hour later had me stumbling to my feet. The doorknob turned as I was crossing the room, and Brady poked his head in, his brown hair dusted with snow. As advertised, my puppy was in a snuggy strapped to his chest—and said chest was clad in a freaking tux.

Suddenly, I really wished I'd skipped looking for my sweater dress and gone to that dance.

"Why was your door unlocked?"

I frowned. "Huh?"

He came inside before very firmly closing and locking the door at his back. "You shouldn't leave the door unlocked, even in the Cove."

My hackles rose at his tone, but I made myself clamp down on my tongue. "You sound very much like a cop right now."

"I am a cop. But even if I wasn't, you shouldn't take chances."

"I knew you were coming soon. I was afraid I might doze off—"

Pancake's sharp bark made me fall silent. I didn't like feeling chastised.

Worse, I didn't like thinking he was right.

"You can't risk leaving the door unlocked. A woman alone can't take those kind of chances. You never know who could be lurking outside." He moved toward the kitchen, setting the bags of Chinese on the counter before he unstrapped my dog and let him free.

Pancake bounded toward me and stood on his hind legs for me to pick him up. I lifted him high and he covered my face with his kisses, making me laugh.

Until I noticed the tension on Brady's face as he unpacked our food and searched for plates.

"Second cabinet on the left." I shifted Pancake in my arms and walked into my galley-style kitchen. "Brady, what's wrong?"

His jaw could've cut granite. "I told you. I just want you to be safe."

"Which I appreciate, but c'mon, you can't be mad over that. It probably wasn't a great move, but nothing ever happens in the Cove—"

"Someone set a fire outside the Town Hall tonight." He banged down a carton of fried rice. "My buddy Austin from the fire department happened to catch it as he was coming in. Luckily, they got it under control quickly."

"A fire at the Town Hall? Who was it? Kids?"

"No. It was Misty Coy, and she set a couple of bushes on fire out front while she was trying to blowtorch the word PIG into the grass."

A laugh bubbled out of me before I quickly controlled it at his flat stare. "Blowtorch?"

"She must've gotten the idea at the ice sculpture demo. Thanks, brother." He blew out a breath and turned to rifle through my drawers until he located my silverware.

"Do you know Misty?" I asked carefully, following a hunch.

His silence told me all I needed to know.

"Jared said he'd ticket her for the infraction, but it'll be a slap on the wrist at the best. There was little real damage. I just don't want you to take chances while she's acting crazy."

"Did you date her?" Is she unstable because you dumped her?

Not that someone dumping you was any reason to do something like that. But I could see a man like Brady being hard to get over.

"Once," he bit off, jamming his fork into the lo mein and taking a bite before dumping it on a plate and shoving the plate into the microwave. He jammed buttons and then stepped back, offhandedly offering a shrimp at a now whimpering Pancake.

"And," I prompted.

"It was six months ago. We went bowling and we had sex. And that was it. She called a couple times—okay, more than a couple—but I was working a lot and our schedules never meshed. For months, there was nothing from her. Then all of a sudden, after the rumors started up about us, she's back. I don't get it." He glanced at me. "Do you know her?"

I shook my head. "I don't get out much, so if someone doesn't live in this building or come to the bakery, I probably don't know them. I try to get to as many community events as I can, but there just aren't enough hours in the day, you know?"

"Yeah, I know." He heaved out a breath as the microwave dinged, but he stepped forward to rub Pancake's head as his gaze searched my face. "I'm sorry I snapped at you when I came in here. I just—after this and the stuff going around, I don't know what Misty could do. I want you to be safe."

"I'm very safe." I leaned up to kiss him softly while Pancake wriggled to get in on the action. "I have a hot cop to protect me, remember?" My attempt to make my tone teasing clearly fell flat.

His jaw locked. "Maybe I should have a talk with her. This is crazy." He braced his hands on the counter behind him. "What am I supposed to do? Never date anyone in the Cove?"

"We aren't even dating. Just having sex."

His lips twisted wryly. "Not sure saying that would help."

"No, but maybe a frank, honest conversation would."

I couldn't believe I was being this mature. The old insecure Tabitha wouldn't feel comfortable sending him off to talk to an ex, but maybe I'd changed. Or maybe the fact Misty seemed inappropriately attached to him took away any possible jealousy.

In any case, all I wanted was for Misty to move past this without any more property getting damaged. For her sake too. We'd all had rough breakups, and the actual circumstances of the situation didn't necessarily dictate the extent of our response. I didn't want to condemn her if there was still a way to deescalate the situation.

"Yeah. Maybe."

"I'm sure you're not in a hurry to talk to her."

"No, not really. But I will. I already have to give a statement to the chief about my previous relationship with her. Because that won't be awkward."

"Ouch."

"Tell me about it." He turned to take the plate out of the microwave and grabbed his fork to sample it before lifting a forkful over

Pancake's head to my mouth. "Good?" he asked as I let out a moan at the same moment my stomach growled.

Still chewing, I nodded and then swallowed. I gave him a sheepish smile. "I forgot to eat dinner."

"I figured. Let me feed you then." He scooped up another forkful and was on his way to delivering it to my mouth when Pancake decided he'd had enough of being a spectator and leaned up to snatch the noodles off the fork.

Brady and I exchanged shocked looks while Pancake noisily chewed his bounty. Then I laughed and he laughed and the tension between us finally broke.

I set my hungry puppy down on the floor with a bowl of his kibble as Brady set down his plate. "Who knew being a parent was this complicated?"

With a grin, I leaned against him and he looped his arms around my waist. "Good question. Seems like everything is really complicated these days. Even casual sex."

He spun me around in his arms and pressed a kiss to the back of my neck just as he had when he'd dropped me off at the bakery earlier in the week, making me melt all over again. "Complicated or not, it's so fucking worth it."

TWELVE

 **BRADY**

OUR DATE CONSISTED OF STARTING TO BINGE A COP DRAMA ON NETFLIX —though I had to say I was rather sick of cop dramas at the moment —and going to bed together full of Chinese in my apartment before midnight.

To sleep. With two dogs, one big and one small, between us.

We'd moved to my apartment since I had the bigger bed. She'd also been a little embarrassed at the current state of her bedroom, which was kind of a disaster zone with clothes and girl crap all over. But she'd barely been home this week, so I understood.

It should've been beyond strange to just get ready for bed and curl up like we'd known each other for months instead of days, prior brief interactions aside. Instead, it felt natural and right to laugh and talk as we cuddled up with our pups. The only parts of us touching under the covers were our bare feet. Hers were cold, so she tucked her toes under my silky pajama pants.

She set her alarm for five am—her version of going in late—and within minutes, I was on my way to unconscious, her soothing lavender scent drifting over me. It must be hand lotion or something.

Did it make me a weirdo I wanted to carry a tube of it around with me so I could sniff it anytime I wanted?

Probably.

That scent was probably a good part of the reason I had the most erotic dream of my life. It involved Tab wearing an apron and me binding her hands with the ties—and her begging me to take her hard.

I woke stiff and aching and breathing fast.

It took me a moment to orient myself. The bedroom was mostly dark, the only light coming from the nightlight we'd left on in the hall for the pups. The pups were gone, and so was Tabitha, though another sliver of light was visible under the closed en suite bathroom door. The soft sound of humming from the bathroom had me hissing out an oath and shoving down my pajama pants to grip my throbbing dick.

So, naturally, that was when she chose to walk into the bedroom, the wide swath of light beaming out behind her letting her see exactly what I was up to.

Let's just say I was reaching new heights—or lengths.

"You're up," she said throatily, immediately dissolving into husky laughter.

I tucked myself away as best I could and rolled out of bed and padded over to her. Her hair was damp and curling riotously and droplets of water clung to her cheeks and neck. I cupped the back of her neck as I lowered my mouth, kissing away the water as I explored her skin down to her shoulder. She rose up on her tiptoes, letting out a soft moan as she scooped me out of my pajama pants. "Can't let all this go to waste."

"Absolutely not." I drew her with me as I backed up to the bed, dropping down on the edge. After a quick yank of her sweats, I pulled her on top of me. She sank down on my erection with a sound of pure feminine pleasure, greeting me with wet warmth that slicked me from root to tip in one slow glide.

I shoved my hands under her sweatshirt, driving it up over her head. She lifted her arms to make it easier, squeezing her thighs and her pussy to grip me tight while we fumbled the material out of my way. I palmed her generous breasts, offering up a prayer to the deities who had blessed me with this offering.

She grinned and captured my lower lip between her teeth as she rocked into me so good, better than even my dream. "Same goes, Hot Cop." She drew back to take a breath, staring down between us to where she was rising and lowering to envelop my shaft, over and over again. So fucking hot. "I could get used to this morning delight."

"Me too, Strawberry. Me too." I reached back to squeeze her full ass, unable to stifle the urge to give her a quick smack. She stopped moving. For an instant, I cursed the impulse, until she dropped back her head, trailing her long curls behind her, tickling my thighs as she panted a single word.

"Again."

I timed it so I surged up into her at the same time as I swatted her behind. She fisted me so sweetly, giving me no warning as she drenched me in her orgasm. I didn't think she'd had a warning either, because she rode me through it, bucking wildly, her eyes shattered and glazed as if she didn't know what the hell was happening.

I wasn't sure either.

I gripped the back of her neck again, bringing her face close to mine, so close I could practically taste the sweat beading on her skin from our frantic pace. I wasn't done yet and neither was she. She tried to shut her eyes and lock me out, but my rough grip told her what I wanted.

What I needed.

"Look at me, baby. Right at me. I want you to remember who's fucking you."

"As if I could forget." Uneven breaths punctuated her words as she clamped her hand on my shoulder for leverage to rise up and down. Every movement trailed her hot wetness over me, and I knew I wouldn't last long. She was so damn tight. I could feel her building to another orgasm already.

I was nearly delirious with the need to go off inside her. To have it coat her thighs just like she was soaking me. Primitive instincts like I'd never known before were roaring to life inside me.

To take. To brand. To own her.

I tested my luck and spanked her firm ass again, even harder than before. She gasped and scored her nails into my skin, marking me too. "You're going to make me come again."

"Good. I want it all over me." I tipped back her head and dragged my mouth down her throat, leaving hot open-mouthed kisses in my wake. "And when I take a shower, I'll take you against the tiles while I'm at it."

"God, Brady, what are you doing to me?"

I filled my hands with her tits, kissing and sucking them like a man possessed. I felt full to bursting and if she flexed around me once more, I wouldn't be able to hold back. "Making you mine," I growled.

She clutched my head to her breasts as she went over one more time, shuddering and grasping me so viciously that I couldn't resist a second longer. She kept right on coming as I joined her, shaking in her arms like a damn addict.

This was what she'd reduced me to. A man who couldn't even take a breath without wanting to be inside her.

As the pleasure ebbed, I threw myself backward on the bed, arms wide.

She giggled at my dramatic display and climbed up my body, dangling the forbidden fruit I'd love to keep in my mouth for the rest of my life. Her nipples were hard and damp and ruby-red from my sucking.

My cock jerked. Damn, I'd be ready for her again soon.

"What part of me are you referring to exactly?" she asked playfully, shifting so that she could rub her wetness over my groin.

"Every part of you. I don't have enough hands to touch as much of you as I want. C'mere." I grabbed her hips and hauled her up my body, making her shriek with laughter as I nearly overbalanced her. I pulled her right where I wanted her and covered her pussy with my mouth, making her laughter subside quickly into moans.

"I can't do this again. Oh, God, Brady. You're ruining me."

Distantly, I heard her halfhearted protests but I didn't much care because I had our salty mixed flavors on my tongue and had much better things to do than chat.

She drove her fingers into my hair, slicing her nails against my scalp. The bite of pain had me arching my hips uselessly against the bed…or so I thought until she realized my plight and reached back to slick her wet hand over my stiffening shaft.

"Such an enthusiastic cock you have," she said throatily as I reared back to take a breath, making me laugh as I dove back down.

"Let's see how enthusiastic you are, Strawberry," I murmured against her drenched folds, flicking her clit in a steady rhythm that soon had her squirming over me. She gasped, her fingers restless in my hair, and I reached back to give her ass a little slap just to taste her response.

She didn't disappoint me, rocking against my face without shame while she held me just where she wanted me. She kept on pumping my cock behind her, but her movements were jerky and uncoordinated. I dipped one finger, then two inside her, searching for that spot that would make her detonate.

"Brady," she begged, and I wasn't sure if she was asking for mercy or release.

I sealed my lips over her clit and sucked while my fingers worked her hard, hoping like hell it was enough to nudge her over.

This one took longer than the others. My neck ached and my hand started to cramp as I simply redoubled my efforts. But when she finally got there, she flooded my tongue and quivered against me with such force that she shot me over the edge just from making her come.

She rolled off and slumped at my side, her long golden-red hair fountaining over her face. She was still panting.

I rolled over to part her curls to find her lips, kissing her desperately even as a laugh caught in my throat. "Still alive, baby?"

"No. Better call the cops." She peeked through her wild hair at me, her dazed blue eyes filled with the kind of joy I'd never forget. "But make sure he puts on pants first, because holy shit."

Her foghorn alarm blared and we both startled, bumping heads with a sharp crack. I didn't think about the pain in my chin as I rubbed her head, making sure she was okay.

"I'm fine. Promise." She sighed heavily. "But I really want to sleep, not go to work. Sex sedatives work so well." She turned her head and nipped the inside of my wrist. "Especially yours, stud."

"I wish we could play hooky for a day." I almost didn't recognize my voice. I didn't play hooky ever—and I wouldn't, not with my job. I knew quite well she wouldn't either. "But we can't."

"No." Her smile was sad as she curled her arms around me. "But I really, really want to suck you off. I love your cock."

I groaned weakly. "Five minutes," I promised, causing her to giggle. "Maybe three if you cup those beautiful—"

She placed her finger over my lips. "We can't. But we can have dinner together." She kissed me lightly. "And dessert."

I tightened my hold around her and rolled her under me, well aware we were both a mess and I'd need to change my sheets after this. Not caring. "Deal."

Then I swore under my breath. "Fuck. Not tonight."

I was supposed to have dinner with the chief's family—if he even still wanted me to join them after we talked about the Misty incident. Even if he did, it probably wouldn't be a relaxed evening, especially if I brought Tabitha. The last thing I wanted to do was make her think I was slotting us into a public dating role already. We hadn't agreed to that. But I wanted her with me.

Far too much.

She looked up at me, questions in her beautiful eyes. Questions I didn't have answers for.

"I like how you make me feel." And then since I was me, I reached down to squeeze her glorious ass. How had I lived before I knew what it was like to have a curvy woman in my bed? Particularly this curvy woman. I enjoyed every damn part of her, inside and out. "I also like feeling you. You're a damn goddess, Tabitha Monaghan."

"I think you're a little biased, Brady McNeill." She reached up to feather her fingers through my hair. "I like how you make me feel too." A frown tugged down her lips. "I don't have time for you, Hot Cop. So if you're thinking you don't have time for me—"

Something akin to panic flared in my gut. I knew this wasn't at all what our original night together was supposed to turn into. Forget no feelings, we were supposed to be just a one and done situation.

I absolutely could not be that guy. Not with her. Not this time.

"Make time, Strawberry." I took a deep breath. "How's Thursday for you? I have the night off."

"I can work with Thursday night." She studied me pensively for a moment before she slipped her hand down to pinch my ass. Hard. "How fast can you fuck me in the shower?"

I jumped to my feet just as familiar paws padded up the hall. "Like lightning, babe."

THIRTEEN

I MOVED THROUGH MY DAY LIKE A WELL-SEXED ENERGIZER BUNNY.

Throughout training the new girls, through making two rush birthday cakes with special fondant requests—including one with a miniature firehouse for Adam Parish's birthday, one of Crescent Cove's Bravest—through a minor scuffle over the last eclair and then another dustup with a crying child who accidentally smashed their upside down cake on the floor, I handled everything calmly and quickly. I might've not moved quite as fast as I would have without the thorough fucking in the shower that morning, but what I lost from chafing, I gained from sheer orgasm relief.

They really were more restorative than any night's sleep. I enjoyed self-administered ones like the next gal, but there was definitely something to having them dispensed by one of Crescent Cove's finest.

"You're humming again," Van said crossly as she hung up the phone after yet another rush order.

I pushed a tray of fresh mini lemon and raspberry tartlets onto the top shelf of the display case. Honey and Mickey had been working their buns off all day, and we were killing it on the production side of things. At this rate, we might've even get a little ahead—or at least be less behind. "Sorry?"

"You're so not sorry. You know how I know?" My sister stepped forward and yanked at the collar of my turtleneck, baring my neck as if I'd been feasted on by a vampire. Which I sort of had been, although mine had sucked other parts of me rather than my blood. Thank God. "That's either a hickey or someone missed lunch."

I slapped a hand over my neck and took a quick glance around. Thankfully, the other employees were busy actually, you know, working.

Besides, my extracurricular activities with Brady weren't even the main hot topic today. Nope, that slot belonged to Misty Coy's pig roast on the Town Hall's front lawn last night.

Poor Brady. I mean, after his performance today and earlier in the week, I had to admit I kinda understood how a woman could go off her rocker after having sex with him. Maybe not to that extent, but if you'd gone long enough without and then you did it with Brady... well, sometimes people snapped. If any dick could cause insanity, it would be his.

Mercy, my personal rose garden had never been tended that well.

I pressed my thighs together and narrowed my eyes at my sister. "Will you kindly hush, please?"

Van let go of my collar and frowned. "You wearing a turtleneck was the first clue. You probably have scruff burn in unmentionable places. That you should be mentioning to me, because I'm your twin and I'm horny as hell and maybe your excess hormones will rub off so I can find someone to make me hum in the middle of a hellish workday."

I glanced around again. Sun filtered through the wide windows, bathing the entire shop in a warm glow. "Hellish? We didn't even have a crazy line for most of the day."

"Sundays are meant for recovering from Saturday night. You knew what I was recovering from today? Cramps. I slept with a heating pad on my front, my back, and an ice pack on my head."

I started to laugh before I recalled my own monthly was due in not too long. Suckage.

"Is that why you've been in such a mood?"

Van's growl made me take a definite step back—and I picked up an empty tray to use as either a weapon or in my own defense.

"Some." Deep lines dug into her forehead as she frowned. Even her normally bouncy curls seemed wilted over her bright red headband, used in a futile attempt to hold the riotous ringlets off her face. "But not only that."

"Do you want to talk in back?"

"No. It's not a secret the police is populated with dickless morons."

I coughed delicately. "Don't suppose you could say things like that at a slightly lower volume?"

"Fine. The police department has one dickless moron and one dickful wonder aka the one who's dicking you so well that you were humming." She opened the display case, used a spatula to pry up a raspberry tartlet, popped it in her mouth, and then banged the spatula on the counter before flouncing into the back.

I affixed a bland smile onto my face and called out to Tiffany that I'd be right back before following my sister. Thank God for afternoon lulls. My customers did not need to hear a Vanessa Monaghan-style diatribe, no matter how amusing it might be.

She was sitting at the desk beside mine in the office, the one I'd given her when she'd started helping out here. Currently, it held a metronome and a phone, the former she was using to bang one ball into the next with enough violence to crack them in two.

She probably wished she could crack real balls, and I was very glad I wasn't a male.

I eased a hip on the desk and risked smoothing a hand over her shoulder. "Talk to me."

"He's a prick. A soulless prick. I tried to flirt with him first. Like any reasonable, attractive woman handles a ticket. Flash your cleavage, hint at your availability for a little stop and frisk of the naked variety. Maybe indicate you like handcuffs more than for what he had in mind. You know."

My eyes were officially saucers. "I don't, but I feel like I'm missing out." I rose and went over to my desk to search impatiently through the top drawer.

123

"What are you doing?"

"Looking for a notepad. I obviously need to take notes."

She scowled at me. "You're not funny."

"No, but you are. Did you really proposition an officer of the law?"

"Not to be obtuse, but I'm going to guess you did the same or you wouldn't look as if you were auditioning to be a vampire's sidepiece."

Idly, I rubbed my neck. "I'm not sure who propositioned who. It was probably mutual. But in any case, he wasn't giving me a ticket at the time."

"Multiple tickets. He's given me several recently. I didn't try to proposition him until I came back after delivering the order to the Chamber of Commerce and found him scoping out the love mobile to yet again defile her with a ticket. And I was in there for no more than seven minutes." She held up seven fingers as if she felt the visual would help.

"So, you decided to flash your tits at him and he turned you down?" I frowned. "That's illegal, you know. If all he did was turn you down and not write you an additional citation, he did you a favor."

"Oh, sure, take the dickless cop's side. I'll have you know that my boobs may not be as stupendous as yours, but mine are pretty damn good. And I don't even need to wear a bra sometimes. So whatever." She rested her chin on her palm and sighed. "But I do suppose you have a point. He could've proven his ultimate dickishness by writing me another ticket and he didn't. So, maybe he isn't truly Satan. Though I did not flash him my breasts, as we were on a public street. Besides, Christian may be objectively attractive, but I have some standards who gets to motorboat these babies." She adjusted her cleavage with a sniff.

"If he'd taken you up on that offer, I'm not even sure you two could actually have sex." I pursed my lips. "Isn't he like 6'3? You're over a foot shorter than him. I can't picture it working." I held up a hand. "Not that I want to."

"Ugh. Well, don't worry, because he's not getting a shot at any of this," she gestured to herself, "unless he bribes me. Heavily."

I laughed and tried to discreetly check my watch but my sister caught me as always. "Fine, fine, let's get back out there. Since you're all focused and shit due to unfairly good sex, might as well keep going until we're finally caught up."

"The late afternoon rush should start anytime." I yawned hugely. "Though I gotta say, I would love a nap. Just 20 minutes would put me back to rights."

"Better yet, why don't you ask Officer Orgasm to come over for another injection?"

"You're terrible."

"Well, if Christian is dickless, Brady must be the opposite. Maverick is the unknown quantity right now. Maybe you should test out both brothers and let us know what's what there."

Shaking my head, I gave her a light shove as she stood up. "Maybe you should stop focusing on being pissed at Christian and maybe consider meeting someone new."

"You aren't seriously suggesting we do a seven brides for seven brothers deal and date brothers? Not that you're dating Brady just getting your back worked by him—" She laughed and ducked back before I could shove her once more.

"I'll have you know we ate Chinese and watched Netflix last night." I didn't mention this morning's activities. "He gives good snuggle too."

"Sure, sure, rub it in. Here I thought after Misty's pig torching at the Town Hall, he'd run the other way from anything approaching an actual relationship."

"Please stop tossing that *relationship* word around."

She rolled her eyes. "Sorry, forgot you're phobic."

"Just don't want to ruin a good thing with a heavy label. Or to get clingy." I let out a long breath. "We both have a lot going on, so I'm just going to enjoy it for however long it lasts."

"Afraid you'll turn into a Brady bat junkie like ol' Misty? Maybe you could sneak a pic for me? I gotta see what this dude is working with to make women all mental. And Misty is cute too. Not the usual sort who you'd think would have to beg for it."

"No pictures. You're twisted, Van."

"Okay, how about you draw it for me—" She giggled as I flashed her the middle finger. "I'm happy for you, little sis. Really. I might also be slightly jealous considering I've been solo for what feels like a millennium but still happy. And you're even successfully parenting together."

"It's been a week," I said drily as I snagged a bottle of water before we headed back down the hall to the front of the bakery. "Still early innings. I'm sure he'll get sick of dealing with puppy shenanigans soon. He's got a busy life too."

"So, you're telling me you're not seeing him tonight?"

"No. Daisy and Pancake are at his place today because he said he'd be home for most of the afternoon. He just had a work thing to handle and then..." I rubbed my neck again as I remembered how quickly he'd shot me down about dinner this evening.

Other than both of us saying we were clean sexually, it wasn't as if we'd had any kind of exclusivity conversation. How could we, when we were just hooking up for fun? Not that you couldn't hook up for fun with just one other person, but maybe that wasn't his style.

Could be Misty was one of many that would be coming out of the woodwork. I knew the rumor mill couldn't necessarily be trusted, but there were a lot about Brady's fickle ways. I didn't choose to believe them, but still, I couldn't help wondering.

And thoughts like that did neither of us any good. I'd just ask him straight out. Let him know that casual was fine with me—even preferred—but that we had to be exclusive or else there was no way in hell I'd be skipping condoms with him or even touching him that way.

Why the hell hadn't I made that clearer the very first night?

Maybe his baton was magic. I couldn't understand why else I'd sailed right beyond so many of my usual protective boundaries otherwise.

"And then...?" Van prompted over her shoulder as she rushed toward the ringing phone.

Mickey got there first, answering in a smooth professional way that caused me to send up a silent prayer of thanks. Honey was doing some of our advance Monday morning prep baking in back, putting us in better position for the new week.

Brady had brought Honey and Mickey into my life, and for that alone, I owed him big time. Never mind the help with my puppy and all the restorative sexual healing.

And the friendship. I really liked having him as a friend too.

Before I could reply, Sage Hamilton strolled in with her adorable daughter Star, who just happened to be walking a very familiar puppy. Pancake pranced ahead of her on the leash as I grinned and came around the counter, only noticing his floppy blue bow tie and the note attached to it when I bent to scoop him up.

"There's mama's boy. Look at my big boy, all dressed up in his Sunday best."

Pancake barked and licked my chin and cheeks.

"He's a cutie." Sage laughed and stroked her hand down Star's silky ponytail. "Go on and pick a sweet, honey. I have to talk to Tabitha for just a second."

Star ran off to talk excitedly to Van, who crouched at her side to point out different desserts in the case. But Star wouldn't be deterred from the flower cupcakes that had been such a hit at the dance I'd missed last night that I'd taken half a dozen orders for them before lunch.

Go me.

"How are you doing?" I asked Sage, shifting toward her with a still excitable Pancake in my arms. "Feeling better?"

"Oh, I'm fine." She waved off my concern, her perfectly glossy blond waves bouncing around her shoulders. "First trimester is always the suck. I'd forgotten to have my crackers and tummy tea and that made it all worse."

I smiled and tried not to gawk at her softly rounded stomach in her clingy top. "When are you due?"

"August. So by the time he or she is ready to come out, I'll be sweaty and miserable. But we tried really hard for this one, so I'm making a baby book and documenting all the milestones." She cupped the slight swell and smiled fondly. "Both good and bad. Including puking in planters. Oliver asked if I could be more discreet next time."

She rolled her eyes. "I said sure, pal, next time I'll just throw up on your fancy shoes."

I had to laugh. Her husband was a decent guy, well-respected in town as part of the illustrious Hamilton real estate family. But he could be a little uptight and I couldn't really imagine how he dealt with animal cracker crumbs on his high-end suits, never mind anything else. Though I'd seen him doting on his baby girl, so obviously, he made do.

Love changed people. I'd seen evidence of that all over this town. It was one of the things I appreciated most about living and working here.

"If you're wondering how we ended up with Brady's dog—and yours, apparently," Sage gestured at me cuddling with Pancake, "we were out for a walk and he was walking his dogs and asked if we could drop off a message to you via pup. Star, of course, was too eager." She shook her head at her daughter, who was currently wheedling a cupcake out of my long-suffering twin. "If her father hasn't adopted a puppy for her by the spring, I'll be shocked. Maybe two. I've heard two is easier than one."

"Maybe you'll have a duo of babies." I nodded to her belly, unsure what the sneaky pang of longing in my chest was all about. "Your husband being a twin and all."

She shuddered. "Mind your tongue. And speaking of twins…" She waggled her brows. "You never know, right?"

"Oh. Yeah. No." I laughed it off and snuggled my puppy. "I'm just newly a dog mom."

"The best houses have a few of each persuasion. Though men always want housefuls because their vags aren't serving as evacuation stations. Star, put that down!" She hurried off to deal with her daughter, who had snatched a sugar butterfly off a tart in the display case.

A sudden chill stole over me. I frowned as goosebumps scattered over my upper arms. To distract myself, I adjusted Pancake in my hold and opened the folded note attached to his collar.

Your guy misses U. Hope you're having a good day. Save me a croquet.

I swallowed hard. My guy—was that Brady or Pancake?

Or both?

I nuzzled my cheek against my puppy's and shut my eyes. Brady was so sweet. We were just having fun.

No matter how fast my heart was racing.

FOURTEEN

 **BRADY**

"I THOUGHT IT WOULD BE BETTER IF WE DID THIS HERE." JARED CLEARED his throat and leaned back in his chair. He was seated at the small desk tucked in the corner of the master bedroom that served as his home office. "Sorry for the tight quarters. Renovations for my new office and the second bathroom aren't starting until the snow melts."

"Perfectly fine." I gave the chief a tight smile. "The environment won't make this statement any more awkward."

"Than it is already?"

"Something like that."

He toyed with his pen. "Look, Brady, many of us have had something like this in our past."

"Have you?"

"Of course not." He looked at me as if I was patently insane. To be fair, Jared employed that particular expression fairly often. He was so rigidly logical that most mere mortals didn't measure up at one time or another.

My mother was much the same.

"Thanks for the support."

"I mean, I spent years focused on Bee, so dating wasn't really a thing for me. Not saying that was right or wrong."

"So, if you weren't dating, how exactly did you make Sami?" At his impatient look, I shrugged. "Just curious."

"There was a weekend." He sighed. "I can't call it a mistake, because it gave me my daughter and I adore her. But at the time, I sure as hell didn't think my dalliance with Trina had been a good move."

"Misty wasn't even a weekend. We went out once."

"Stayed in?"

"We went bowling and then we had sex in my car. End of relationship. We talked about going out again sometime, but we never managed to line up our schedules and then we just moved on."

"You moved on."

"Yeah. I assumed she did too. I didn't make any promises, Jared. It wasn't like that. Honestly, I didn't hear anything about or from her all these months and then soon as the thing with Tabitha happened, she popped out of nowhere like a damn groundhog."

"It is February."

"She was saying some shit about dumping me and how I went for Tabitha as revenge. I mean, what the actual hell?"

"Convoluted." He leaned forward and lowered his voice. "God knows I love women, but their thoughts at times can be a winding road."

I just sighed.

"You're a straight shooter, Brady. I can't see you leading her on."

"I didn't."

"But that also doesn't mean that sometimes we don't put out signals we don't even realize. Or maybe she made herself feel better by deciding she cut you loose."

"Yeah."

I'd thought much the same during my shower this afternoon after I'd gone for a run with Daisy and Pancake. The puppy had slowed me down to the point I'd fobbed him off on Sage with a note for Tab. The note had actually been on my mind as a cute thing to surprise her with at the bakery, and the bowtie had been an impulse buy the last time I'd gone to the pet store. "I'd intended to stop by to see her today."

"And?"

"I didn't want to."

The chief laughed. "Straight shooter, all right. Well, if your gut says stay away, could be that's wise. Misty doesn't have a record, but I have to say, I don't have good vibes about her. She seems jittery. Off. Could be on something or just may be wrapped up in the situation and when you move on, she will too."

I frowned. "I just said I moved on six months ago."

"Not from that situation. I mean from Tabitha. For some reason, her presence in your life seems to have aroused her anger."

"Now I'm supposed to 'move on' from Tabitha because Misty doesn't like it? Why can't people just stay the fuck out of our business? Why is that so hard?" I paced to the trio of windows overlooking the lake. Sunlight glinted off the ice, almost blinding in its intensity.

Jared's chair squeaked as he leaned back. "Small towns have a rhythm, Brady. I know it gets annoying sometimes, but people look out for each other here."

"If someone sneezes in their house, someone outside has a tissue. Yeah, yeah. I get that. I even appreciate everyone cares so much. But it's a lot when you're just trying to get to know someone."

"Well, you could try being a little more circumspect."

"You mean not do it on the bakery tables? Yeah, I'll take that under advisement." I swore under my breath. "Shit, Jared."

"I don't judge. Your life is your life. Just the less people know to talk about—"

"We didn't do ninety-nine percent of what's been said in the way it's been said. I didn't even kiss her in the café. This town you love is full of damn perverts."

"Now you hold on there. The Cove is a lot of things, but I won't stand for you calling the good, law-abiding people of this town perverted."

"Nosy, busybody perverts." I crossed my arms. "I feel like we're in a damn knitting circle rather than officers of the law."

He gave me a cool glance. "You chose to move to the Cove. If you're finding it doesn't suit you—"

"No, dammit, I'm not finding that. I love the damn Cove. I love my job. I even love Mrs. Gunderson." Hearing myself, I frowned. "Okay, I'm fond of her. But I'm not moving on from Tabitha."

"You're not?"

"No, I'm damn well not. I wanted to invite her to dinner."

"Well, now."

"Will this be tomorrow's gossip?"

"Really? You're accusing me of fueling the town's gossip machine?"

On the verge of giving his desk a bad-tempered kick, I made myself sit back down in the chair opposite it. "No. I just don't like my hand being forced. So, I guess I will be talking to Misty."

"Be careful there, Brady. If she's unstable..."

"I'm hoping she just got her wires crossed, and if I talk to her, it'll all get resolved. She seemed like a nice enough girl. Most importantly, I don't want any of this to touch Tabitha. She's already running on empty and doesn't need anything else on her plate."

"You really like her."

"Yeah, I do. Why is that so hard to believe?" Before he could speak, I rested my forearms on my thighs and leaned forward. "Let me guess, because I'm the gigolo of Crescent Cove."

His lips twitched. "I wouldn't say that. I didn't know any money had changed hands."

"Funny guy."

"Look, gossip around here is mostly harmless, but not always. I'll do my best to squash or divert what I'm made aware of, but the best thing to do is to try not to make a spectacle." At my snarl, he held up a hand. "Not saying you are. Just be careful for a while, okay? For Tabitha's sake, if not your own. Let things die down. Give people's memories some space so they get onto the next thing and forget all about what you can do on a three-legged table."

I snorted. "Those damn tables wouldn't even hold me if I didn't move, never mind thrusting."

"I know the mechanics, McNeill." He folded his hands together and leaned forward. "Though I'm glad you told me you're...invested in

Tabitha. Bee told her mother she was going to invite Polly from the diner to dinner because 'she's single and looking to mingle.'"

I groaned and dropped back my head, closing my eyes. "God, no."

"Bonnie told her not to, that you would be cranky as hell about being set up."

"Score one for Bonnie."

"She also said she worked her magic first."

I lifted my head and opened one eye. "What?"

Jared nodded gravely. "Apparently, she's taking credit for you and Tabitha getting together."

"Of course she is. Should we invite her to the wedding now?"

"I dare say she'd be thrilled."

"She dispatched me to the bakery when Tabitha's call came through. That's literally all she did. And Tabitha and I had met before that night. We live across the hall from each other. It was bound to happen someday."

"Just repeating what I was told. She could be your mother-in-law-to-be and then you'd have real problems." He appeared to make the sign of the cross. "I mean, I adore her. She's a lovely woman."

I sighed heavily. "She's not coming tonight, is she? Please say no. If she asks me one leading question—"

"No, you're off the hook. She went shopping with Erica. Buying baby clothes is her life. I swear, she'd love a fleet of grandchildren."

Gina knocked on the bedroom door and stuck her head in. "Jared, can I see you, please?" Her voice sounded unusually strained.

I hoped dinner hadn't met a misfortune. The actual food, not the act of breaking bread with these fine individuals.

At the moment, I'd prefer to sit in a dark closet with a paper plate than try to converse with people who were probably imagining what lewd positions I'd been in at the bakery.

Jared was already halfway out of his chair. "Sure thing. We're done here." He glanced at me. "Please tell me we're done."

I raised both hands, palms out. "For the rest of my life, I hope we never have to discuss this subject again."

135

"Me too," he agreed fervently before crossing the room to his fiancée. "Just give us a moment."

"Take ten. I'm just sticking around for the roast chicken. And the pecan pie."

The door closed behind him and I heard a lot of furtive whispering too low for me to make out. Then came a shout.

"Holy shit! No fucking way!"

I frowned. I really hoped my chicken dinner wasn't in peril. I'd held it out as the fowl pot of gold at the end of a craptastic day. Minus the part with Tabitha. That part of the day had been pretty awesome, but it had ended far too early.

I tugged out my phone and pulled up the menu for Bucket of Love, the new fried chicken place in town. Thank God their Sunday hours extended late into the evening. I could take care of my own chicken needs if necessary.

No thanks to you, Chief.

Before I could scroll down to the combo meals, the door burst open and a laughing Gina flailed at Jared, who had her in a fireman's carry. "We're having a baby!"

I stared at them. Granted, my mind had been centered on chicken, but the thought shouldn't have been that foreign, especially in a town like the Cove. "You have a baby already, right?"

From Jared's cross expression, I supposed that wasn't the proper response. Gina, being the wiser one of their duo, didn't seem to hear me or care about my opinion.

Quickly, I cleared my throat and rose to my feet. "Wow, that's awesome. Congrats, you two. Were you planning on expanding your family? I suppose it's like puppies, if you have one already, same work as two."

I could say that was actually not true considering recent events in my life, but I was all about being friendly and polite.

"Um, babies are a little more involved than puppies, but we practice a lot and Sami wants a sibling. But this took some special Cove intervention." Gina poked Jared and he set her down. He hooked his arm around her waist and hauled her against him, burying his face in the crook between her neck and shoulder. She giggled. "You're tickling me."

"Intentionally." He tightened his hold and lifted his head to beam at me. I'd never seen him this overjoyed. "Listen, man, I hate to do this to you, but we gotta celebrate."

Celebrate being code word for screw, I was guessing, and hey, they didn't have to worry about condoms now. No wonder they wanted to take advantage.

Laughing, Gina poked him again. "You can't disinvite someone after they're already here. The chicken just finished cooking."

"Trust me, McNeill understands. Especially if you bag up his chicken. He didn't want to have dinner here anyway."

I debated responding then decided he had a point. Free chicken dinner? Without having to get advice on my love life, which I wasn't even allowed to have in case some busybody in town got too excited about it? Sounded like a win to me.

So, I smiled and nodded, although they were too busy squabbling to wait for my input.

"This is a moment I'll never forget," he interrupted Gina, effectively stopping her Martha Stewart-style hospitality rant in its tracks. "We're having a baby. Our baby. Sami is too, but God, Bee. We weren't sure it could happen and this is the best gift ever." He cupped her flat stomach in his big hand, his voice wobbling. "I love you so much."

I took a step back, surprisingly moved. This was not something meant for my eyes. The chief was so fucking happy, it practically emanated from him in waves. And Gina's chin wobbled as she linked her fingers with his over her belly and stared up at him, tears hovering on her lashes.

"I have to tell my mother," she said between sniffles.

"After," he growled, lifting his head to give me a pointed glance. "Next two nights off of your choice if you take your bagged chicken and scram."

"Brooks, you're terrible." Gina laughed helplessly.

I considered. "Three and we have a deal."

"Damn FBI," he muttered before grinning. "Totally worth it."

I shook his hand and pulled him in for a hard one-armed hug. "Happy for you, man. You too, Gina," I added, moving back. "And hey, I'll even drop off some of Tabitha's primo baked goods on those nights your man is working for me."

She laughed. "Thanks. Sorry about all of this."

"No problem. Babies trump all in the Cove." I grinned and resisted the urge to rub the heel of my hand over the strange ache in my chest. Probably hungry. My chicken craving was becoming an imperative.

"Go bag up your dinner and get out of here, McNeill."

"Going. Congratulations again." I headed out of the bedroom, pulling the door shut with a definitive click before hightailing it downstairs. I really didn't want to hear anything I couldn't forget. The dude was my boss.

I followed my nose to the kitchen, my mouth already watering. And I clearly wasn't the only one. Lola, Jared and Gina's big gold dog, was standing beside the stove, staring upward with a look of clear consternation. The covered dish was so close and she so obviously wanted it, but she was clearly facing a crisis of conscience about nosing her way into her family's dinner.

I didn't have any such compunction.

"Hey there, girl," I said, ruffling Lola's soft silky ears before grabbing some paper plates and going to town on the aromatic roast chicken with peas and delicately sliced new potatoes with shallots and other unidentifiable vegetables soaked in gravy. I loaded up one plate, apologizing to a broken-hearted Lola, then went back for a second one before I even realized what I was doing. Tab would be working late tonight. She always seemed to lately. I couldn't in good conscience leave her hungry while I was chowing down on this good stuff. Sage had texted to let me know she'd left Pancake at the bakery at Tab's insistence, so she'd probably gotten behind at work. Our puppy was adorable, but he demanded a lot of attention.

Doing great on steering clear of Tabitha, aren't you, son?

I ignored that internal voice as I scooped up more peas. Green vegetables had vitamins and shit and Tabitha needed extra with her schedule.

Besides, I wasn't going to do steer clear. I didn't care who gossiped about us. I was having fun with her, and hell, I missed her already. The sex was phenomenal. Anyone who didn't approve could go hang.

Including Misty.

I wrapped up both plates in aluminum foil and sneaked a piece of chicken to the woe-begotten Lola before heading out. And if something that sounded like a scream of ecstasy followed me outside, I ignored it.

Good for the chief. His boxers were usually a little too tight.

And I wasn't jealous—about getting some, of course. Not over his growing family. That would be ludicrous.

I drove over to the bakery and parked in the back, noting the lot was empty except for Tabitha's sedan. Bingo. Then I frowned. If she was trying to get some work done, she didn't need me hanging around. But I'd inadvertently dumped Pancake off on her, so I'd be helping her out by taking him back. Plus, I'd make sure she got a good meal into her. She was probably falling over from fatigue by now. She just hadn't been resting enough.

Partly your fault.

On the bright side, there weren't any customers around now. Most people were home with their families at this time on a Sunday, not trolling the closed or soon to be closing shops on Main Street. Valentine Fest had ended today so I hoped that meant Tab would get some breathing room.

Maybe we would too, without so many prying eyes.

I grabbed the foil-covered plates and Pancake's spare leash and went to the back door, rapping quickly. She didn't respond for long enough that a niggle went down my spine.

I backed up to assess the building. Maybe she was in a store room or something? Possibly put in headphones while she baked? If she didn't answer soon, I'd text her to make sure she was okay.

Damn, McNeill, becoming a nervous ninny or what?

Another knock later and I glimpsed Tabitha through the thin pane of glass on the door rushing to answer with Pancake tucked under her arm. She'd put up her hair and had flour or something dusting her nose and her freckles stood out even more against the paleness of her skin.

My heart freaking flopped in my chest like a trout at the end of a really big, really sharp hook.

She opened the door, her wide smile at the sight of me almost distracting me from the deep shadows beneath her eyes. Almost, but not quite. "Brady." Pleasure flowed through her voice like wine. "This is unexpected."

Questions flew through my mind.

Have you eaten?

Are you going home to get some rest soon?

How about just taken five minutes off your feet for a change?

But I didn't ask them. Instead, I just stepped forward, softly cupped her chin with my fingers, and drew her mouth to mine. I kept the pressure gentle, easy. But there was no denying the need that had me lingering for longer than I'd planned as I tilted her head to take and take some more. She made a low noise in her throat, eliciting an answering one inside me. Not one to be outdone, Pancake whimpered and stuck his wet snout between us, forcing me back whether I wanted to go or not.

I laughed and turned my head to kiss him too. "Missed me? Or don't want to share your mama?"

A big slobbery tongue lapped over my face while Tabitha giggled.

"Sorry about dropping off the kid without warning." I rubbed between Pancake's ears and he wriggled in canine joy. Apparently, he'd grown to tolerate me during this week we'd spent so much time together.

"Seeing him was the highlight of my day." She grinned and tapped her lower lip with her free hand. "Until now, anyway."

"It's the bowtie, isn't it?" I straightened it around Pancake's neck, juggling the plates in my other hand. "Maybe I should get one."

"You should. Matching. Oh my God, what is on those plates? That smell is making me lightheaded."

"Gina makes one hell of a chicken. At least according to smell and Lola's taste buds."

"Gina?"

"Yeah, I was at the chief's. Gina's having a baby." I frowned as Tabitha shot me a look. "That may be a secret. So, you didn't hear it from me."

"Having babies in the Cove isn't much of a secret. It's rarer for someone to *not* get pregnant."

"You do have a point."

"Is one of those dinners for me?" Hope lined Tabitha's tone. "I'm starving."

"It sure is. I'm sure you didn't even have lunch."

She didn't answer, but I suspected that was because she was too fixated on the chicken. "You're going to eat with me, aren't you? You can't drop this and run." Her lips tugged downward. "Though you indicated you were busy for dinner today..."

"Dinner with the chief turned out to be a bust. Well, not for them. They're overjoyed about their new addition."

She smiled mistily. "Gina loves babies. I'm happy for them. She's so good with Sami."

I didn't know what to say to that, so I fell back on my old faithful chicken. "But I got a home-cooked meal out of the deal, so no complaints. I wanted you to come to dinner with me," I said quickly, and she lifted her head in surprise. "Just I had to talk to the chief about Misty and I didn't know if that kind of dinner was crossing the line for our agreement."

"I don't know. Is it?"

"You tell me."

Pancake let out a yelp as he strained toward Tab's chicken dinner. She told him *no* in a surprisingly stern voice and he let out an all too human-sounding sigh. "After I destroy this chicken."

I couldn't help laughing. Being with her just made me feel good.

Happy. Sappy. And probably a dozen other emotions I had little experience with and wanted to drown in.

That wasn't even mentioning wanting to peel off her apron and her intriguing turtleneck to get another glimpse of her in that wine-red lace bra and panty set she'd slayed me with this morning.

She cocked her head. "I'm ruining the whole female mystique, aren't I?"

No, you're ruining me for anyone else.

I swallowed hard, swapping the plates for Pancake before he took a flying leap at them. "I say we make the rules. Eating together isn't anything but what we make it."

"I like how you think, McNeill." She pried up a corner of the foil on one of the plates and inhaled deeply. "This smells obscenely good."

She shifted and her frosting scent wafted over me, making me think about something much different. "Do you have time to take a proper dinner break? I'm a greedy bastard and want more than fifteen minutes with you."

She gave me a slow smile. "For you, Hot Cop, I'll take thirty."

FIFTEEN

We had dinner every night that week. And almost every night the next week too. We didn't talk about what it meant.

Better not to overanalyze, Tabitha.

Nor did we discuss what it meant that he came home to my apartment when he got off late shifts, where Pancake and Daisy and I were usually sprawled on the couch with popcorn and something on Netflix. Some nights he brought Chinese because he always got hungry when he worked late.

I supposed I always got hungry when he worked late too. I sure as heck didn't turn down the egg rolls and lo mein he brought with him. Or the occasional spicy pork with crab rangoon on the side.

Sex was on the menu nearly every night, except the ones where I passed out before he could say post shower nookie. Not that he ever would say that particular phrase.

We both enjoyed heavy doses of dirty talk. At this point, I was so primed by him I could practically come just from him whispering how much he'd fantasized about fucking me all day long.

He said that a *lot.*

Pancake and Daisy liked our routine too. I would be forever grateful that Pancake hadn't been too small to start off on regular puppy food. I had no clue how Brady and I would've dealt with formula or bottle feeding. Thankfully, we hadn't had to worry about any of that, and for any other mom needs he had, Daisy was doing a great job.

They curled up together and snuggled happily and hardly ever squabbled, except when Pancake dared to steal some of Daisy's kibble. A sharp growl and a nose nudge later and Pancake was relegated to his rightful space as the junior member of the household.

Households, plural. We weren't living together. We had our own spaces, our own lives. Just it was handy as hell having my Hot Cop just across the hall.

Even if I was well aware that the talk about us hadn't died down. Au contraire. It had just gotten sneakier.

My notoriety had led to some fun new things though. Macy and Vee over at Brewed Awakening had offered to put some of my desserts in their case in return for featuring a brew of the day from Macy's shop. I fully understood this was Macy giving a leg up to the new kid, because she surely did not need my product placement. She had more business than she could handle.

To be honest, lately I did too, and if I hadn't had Mickey and Honey working for me now, I would've drowned days ago. They both worked long hours without complaint, although Mickey was still taking some class for her degree and needed time to study. Honey volunteered with kids and needed time for that too, but they were both eager to make their schedules mesh with mine.

If Brady's enthusiastic nightstick wasn't gift enough, his sister and her friend coming into my life had been a godsend. I was still getting tons of orders from displaying my flower cupcakes during Valentine Fest. But I enjoyed the work, even if I dropped into bed each night as if I'd been running since sunrise.

Which I had been, and usually before.

Sunday morning, Honey and I were working side by side, her on flower cupcakes I would then hand decorate and me on a three-tier birthday cake for a two-year-old. I was hitting the coffee hard this morning because I couldn't seem to get going—and that was after a full eight hours' sleep the night before. I'd conked out during some slasher flick Brady had wanted to see. He'd teased me I was probably too much of a wuss to make it through.

He'd been right, but not because I was a wuss. I'd drifted off sometime after the slasher dude had placed the neighbor's head on a stake. Yeah, I had trouble believing what had lulled me to dreamland, but leave it to me. Then instead of dreaming of mayhem, I'd ended up drowning under a spilled vat of buttercream frosting.

No figuring that one out. Nope.

"Hey Tab, can I ask you something?"

I kept frosting the cake, my hand sure and steady even if I didn't feel that way on my feet. "Sure."

"You and my brother."

"Yeah?" I tried to keep my tone even.

"You're new, right?"

"It's been about three weeks since we started..." I cleared my throat. "Uh, yeah."

"How do you balance it? Like you work all the time. And he works all the time. How do you make it work?"

That was a question. I still wasn't sure. "Well, we don't really go on regular dates."

She snorted. "Does anyone? I mean, Netflix and chill is a thing. But don't you get, I don't know, itchy? Need time for yourself?"

"Well, we're new, as I just said, but truthfully, I've had a ton of time for myself in the past. I've been single a long time, minus a few brief detours. And it's not complicated with Brady. He doesn't make things difficult."

Honey wrinkled her nose and focused on pouring batter into the cupcake molds. "I just bet."

I sighed. "Let me guess, grapevine gossip again?"

"Everyone knows what my brothers are about. They're honest about it, so far as I'm concerned, it's not an issue. As long as they don't lie."

"No, your brother is exceedingly honest. I'd like to think I am too."

"Good." Carefully, she scraped batter off the sides of the bowl. "I bet that's why he's hanging around. Not everyone is as honest like he is. His ex Liz was—" She broke off and cleared her throat. "Anyway, you probably don't expect anything. Do you?"

"All I expect is we have fun together. As long as that's the case, we're good."

"Do you?"

I didn't have to paste a smile on my face. It just came naturally. "We do. What about his ex Liz?"

"Crap, me and my big mouth."

"Don't worry about it. If it makes you uncomfortable—"

"She just put some ideas in his head that kind of reinforced he wasn't father material. Or husband material. Since then, he's just been so sure he's Mr. Lova Lova man and forget anything else more...substantial."

"Did he love her?"

She angled her head. "You don't seem like you're jealous. Or pissed he had a life before you."

I didn't have to fake my laughter. "Why would I be? He's a great guy. Of course he dated."

"No, I don't think he loved her per se. He never stuck around that long. But he valued her input—and her opinion of him."

"Are you worried about your brother? That maybe I'll do the same as Liz and fill his head with my opinions?"

"No. Already I can tell that's not your style. Besides, it's usually the woman who gets hurt with him, not vice versa." She pursed her lips. "He gets bored easily. They both do. Mav too," she added.

"So you're worried about *me?*" I couldn't keep the surprise out of my question. "No one ever worries about me."

Except Brady. He always seemed to be concerned if I was eating enough or sleeping enough. As someone who'd carried a few extra pounds—and sometimes more than a few—for most of my life, his insistence on regular meals was both exasperating and impossibly sweet.

Clearly, he was genuine in his concern, since he never left me wondering if he embraced my curves. That man left me feeling worshipped in a way I'd never imagined.

It was kind of terrifying. After being with a guy like him, how would I ever go back to a regular dude?

More likely, I'd have to accept life with the Hulk and use my very detailed, very explicit memories of Brady as fantasy fodder.

"Van worries about you."

I chuckled. "Van was worried I was going to die a reborn virgin until I started getting a lot. Now she worries I'll sprain something. Sorry, TMI."

Honey didn't reply for so long that I looked up to see her staring off in the distance with a wistful expression on her face. "I always wanted a sister. Not two smelly brothers."

I laughed. "Your brothers are the exact opposite from smelly. They both always smell as if they should be in a damn GQ shoot."

One of Honey's perfect brows climbed. "You've been smelling Mav too?"

"Only on accident."

"Hmm."

I shook my head, laughing. "It's not like that. And trust me, I already know everyone in town is waiting for Brady to get bored with me and find someone else at the bowling alley."

"God, no. Not her. She's an ounce of sour cream short of a burrito bowl, that one."

I didn't mean to laugh. I truly didn't. I was just happy all had been quiet on the Misty front since the night of the dance we'd never made it to. "It's not easy when someone decides to move on before you do. Or if they seem happy and you're struggling. If that happens with Brady—" My head swam and I broke off to grip the edge of the counter.

"Hey, are you okay?" In a blink, Honey was beside me. "You're awfully pale. Maybe you should sit down."

"I'm fine." I flashed a smile I didn't entirely feel. "Just tired."

"He needs to stop keeping you up all night. You work too hard and need your rest."

I flushed. There was simply no helping it. Talking about having sex with Brady's baby sister was just two steps away from squicky to me. Even if Honey was impossibly mature. Sometimes I forgot she was even younger than I was, never mind that she was related to Brady.

"I slept all night last night."

"Well, then, you need a day off. You haven't taken one since I started."

"I will when things quiet down—"

"Tabitha," Honey shifted me toward her, then gripped my shoulders and peered down into my eyes, "things will never slow down. Your bakery is the talk of the town. You can't keep anything in stock. Even your blueberry-apple dog cookies are flying off the shelves."

"Brady talked them up at the station," I said faintly as her words sank in.

Talk of the town? Really? I knew we'd had a ton of growth lately, but Honey made it sound as if we weren't just some flash in the pan. That maybe this suddenly overwhelming success could last.

Yeah, if you keep working 7 days a week and twelve hour days. Like that's sustainable.

"How about I give you a yogurt with some flax seeds? Maybe a nice ham sandwich on wheat? I bet you haven't eaten. You're too pale."

"I'm okay. I had a banana." I took a deep breath and forced a smile as I eased back from Honey. "I just want to finish—uh oh." I gripped the counter again as Honey shimmered in my vision. "You know, maybe a girl can't live on coffee and a banana alone. That sandwich and yogurt sound great, thank you."

"Sure thing. Wait here."

She led me around the counter to one of the empty café tables. We were in the mid-morning lull before customers started arriving after church and other early morning activities. A couple came in as Honey led me to the table, but Lea appeared from the back, laughing with Tiffany, and they took their spots behind the cash register and counter. Mickey would be in later, but she was studying this morning for some big exam, and Sundays weren't typically busy until later in the afternoon. Van was out making a couple of deliveries for us, but she'd be back anytime now.

Basically, this was the best possible time to take an unscheduled lunch break.

As Honey started walking away, I reached out to snag her arm. "Wait. I'm not taking your lunch, am I?"

She waved me off. "No big. I'll just make one of those fab chicken salad croissants Brady is always stopping by for. Though I suspect he is fond of the chef." She winked at me before circling the counter and disappearing into the back.

I relaxed in my chair, frowning at the knot in my lower back. Admittedly, I'd bought these chairs mostly for form over function—they were so cute and reminded me of ones you'd find in a Paris bistro—but this one was super uncomfortable. Or else my exhaustion was adding some aches and pains as well.

Discreetly, I tried to roll my neck and my shoulders to get some of the tension out of my muscles. It didn't seem to work. I wanted nothing more than a hot shower and a warm bed where I could snooze the afternoon away. Brady spooning me would be a bonus.

That man gave exceptional spoon, whether or not he'd admit it. I wasn't even sure he entirely realized it. We never started out cuddling, but by the middle of the night, I was in his arms, and his hold around me was unbreakable. I'd gotten hot the last few nights, but I hadn't made a peep.

I liked the way he held me. Liked the way he did everything, and that was kind of a problem.

Don't go there, Monaghan.

"Okay, here we go. Sandwich, soup, and yogurt for dessert." Honey carted out a tray to me with the meal arranged prettily. Even the yogurt had been scooped into a dessert cup.

I teared up. I looked up at her with them in my eyes, and she backed up as if my head had just revolved.

Since I understood that reaction all too well, I sniffled out a laugh. "Don't mind me. Overtired or something. Thank you. Soup too?"

"Yeah. Today's special is three bean."

I blinked. "It is?" We only did soups a couple of days a week, usually on Thursdays and Fridays. But my new employees were clearly industrious, and I didn't mind one bit. It was exhausting handling everything all the time.

"It is," she confirmed. "Van approved it. Tiffany whipped up the recipe."

I dipped my spoon into the bowl and sampled it, letting out a wholly inappropriate sound. "Holy crap, this is good." Between that and the scent of the ham and cheese sandwich, I was going to need a moment alone.

"Right? What I told her. We may have to go to soups seven days a week." She tugged her apron tighter. "I mean, if you okay it. You're the boss, of course."

I waved off her concern, too busy eating to say anything. Damn, I needed to put up a sign to try our new soups. This stuff would fly out the door. Hopefully with a crusty roll or a dozen purchased on the side.

Yeah, so much for me not working seven days a week. The bakery was what I thought about morning, noon, and night. When I woke, it was the first—

I frowned. Actually, no, the bakery wasn't my first thought when I rose anymore. Now I thought of Pancake first, which led to thoughts of Brady. Occasionally, Brady came first, especially if his morning happy cock was nicely nestled against my backside.

This development would probably rate as progress if I had a therapist. I did not have a therapist, but I had a healthy sense of self-preservation.

Don't fall for the player.

I spooned up more soup. Really quickly.

"Guess you like it, huh?" Honey laughed.

I gave her a thumbs up and reached for the half sandwich.

"I'll just get back to work then."

"Thank you," I said between bites. "You saved my life."

She lifted a brow but just grinned before she went back behind the counter. I devoured the delicious sandwich and was just digging into the yogurt, topped with fresh blueberries—God, I was giving this girl a raise—when the door swung open.

A whirling ball of chaos otherwise known as my sister shot inside, her flaming hair springing out in every direction from her headband as she whipped her head back and forth. Clearly, she was looking for someone.

Her eyes narrowed as her gaze landed on me. I lifted my dessert cup in a futile attempt to block my face, but her screech told me I was unsuccessful.

"Dude, you gotta see this shit!" If she thought it was strange I was sitting at one of the tables eating lunch, she did not say. I never had before, but hey, she obviously had bigger fish to fry.

Or cake boxes to sling on the table, upending my tray and toppling my empty dishes to the floor. Minus the dessert cup, since I had that in a death grip as I shoveled in blueberry-accented yogurt as if it was my job.

Yet none of those things slowed down my oblivious twin.

"Look at that. Just look," she demanded, jabbing a hot pink nail at the decorated round single layer cake that did not look as if I'd designed it just yesterday. The frosting was all smeared, way worse than it would've been from Van's inelegant toss, and the sweet greeting I'd put in purple frosting was obscured. A new one had been put in its place.

Fuck you, Grimace.

At least I thought the last word was Grimace. The c and e were seriously smudged. But Van wanted to make sure I got the message.

"Someone sabotaged your cake."

"I see that," I said tiredly, still eating yogurt although much more slowly and sadly now. Partly because the yogurt was almost gone.

"Whoever it was must've gotten into my van while I was parked making deliveries."

"Don't you lock it?"

"Usually."

I sighed. Good to know my sister was taking such precautions with my products.

"Someone took a shot at you because you wore purple yesterday. And that someone needs to meet my fist." Van braced said fists on her hips and looked around as if she was expecting the culprit to reveal themselves. "I'm about to catch me a charge. And that dickless cop can just take out his ticket book, because this time, he's going to have to cuff me and bring me in."

I glanced down at myself, belatedly realizing that today I was not wearing purple. But she was right, I had been yesterday. Was that what Grimace referred to? That huge purple character from McDonald's a million years ago? Who would even get that dated reference?

My sister, apparently. And me.

I scooped up the last bit of yogurt and gave my sister a bright smile. "Just living up to my title."

She frowned. "Are you okay? You're pale."

"So I've been told."

"You're too calm. Why are you so calm?" Her frown grew as she crouched at my side. "Why didn't you tell me you're sick, you jerk?"

"I'm not sick. I'm just—oh, shit." I scrambled to my feet and raced for the bathroom, darting around the handful of customers who had just trickled in. I made it into the room and shut and locked the door, beyond grateful the bathroom only had one stall.

And that I'd tied my hair back, so I didn't throw up all over it.

Van banged on the door while I retched my entire lunch. Every time I thought I was done, more came. By the end, I was sweaty and shaking and washing my hands and face was a task of epic proportions.

Somehow I summoned the energy to unlock the door for my sister. She took one look at me and cupped her hand over her mouth. But that didn't obscure her exclamation, since an indoor voice was obviously optional when it came to my twin. "Oh my God. You're so knocked up!"

SIXTEEN

 **BRADY**

THE CALL CAME IN JUST AS I WAS FINISHING UP AN UNEXPECTED evening shift. I'd been called upon to accompany Mav on his second ride-along, and instead of getting annoyed at losing my regular Sunday night off, I'd decided to try to enjoy showing the ropes to my little brother.

The shift had gone well. A few nuisance calls, an attempted breaking and entering, the standard rogue duck blocking someone from exiting their driveway.

Normal day all the way around.

"Dad wants you to come to dinner next Sunday."

I tried ignoring him, but he only repeated the question. My shift was almost over. The day couldn't go downhill this late in the game.

I hoped.

"Pretty sure I have plans," I muttered.

"With Tabitha?" My brother didn't rub his hands together but it was damn close. "Even better. He wants to meet her. Trust me, it's better if you bring her of your own free will."

"Right, so he can pelt her with weird questions, and Mom can grill her as if she's the number one suspect in an armed robbery."

Mav laughed. "You know that's the drill. It's well within their parental rights, as Dad always says."

"When was the last time Dad asked your girlfriend if she believed in UFOs?"

His laughter deepened. "Well, does she? It's an important question. And dude, girlfriend?" I looked at him in time to see his eyes widen. "Have you actually ever had a real girlfriend?"

"A couple."

"Plural?"

"Okay, more like one or two." I scratched the back of my burning neck. "Besides, it's not like she knows I just called her that. It's not a big deal."

"So, you're catching feelings for once. Figures. She screams unavailable so pointer dick is engaged."

I was not having this conversation with him. "I'm not bringing Tabitha because I'm not coming to dinner."

"So, you're scared. Gotcha."

"I'm not scared, just it doesn't seem right to subject her to that when—"

"When chances are good you're going to cut her loose anytime now. You probably know best."

"You're an asshole."

"An asshole who speaks the truth."

"That's not it at all. Just I haven't even been to dinner with them for a while. Why would I put Tab through that?"

He scratched his stubbled jaw and the sandpapery sound made me want to pull over and shove him out on the nearest street corner. I didn't do it, because I was a saint among men. "Well, just speculating, but I'd say because they're your family who loves you and they want to meet the woman you care about. And if you introduced Tab to them, she might get an indication you think enough of her not to do your famous drive-by dick routine."

I hung a left on the outskirts of town and did a U-turn to head back toward the station. Maybe he had a point.

"Look, we agreed to keep things loose."

"And family dinner isn't that."

"Not exactly." I rapped my fist on the wheel, on the verge of tapping the horn at a pair of kids walking up the damn middle of the street. They hurried to the sidewalk, and I curbed my impulse. But apparently, I wanted to vent or some shit. "I want more. I just don't want to be the one to say it."

He didn't laugh. It was a minor miracle.

"I knew it when I first saw her."

I slanted him a glance. "Knew what?"

"She looks like forever, man. You know those forever girls? The ones you don't mess around with. Rare. Special." He popped his knuckles. "She's just got her forever in her bakery. Seems to me she doesn't have a lot of room for much else."

"How the hell do you know that already? You just met her recently, you said it yourself."

"Yeah, well, you just got to know her better recently too, and you're in love with her." He jerked a shoulder while my brain pinwheeled as if I'd had too much to drink—and I was stone-cold sober. "Just an observer. What the hell do I know?"

"Nothing. Nothing," I repeated. "And I'm not in love with her. No more than halfway," I added under my breath.

Maybe three-fourths.

"Honey works for her, right?"

"You know she does."

"Have her invite her to dinner. Then it's not saying anything on your part, but you're kind of…maneuvering her into position."

I barked out a laugh. "Position for what? Do you get any pussy at all or is this just crap you get off Dr. Phil?"

He yawned and stretched out his long legs as if he didn't have a care in the world. "Don't worry about me. Worry about your own problems."

"What problems? I have no problems." Signaling, I swerved into the cop shop's minuscule parking lot, snagging a space right in front. "My life is frigging golden."

It was, dammit, and I was done with this conversation.

I was already imagining the steak I intended to grill for dinner on my tiny balcony. It wasn't exactly grilling weather considering it was the end of February and about forty degrees, but I didn't care. If I got lucky, Tab would be done with work. Maybe we'd open a bottle of wine and see where things led.

While one or both of us struggled to keep the dogs from stealing a steak and eating it in one gulp.

The radio squawked to life as I grabbed the door handle.

"McNeills, call for you." Bonnie sounded like her usual businesslike self. She didn't even have a hint of remorse in her voice for tagging me just as freedom loomed.

"What is it?"

Mav cut me a look. "Brady's going off-duty, but I can take it."

"Oh, he'll want to take this one, guaranteed." I exchanged a glance with my brother. "Call came in from 2200 Main Street, Apartment 212."

My heart thudded in my ears. "That's my building. Tabitha's apartment. What's going on?"

Why the hell didn't she call me?

"Call is for property damage and tampering."

"On it." Before she could say anything else, I silenced the radio in a direct violation of protocol and reversed out of the parking space. Then I slammed on the brakes and glared at my brother. "You can stay here."

"And miss the show? No way."

"Did I say you were an asshole?"

"Only since I was in diapers. Still staying." He gave me a sunny grin. "I'm your backup, pal."

"What kind of backup could I need with Tab?"

While he waggled his brows, I bulleted out of the lot to keep from committing an act of violence against a fellow cop.

We were at my apartment building in two minutes, thanks to most of the important businesses in town being located on or near Main Street. I tried to shove my worry in a box and led the way upstairs to Tab's apartment, well aware of my brother right behind me.

I knocked and the door immediately swung open.

"About time." Van gripped the edge of the door, casting a quick glance behind her. "She's upset."

"I'm not upset. I'm just fine." Tabitha appeared at her side, her face completely devoid of makeup and her eyes ringed with dark circles. Her cheeks were blotchy. She'd obviously been crying. I took one look at her and my gut lurched.

"Tab," I said softly, holding out a hand to her she didn't take. She just stared at it. "What happened?"

She opened her mouth then shook her head and turned away.

"She's had a rough afternoon."

"Afternoon? It's almost seven pm."

Van pressed her lips together and pointed at Mav, who wisely stayed silent. "Why is he here?"

"We were on patrol. Tab didn't call me. She called the station, so dispatch contacts whoever's on duty." I tried to keep the annoyance out of my voice that Tabitha hadn't seen fit to call me specifically, and that she still wasn't telling me what was going on now. That wasn't as important as helping her with whatever had happened.

Van glanced over her shoulder at where Tab was sitting on the edge of the couch, clasping her hands together. "Can we have some privacy?"

At that exact moment, both Pancake and Daisy started barking up a storm from my apartment.

"You're asking us to leave?" Baffled, I raked a hand through my hair. "She called in a property damage and tampering complaint."

"You can stay. He can leave." She propped her hands on her hips. "You aren't needed, GQ."

Mav arched a brow. "I don't think that's your call to make, Pocket Plus."

"Oh, really? You want to start?"

"No, he does not." I turned toward Mav. "This is about Tab," I told him quietly, and he blew out a breath and nodded.

"She started it."

Van snorted. "Yeah, and believe me, I'll finish it."

157

"I'd like to see you try."

I tipped back my head as the dogs decided howling was a more effective way of garnering our attention.

"Can you bring them over here?" Tabitha's voice carried to the doorway but just barely.

I pulled myself back in line. This is about Tab.

"Sure."

I crossed the hall to my door and unlocked it, fully prepared to be bowled over by two overexcited dogs on their way to see their other owner.

Well, Pancake's other owner. Daisy was mine. Even if it was beginning to feel as if we shared her too.

But Daisy only rubbed against my hip until I patted my thighs, indicating she should stand on her hind legs for our standard hug. I needed it way more than I expected. "There's my big, beautiful girl." I hugged her back and gave her a brisk rub before turning my attention to Pancake, who was scrabbling at my legs for the same treatment. I lifted the puppy into my arms and he licked my cheek as I gave Daisy a questioning glance. "Across the hall like a good girl? No leash?"

She sat back on her haunches in her version of acquiescence—a lone holdover from training many moons ago—and I turned to carry Pancake across the hall, trusting Daisy would follow. Instead, she rushed ahead and beelined right into Tabitha's apartment. She hurried right over to where Tab was sitting on the couch, immediately gently resting her head in her lap.

I frowned. Daisy normally nearly knocked Tabitha over with her excited greeting too. But today, she was being so careful. Almost reserved.

"Aww, there's a love. Hi, my sweet Daisy." Tabitha's voice sounded uncharacteristically thick as she bent to rest her cheek against Daisy's head.

Pancake, however, had no such reservations and scrabbled out of my arms to leap to the floor, his stubby black and white legs splaying out beneath him. Even so, he managed to elude both Van's and Mav's attempts to slow his flight toward Tab. He hoisted himself into the air with more speed than grace but stopped short as Daisy gave him one sharp bark and nosed him back.

"She knows," Van whispered and I gave her a sharp look.

"Knows what?"

Van and Tabitha exchanged a look before Van again looked at my brother. "Can you go? Please," she added, her expression fierce despite the soft plea.

He nodded and glanced at me. "If you need me, I'll be in the car."

"Thanks."

The sensation of ice coating my spine didn't make sense. I didn't know why I was scared, but fuck, I could barely breathe through the crushing sensation in my chest.

God, was something wrong with Tab? What was going on?

The second the door shut behind Maverick, I stared at Tab. "What's happening? Please tell me, baby. I'm worried as hell here. I won't be mad, if you somehow think I will."

"She's the one who should be mad, not you, pal."

"Van, shut it. Please." Tab nudged aside the dogs and reached over them to the side table. She picked up a white stick and held it high so the dogs didn't grab it before holding it out to me.

Frowning, I reached for it before realizing what she'd given me was a pregnancy test.

A positive pregnancy test.

I cleared my throat. "Is this yours?"

"No, she got it off eBay, genius."

This time, Tab ignored Van entirely. "Yes. It's mine. First response. Earliest one out there." She blew out a breath. "So, about that vasectomy…"

SEVENTEEN

"WHAT KIND OF GUY LIES ABOUT HAVING A VASECTOMY?" VAN demanded while I debated tying her up and shoving her in the coat closet. What had I been thinking letting her come home with me in the first place?

Oh, yeah, I'd been on the verge of yet again tossing my soup—it had been great going down, not so awesome coming up—and/or sobbing into my tenth tissue. Van had offered to stay with me while I called to make a report about the sabotaged cake, and she'd even run into the drugstore to buy two early response tests, both of which I'd already taken.

Then I'd thrown up again, but I was pretty sure that had been for dramatic effect at that point. I hadn't been nauseated at all before today, so how could my body have realized I was pregnant all at once? It was like a full-scale revolt was happening throughout my battered system.

Or else I'd been ignoring the signs like I'd ignored so much else.

I'd just told the father I was having his kid and he was saying absolutely nothing at all. Better, he wasn't even standing any longer. He'd sank down on the coffee table to stare at the test I'd handed him.

The cheap table was groaning under his weight, but he didn't appear to notice.

Since I was still in a state of shock myself, I couldn't blame him. But he wasn't sick to his stomach even now, so I could blame him for that.

"Or did you go to some disreputable scam joint that doesn't even know what to snip?" Van went on. She probably didn't even notice that she was the only one talking.

Possibly breathing too. I was getting lightheaded the longer Brady and his wonder penis stayed mute.

He finally looked up from the stick he was clutching and gazed at me as if he'd never seen me before. "Maybe your sister has something she forgot to tell me."

White noise filled my ears. If I'd had more energy, I would've picked up the book on the side table and thrown it at his stupid block head. "I can't even get up to hit you right now, and you know why that is?" I fumbled for the book anyway. If this was the last thing I ever did, I'd make this shot count. "Because I'm pregnant with your baby, you complete and total piece of—"

"Yeah!" Van cheered as if she was at a sporting event.

Both dogs looked back and forth between us as if they'd bought tickets at well.

Brady leaned forward and plucked the book out of my hand. Which only pissed me off more so I kicked out at him, missing him entirely and hitting the coffee table. I let out an unholy howl, and Pancake scampered onto my chest to render aid—or squash my internal organs, whichever happened first. Van hurried forward to pluck the dog off me and Brady sat at my side, bending to check my toes as if he hadn't just accused me of being unfaithful.

So, I grabbed the book and took advantage of the angle to whack him in the back of the head. And I did not feel guilty.

It was his turn to let out a pained noise as he reared back and stared at me. "Now I really believe you're knocked up, because you're behaving irrationally."

From where Van was holding a wriggling Pancake, her blue eyes widened. "Oh, no, he didn't. I better tell GQ to get his fine behind up here again. This shit is going down. You ever had your ass whooped by twins, McNeill? Get ready for pain."

I wanted to admonish Van and yet I did not, because maybe she'd whoop his ass where all I could do was the most terrible, awful, horrible thing I could have done at that very moment.

No, not throw up on myself or him. At least I hadn't suffered that indignity.

I burst into tears. Again. Or still, since I'd cried more today than in the last ten years combined.

Brady shut his eyes. His expression was so pained I half wondered if he'd leap to his feet and get the hell out of there. Pancake was now howling, and Daisy was frantically licking my hand as if she could heal me through the power of her tongue. My toes were throbbing. And my sister was issuing threats that would've gotten her hauled off to jail if anyone was paying attention.

Then he shocked the hell out of me by sitting beside me on the couch and pulling me into his arms. He cupped my head and drew it to his chest, murmuring soft, sweet things that were just like the Brady I'd fallen in lo—

The Brady who'd impregnated me, the rude pig.

"Strawberry, I'm sorry. I didn't mean to make you cry. Don't cry. You can't. You know it kills me."

"Strawberry?" Van interjected. "You can't call her some hokey pet name. You just called her a ho."

Good point. I was not going to soften toward him ever again. He'd hurt me when I was weak and vulnerable and at the risk of throwing up at any blessed second. On top of that, my stomach continued to growl even as I wondered how long I'd be able to resist yet again making friends with the john.

I was officially in baby hell. And it had just happened. I had eight plus more months of this.

"I'm going to die," I moaned forlornly, clutching his vest because even if he was a pig, at least he was solid and warm and smelled good.

"Huh? What? Why? Pregnancy isn't fatal. Why would it be?" He was starting to sound as incoherent as I felt.

I had a feeling we were not doing this pregnancy reveal as smoothly as others in the Cove. In fact, we were probably the least smooth parents-to-be in the history of childbirth.

Dear God, Brady would probably make big babies since he was tall and broad-shouldered. I wanted to frost cakes, not scream in agony.

"The only pain I like is when you spank me. I can't do this." I buried my face in his throat and pretended I hadn't just admitted that in front of my twin.

Who would not let me forget it until the end of time, forever and ever amen.

Van whistled. "Damn, you go, girl."

Maybe she was done. Please God let her be done. But I wasn't lifting my head in case any encouragement made her continue.

"Did you turn my sister kinky before you knocked her up? I kind of hate you even more. Now what's she supposed to do with all of those needs you stirred up? Be happy while she's the size of a house with sitting on pillows and watching bad TV?"

"Why would she sit on—"

"Hemorrhoids!"

"I'm going to die," I moaned again, but no one cared.

Brady's chest rose and fell a few times underneath me and I gathered he was trying to get control of himself. Because he damn sure wasn't getting control of this situation.

My sister was still ranting. I swore I heard her mention butt plugs, although I didn't know why. Didn't want to.

At least I wasn't crying anymore. I'd gone into baby-induced shock.

He stroked my hair and slid his fingers underneath my chin to tilt my face upward. "I didn't lie about the vasectomy."

I hiccuped and vaguely gestured to my pee stick which was probably a chew toy for the puppy at this point. I didn't have the bandwidth to see where he'd disappeared to right now. "Well, explain that." He opened his mouth to respond and I shook my head. "Please don't say something I can't forgive you for. I really don't want to end up a statistic tonight."

"What kind of statistic?"

"The murdering kind."

His lips twitched and I felt my own doing the same before I remembered the whole ho thing. I took a shaky breath. "The last time I had sex before you was," I did the fuzzy math, "sixteen plus months ago. And I do pray, but not that religiously that I could expect some kind of faith-based intervention. It's yours, trust me."

Deep furrows lined his forehead. "But how?"

"How the hell should I know? Ask Van. She knows everything." That was entirely sarcasm, but when I glanced up to see her reaction, I discovered to my complete and utter shock she'd left the room and taken both dogs with her.

"Something's wrong with my sister. She never cares about social niceties. Hey, maybe she's nauseated too. Twin thing. That's payback for some shit she put me through over the years, let me tell you."

"You're sick?"

"I've been throwing up on and off since lunch. Honey gave me this amazing sandwich and soup and she even put blueberries in my— wait, what are you doing? Brady, put me down! Van, help me," I called as he plucked me off the couch bodily and carried me to the door.

My sister hurried into the living room just as he reached the door with me in his hold. Though even in my dismay, I could've help noticing he wasn't breathing heavy at all. I wasn't anywhere close to light, and the dude was carting me around like a stuffed animal—who was going to be even more stuffed soon.

Heaven help me.

"Van, help," I called again. I wasn't going to be swayed by his manly displays of muscles. "He's going to kill me just like that dude on Asher's podcast. The Pregnant Ripper episode. I think it was episode 200. The anniversary one."

"Pregnant Ripper? You have a truly disturbing mind." Brady jockeyed me enough to point at my twin. "Van, don't start."

"Unhand her right now. Where do you think you're going with my sister? You will not harm one hair on her head, mister." She drew her phone out of her pocket and quickly snapped a photo. "Now I have proof of your dastardly plans. You have one last chance before I turn you in." She smiled wickedly. "Or else I can take the law into my own hands. Trust me, you do not want me to do that."

"I'm taking her to the ER. She shouldn't be throwing up so much."

"Um, she's pregnant. I'm not an expert, but that's kind of typical, Hero Pants."

"Not this much. This soon? It's only been a few weeks."

"Hello, I made an appointment with my doctor already. I'm going in on Friday—"

"Friday is days from now," Brady informed me as if I wasn't familiar with the days of the week. "You'll get dehydrated at this rate."

"Oh, stand back, mighty penis has arrived."

I sighed. "He does have a point. Besides, I haven't been pregnant before."

"And he has?"

"No, but he has specialized training."

"In implantation?" Before I could reply, Van threw up her hands. Literally. No one could accuse my sister of not having a flair for the dramatic. "Whatever. Go to the ER. Have them poke and prod you. I'll watch the dogs and make a list of all the reasons I'm never letting a man knock me up. No matter how well-endowed." She strode down the hall, adding over her shoulder, "And I'm definitely not letting one spank me while he does it."

"I liked the spanking," I said woefully to no one in particular.

"Me too."

"You like to be spanked?" I cocked my head as I looked up into his disturbingly sexy face. If I was going to be murdered and my baby harvested, I supposed he was the best possible one to do it. "I never guessed."

"Not me, baby. I liked spanking you."

"Oh. Yeah, that was nice." I let my head rest on his shoulder. I was so tired all of a sudden. "Just gonna have a little lie-down. Sorry I'm so heavy."

"You aren't heavy at all. You're absolutely perfect." His lips touched my forehead. They were so cool, which was weird because normally his mouth was so warm. Or else I was hot.

Really hot.

"Tabitha? Hey, Tab. Strawberry? Open your eyes for me, please."

I wanted to. But I didn't have enough energy. "Just sleep now."

He called for Van. I heard that quite clearly. I also heard him whisper for me to come back.

Then I didn't hear anything.

EIGHTEEN

THE NEXT TIME I OPENED MY EYES, I FELT HUMAN AGAIN. LIKE...ALL the way human. Not tired, not achy, not nauseated. None of that.

I was even smiling as I opened my eyes. Until I realized I was in a hospital room and had a bag of fluid attached to my arm and a broken-looking Brady asleep in a chair beside my bed.

What the heck had happened?

I tried to think back. All I could remember was shouting insults at Brady and him cradling me while I cried and then while he carted me down to the squad car. I'd drifted in and out while he talked to his brother, and they both had sounded so tense. My sister had too.

Van, who wasn't ever afraid of anything, had been scared for me.

But I was okay. Still a little tired, but I felt pretty damn—

You're pregnant.

I'd kind of forgotten that part. Maybe partially on purpose.

I reached down to stroke my stomach in my thin hospital gown. I couldn't feel anything. There was a small slope, but that had been there since...well, always. Saturday night's Chinese food extravaganza with Brady certainly hadn't helped. I was probably retaining water too.

Too much salt. Too much baby.

I frowned and widened my explorations. Still nothing. Maybe it was all a mistake, and I'd had food poisoning.

Instead of that making me feel better, a bolt of fear lanced through me that the baby was gone. Maybe I'd lost it. How long had I been out? I needed to talk to the doctor.

God, I couldn't lose my baby. Not when I'd just come to terms with having it.

Well, I hadn't come to terms with it. Not even close. My mind was in chaos. I couldn't figure out how I was going to do this—how we were going to do this—but I was having this child. If he or she was still there.

"I can't tell you what a sight for sore eyes you are," Brady's gritty, sleep-roughened voice had me shooting him a glance just as tears filled my eyes for probably the thousandth time.

He rocketed forward, instantly in protector mode. He was so good at that. "What is it? I can get the doctor. Are you hurting? Sick?" He tried to stand, got his feet tangled up, and nearly upended his chair as he fumbled for the nurse's call button. "Let me just—are you laughing or crying?" he demanded as I snuffled into a tissue I'd found beside me, caught between tears and laughter.

"Both." I reached out to grip his hand, hauling him close to pull it against my cheek. "I'm fine. I'm just fine. I feel great."

"Thank God."

"Is the baby okay?"

He nodded, an emotion I couldn't name flitting through his expression. "They wouldn't tell me much of anything other than what I wheedled out as a cop. Which wasn't much. But they told Van as next of kin. You're definitely pregnant, and everything seems fine." He flashed me that crooked smile I loved so much. "Other than his or her parents being raging idiots, that is."

"Not using condoms as practically strangers sealed that fate." I narrowed my eyes. "How did I end up here? Did I pass out or what?"

"Yeah, partially by running yourself too hard." His jaw locked. "Not getting enough sleep or fluids or nutrition." His gaze dropped to my belly, and I couldn't decide if I liked his examination or if I wanted to pull up the sheet. "Your body couldn't handle all that along with growing a baby."

"I didn't realize I was eating for two."

"Yeah, well, now we know, so things will be different. You can't keep working so hard. It's not good for either of you."

I didn't say anything. I appreciated his concern, truly I did, but who else could do for the bakery what I did? This was just part of running a business.

But a baby changed things. Would change me most of all.

I took a deep breath. I couldn't let myself spiral. "Where are the dogs?"

"At my place. I've checked in on them. So has Caleb and Lu. Even Bess stopped down to play with them for a few minutes." He gripped my hand hard enough to bruise, but I didn't mind. I needed him holding on to me right now. "Can I get you something? Water? A sweater? Are you hungry? The nurse brought juice." He stopped. "You're laughing again."

"Yeah. I can't help it." I reached up to cup his beardy cheek. Clearly, he hadn't shaved in days, and his eyes were heavy and lined from lack of sleep. The wrinkle between his brows made him even cuter. "When did you get so cute?"

"Now I know you're not all the way better, because the last time you were awake, you thought I was the Pregnant Ripper. I've never listened to Asher's podcast, and I don't think I ever will."

"It's so good. Just I don't recommend it after midnight. We can listen to it when—" I cut myself off and shook my head. "Sorry. I forgot we broke up."

"We did not break up." His vehemence made me lift a brow.

"Sorry, we weren't even officially dating to break up."

"Says who?" He narrowed his eyes at me. "We were fucking dating."

Some hormonal part of me swerved toward him and threw her legs in the air. Though that was what had gotten me in this predicament in the first place. "You're the one who didn't want labels."

Instead of continuing to argue with me, he growled, "Now I do. We're fucking dating."

Now my nipples joined in the fray. I didn't understand why my body parts had absolutely no restraint toward this man. Besides the fact he was so strong and protective and sweet and fucked like an absolute god, when he wasn't being a clueless dolt. "What, now you've decided I didn't cheat on you?"

"It wouldn't have been cheating, because we had no firm commitment."

"Oh, okay. Good to know. So, if I'd decided to blow Christian, you would've been cool with it."

He lurched forward, cupped my cheek in his huge hand and just shifted me up to take his mouth. He didn't go easy on me either. This was a kiss for the ages, full of heat and need and the inherent gentleness he always touched me with.

Except when he was spanking me, of course. But that wasn't really the time for delicate touches, so I had no complaints there.

Absolutely none.

As we broke apart, breathing hard, he stroked his thumb over my lower lip. "No, I wouldn't have. I would've hated every second. But my mistake was not getting you on lockdown the first time you told me you didn't fit me. Baby, you fit me better than anyone ever has or ever will. Every part of you. Your heart, your mind, and your gorgeous curves. I—"

My heart shot straight into my throat, beating crazily. I would've sworn he was about to say he loved me. That was insane. That couldn't be possible.

Even if I was pretty sure I loved him too. Maybe. If I let myself.

I wasn't ready to do that. To say those words and follow through on the commitment they meant. I'd already committed to Sugar Rush. Succeeding at this one thing was what I'd pinned everything on in my life for so many years.

Love wasn't on my agenda right now. Dammit.

"You had a vasectomy." My voice was shaking. "Of course you'd think I could've done it with someone else. Isn't that fail safe?"

"Nearly so, if it's been long enough. I called my doctor. Evidently, I neglected to get a few things clear. Or he told me, but I didn't retain it. There's a very small failure rate too, about 1 to 2 men out of 1000. At the time, I wasn't even thinking about it, since I was single then. But you know in the Cove, we always break the curve."

"Oh my God, did you go bareback with Misty?"

"Hell no. Are you kidding me? I always used condoms even after the vasectomy. Except—" He frowned. "You were my first."

"Good thing, because I'm not sure how many kids you could support on a cop's salary. Clearly, you're shooting full rounds."

He didn't laugh, just swallowed hard and leaned forward to rest his cheek on my belly. "I want to name her Strawberry."

Now I laughed. He sounded as if he was beyond running on empty. He probably had no clue what he was even saying right now. "Strawberry Monaghan. There's a name."

I wasn't going to get starry-eyed over this man. I couldn't. Not until I knew this was more than the weird baby mojo that seemed to overtake men and women alike in this town once a child came into the picture.

He'd been worried about me. He was a good dude. Fear and impending unexpected fatherhood when he'd believed it couldn't happen for him could do strange things to a man. At least I assumed.

As for me, I felt more clear-headed than I had in weeks. It helped to know what I was dealing with, even if I didn't have one blasted clue how I would handle everything.

"I want her to have my name."

"Her?"

He nuzzled my belly and I swallowed hard. "Her. Him. Whatever. I'd like a McNeill."

"Well, I'd like the baby to have whatever name I have." His mouth tightened and I reached up to brush his hair away from his forehead. "Maybe we can do a hyphen."

"Yeah. I'd appreciate that. Thank you."

"Sure. We made this cake together." I trailed my fingertip down his slightly crooked nose to go with his slightly off-center smile. Somehow the imperfections just made him more handsome.

And I wasn't the only one who thought so.

Misty.

I'd intended to report the sabotaged cake. Obviously, that had not happened. I should've just gone down to the station, but I'd been all out of sorts.

Yet I still was not opening my mouth to Brady to confess all. In his current state, I wasn't sure what he'd do. He'd probably try to put me under witness protection then go after Misty. I wasn't going to risk that when he wasn't in his right mind.

Accidental pregnancy mania had to be a thing.

But I couldn't just ignore what had happened. I just needed time to come up with a plan. Maybe even talk to my sister to get her opinion, God help me.

I frowned, my fingers stilling in their exploration just above his lush mouth. "Where's Van? Did you kill her?"

"You really need to stop with those podcasts."

I laughed. "They wind me down before bed."

"She's fine. She was here all night and was dead on her feet. Mav drove her home."

"No way. She allowed him to?"

"It was late and she was falling asleep standing up. It was a shock to see. To be honest, I wasn't sure she ever slept. I kind of thought she just dropped into a coffin until sunrise."

"You are not funny." I poked him and grinned. "Okay, maybe a little. Besides, I'm the one with the bloodthirsty listening habits."

"Apparently." His eyebrow rose as he straightened and sat back in his chair. "I'd rather put you to sleep a different way than those podcasts. Besides, you have to think about the baby. That can't be good for him or her."

"Or both," I said flippantly.

I was just kidding. Of course I was. Who would ever put that thought in their head voluntarily, especially if they were the one who had to birth him or her?

Them. Oh my God.

Our eyes met. "You don't think..." His voice was almost inaudible.

I shook my head violently. "No. No. Of course not. I was just kidding. I mean, how could that be possible? If one was a shot in the dark—"

"Har-har."

I ignored him and his peacocking about his prowess. "Two would be impossible, even in the Cove."

"No, it wouldn't."

"No, it wouldn't," I echoed, lowering my face into my hands. "I'm never having sex with you again."

"Why? We're in the bonus round now, might as well enjoy it." He tugged my hands away from my face, and for some reason, the moron was on the verge of a grin. "C'mon, the chances can't be that high."

"I'm a twin, Brady. Fraternal twins carry the tendency through the female."

His grin disappeared as if it had never been. "Oh, yeah."

"Oh, yeah." I blew out a breath. I was about to hyperventilate if I kept thinking about the possibility, and I already had enough to deal with, thank you.

Like how I was going to keep my bakery going while I was pregnant and exhausted, never mind once I actually had a baby. If I'd thought a puppy was too much for me alone, forget a baby. And no matter how invested Brady seemed now, I couldn't trust that. We were too new.

He also didn't have a good track record. The one he did have only involved sex. This would be late night feedings and bottles and diaper changes and screaming. And maybe still managing to have sex now and then, if that part of our relationship survived the rest.

As far as the Misty situation or any of the other things ahead of us, I couldn't dwell on any of that right now or my brain was going to explode.

Forget twins. I was definitely not going there.

"I have an appointment with my doctor Friday. I'll get tested or whatever is necessary just to make certain. I'm not sure if they can even tell this early, but I bet they have ways of finding out. Hormone levels or—are you okay?"

He jerked to his feet and paced around the small space, shoving his hands through his hair. "This is like 20/20 type shit."

I didn't laugh. "Tell that to the resident of my uterus."

"But I can do this." He stopped to grip the back of his chair. "I can be a good dad."

"Of course you can. I know this is your worst nightmare, getting saddled with a kid you didn't want—"

"I want our kid, Tabitha," he interrupted. "It's not a nightmare for me. I just…" He shut his eyes. "When one of the nation's top criminal profilers tells you that you may not be father material, it sticks."

The conversation I had with Honey came roaring back in vivid Technicolor. "Yeah, if you're a serial killer."

His head lifted and his bleary, emotional eyes zeroed in on mine. "Huh?"

"Criminal profiler," I said slowly. "Doesn't sound like labor and delivery was her area of expertise. Besides, being a profiler doesn't mean she knows everything. You are the one who decides what kind of father you'll be. Not some woman who may or may not have had her own agenda."

His jaw relaxed and he managed a small smile. "So, I guess you really enjoyed being spanked."

It was my turn to do a double-take. "Say what?"

"You mentioned it in front of Van."

"I was feverish," I mumbled, tucking my hair behind my ear. My face was hot again right now, coincidentally enough. "And pregnant."

"Is that going to be your excuse for everything now?" There was no mistaking the fondness in his voice, so I did my best to control my irritation. And my tongue.

I'd done pretty good the last few weeks at not letting it rip with the inappropriate comments meant to unerringly drive men away, but I still had the latent talent. Add in that my defenses were lowered, and Brady didn't realize what bear he was waving a stick at.

A hungry bear with a growling stomach, apparently.

"Let me get you something to eat. In a minute. Oh, and speaking of eating—"

I frowned. "Eating is a good idea. Now."

"It is. How do you feel about dinner with my family next Sunday?"

I was already shaking my head. Vehemently. "Unless you just mean Mav and Honey, no. I can't do that. Not now. Family dinner? Ugh." I clutched my midsection and rocked.

"Why? They're not that bad. Well, they kind of are, but they mean well."

"Your mom was in the FBI. I'm the hussy who got knocked up by her son without even properly dating him first. It's only a month, and I could be having twins." The rocking intensified.

"My mom isn't an ogre. My dad will take one look at you and hug you for ten minutes. They both dream of grandchildren. I'm pretty sure they'll canonize you for doing the impossible."

"Breeding with the player of Crescent Cove?"

"I'm not a damn player. I've never slept with two women at one time. Not ever."

"You're just fickle."

"Maybe I just hadn't met the right woman. You ever think of that?"

I frowned as he dropped back down into his chair. "No," I admitted.

"Truthfully, me either. I assumed I wasn't made for that. But how do I know what I'm made for until I try? Until we try?" He leaned forward to take my hand, lacing his fingers with mine. "We have something special, Tab. You feel it too."

Pressing my lips together, I nodded.

"We didn't expect it and it's not convenient, but I'm damn sure not going to walk away from it until we see what we can do together. All I'm asking for is a chance."

I took a shaky breath. "Family dinner is a lot."

"I can go to dinner with your family first if you'd rather."

"I don't have a family. Van and I were hatched by changelings in the woods."

He didn't laugh. "If you don't want me to meet your folks, fine. If

177

you're not ready to meet mine, that's okay too. We'll take it day by day."

I didn't want to hurt his feelings. That was the last thing I wanted. But the idea of facing expectations so soon from people I didn't even know when I was still trying to come to terms with my new reality...

"What do we tell them, Brady? That you came to help me with the power outage and the puppy I found, and we made a baby before we even knew each other? Or do we make up some pretty story that isn't so messy?" I almost didn't even realize the persistent waterworks had started again until he dragged his chair closer to the bed and cupped my cheek.

"Messy and beautiful. It doesn't matter how we started. It matters how it is right now, and right now, we're happy. I'm happy to come home from work to you and the dogs. I'm happy to wake up with you curled in my arms. And I'm sure as hell happy when I slip inside you, and you remind me what's so amazing about being with just one incredible woman." He kissed my knuckles. "I want to go out with you."

"What?"

"I want to take you out on a date. Fancy clothes, no dogs, no takeout." He rubbed his thumb over my fingers. "We'll get ready in our separate apartments so I can kiss you at the end of the night as if we've never kissed before."

His grip on my hand tightened as he waited for my reply. Asking me out was hard for him, I realized. I wasn't sure why because he certainly had enough experience to—

No. I wasn't going to think about anyone else but us. He was tiptoeing out on a limb so I could too.

I smiled. "Yes. I'll absolutely go out with you, Hot Cop."

NINETEEN

 BRADY

I kept waiting for the other shoe to drop. One of many.

Namely for the word to get out about our love child. Which had to be the stupidest phrase in the history of the world. Why were babies born out of marriage any more love children than those made at other times?

Anyway, there were many months before the baby was born. Many months. Who knew where we would be in our relationship by that time?

God, just eight. And if there were twins...

We'd agreed to kind of give ourselves space this week before our date. We still saw each other to do the usual Pancake handoff and occasionally texted or she bagged up cookies and lunch for me, but for the most part, we stayed in our separate lanes.

I didn't like it. My lane had included her only for a short time, but I'd grown to anticipate being with her more than anything. Not eating a late meal with her before watching something on streaming and crawling into bed made my whole day feel off. Wrong.

And I worried. Was she eating enough? Was she working herself too hard? How was she sleeping? How was the nausea? I'd read tea, crackers, and soup helped some women. Had she tried those?

I wanted to ask. I wanted to know everything about how she felt and what was happening.

Could someone become a helicopter parent while still in the first trimester? I was on my way to finding out.

Her first doctor's appointment was tomorrow. I still felt as if this was all some strange cosmic joke. How could she be pregnant when she looked exactly the same? I understood that was nonsense reasoning since it was so early, but nonsense reasoning was all I was capable of at the moment. I needed to hear her doctor verify the baby was actually there with my own ears. Actually okay.

Somewhere along the line I'd gone from being concerned the baby existed to what if it didn't. And I had no clue what to do with that fact.

She wanted to not tell anyone yet. It was too early. I assumed she didn't want questions. I could see how that would be annoying. Second-guessing her decisions was the last thing I intended to do at this point. This was her show.

I just hoped she'd invite me to her doctor's appointment tomorrow. I wanted to take her, not be assumed to be a deadbeat from the jump by the doctor. When in reality, I wanted nothing more than to hold her hand.

Or she could hold mine, but same difference.

I just missed her so much and it fucking sucked. But I was trying not to crowd her. She probably needed room to process all of this. Having an unplanned baby was a lot to absorb, and she was dealing with endless changes in her body too.

So, I went to work and I took care of the dogs and waited for the precious few moments I could see her like a starving man waited for crumbs.

Thursday evening while I was volunteering at the learning center, twin thoughts assailed me once again. As my breathing shortened, I bent to put my head between my knees. I'd taken to assuming that position when thoughts of impending parenthood nearly sent me into a personal crisis.

Which was often.

I couldn't say I breathed better in that position, but I definitely got some interesting comments from witnesses.

"Hey, Brady, did you lose your keys?" Connor Jackson sat on the bleachers beside me and mimicked my position, looking between his legs. "I don't see nuthin'."

"Nah, I'm just being silly." I had to laugh as I reached over to ruffle his shaggy blond hair. He needed a trim.

Would our baby have blond hair like Tab? Or the more sunset color her hair turned sometimes in the sunshine?

Would I ever stop thinking in circles every moment of every day?

Connor grabbed the basketball he'd set beside him on the bleachers and started to dribble. "Haven't seen you this week."

"Yeah, sorry, been really busy at work." Lame excuse, man.

But I couldn't tell him the truth. Then again, he was nine, so it wasn't as if he hadn't heard of babies. He even had a little brother.

God, we could be having a boy. I could have a son.

I swallowed hard. "Listen, can you keep a secret? I'm only telling you."

Connor's liquid brown eyes went huge. "Dude, really, me? Like I'm the only one?"

"One and only," I confirmed, lowering my voice. "Well, beside the parties involved. The girl and her sister. They're twins."

Twins. There went my pulse rate again, skidding right into the danger zone.

He stared at me, not understanding.

Get to it already.

"So, I'm, um, having a baby. I mean, the girl is. My girl." My face was flaming so hot I wanted to stick my head between my knees again.

"Oh. Like Leo, my baby brother."

"Yeah. Maybe. She could be a girl. We don't know yet. It just... happened." I sounded entirely clueless about this whole process, which actually wasn't too far from the truth. I just hoped I hadn't opened a box of worms I couldn't close.

Please God let him know the birds and the bees.

Hell, maybe he could give me some tips, because I felt utterly inept.

"She's your girlfriend? Did you buy her a ring? My uncle Steve said girls like big rocks." Connor poked at the hole in his jeans. I knew that was the style nowadays, but Connor's clothes in general were on the overly worn side. "He's had three wives."

"At once?"

His giggle was so childlike and sweet it made me grin. "No. One after each other. No babies though."

"Do you like your baby brother?"

"He's okay. He poops a lot." He clipped his fingers over his nose. "Otherwise, he's pretty cool. Especially after a bath."

"I can see that."

"Do you have a brother?"

"I do, and a sister. They're younger than me. Not babies though." I snatched the ball out of his hand when he wasn't paying attention, and he tried to grab it back as I danced out of reach and dribbled. "My brother is an officer like me now."

"Really?" Connor stopped trying to grab for the ball. "Hey, maybe I could someday come down to the station."

"Sure." I bounced the ball back to him. "We could do a field trip. As long as no dangerous criminals are around that day." It was hard keeping my face straight.

He stared at me so hard he forgot to dribble. "Really? Like on Law & Order?"

"You watch that show?" I wasn't sure that was age-appropriate, but then again, I'd started sneak-watching horror movies at age 8, so who was I to judge?

"Sometimes when my mom falls asleep on the couch breastfeeding Leo."

I tried not to look aghast. I'd forgotten breastfeeding. I didn't know how to deal with sharing Tab's stupendous breasts with an infant. Of course his or her needs would come first.

If Tab even intended to breastfeed. I should ask.

Not on our date though. I'd wait until after. I wanted her to just enjoy herself that night, not think about upcoming motherhood. She'd probably want to drink heavily and she couldn't, so I'd help her have fun.

Damn, her breasts would be getting bigger. I already was in love with them. How was I supposed to hold down a job if she went up a cup size or two?

I did have some time off saved up. I could use it to praise them properly—assuming she still wanted to have sex with me.

"Brady?"

"Hmm?"

"When can we have the field trip?" Connor peered up at me, his hair hanging into his eyes.

"Soon." My mind was whirling. "Maybe really soon. What about a haircut and some new clothes too? Don't you have that Black and Gold school dance coming up?"

"Yeah." He shifted back and forth, halfheartedly dribbling. "I wanted to ask Danielle to go with me. I mean, just be there with me. I can't drive."

I nodded soberly as if this was news to me.

"But my mom can't afford new clothes." He twisted his mouth. "Mine are okay."

I imagined he was used to making do. Maybe I could help him have a few hours with no worries either, just like Tab. It wasn't much but it was something.

"No big. I can handle it." Frowning, I looked toward the side of the learning center's gym where some of the other kids were jumping rope and doing exercises on a padded mat. "We'll have to ask your mom first. Is she here today?"

"No. She dropped me off." Connor's expression went from hopeful to dejected in an instant. "We'll go some other time."

"Yeah." I clapped his shoulder. "Soon, buddy. I promise. I'll call her tonight, and we'll make plans."

"You won't forget?"

"I won't forget. Now let's see if you can score on me today." I darted forward and snagged the ball out of his hold, making him laugh and chase after me.

Later, during the drive home, I called his mom and made sure she was okay with me taking him to the police station and to the mall for a cut and some shopping. Mrs. Jackson was profusely grateful, and she kept thanking me over and over.

"It's so hard raising kid as a single parent. You just have no idea. Good people like you make it easier. Thank God for you, Brady McNeill."

Her words kept echoing in my head. As a cop, I'd always stayed on the right side of the line. Helping people made me feel good, so it wasn't as if I didn't get anything out of it.

But the situation with Tab was so different. I didn't know where to put the need to do something for her and the baby. Taking care of them was my job just as much as it was to show up for shifts on the force, and I felt as if I was just calling in sick every day.

I couldn't keep doing that.

As much as I wanted to respect her boundaries and her space, I couldn't not know how she was all day long. I didn't need her to check in hourly—though with my current state of preoccupation, most days I wouldn't mind—but I needed more than *this*. A date once a week didn't cut it. Maybe if we'd started slower, maybe if I didn't already love her...

Sighing, I stopped at a light and scrubbed my hands over my face. What was the point in denying it? I might not have ever been in love before, but I was crazy in love with Tabitha Monaghan. One way or another, I had to get her to love me back.

A sharp rap at my window had me dropping my hands, instantly on guard. Misty's slightly manic smile filled my window.

Just what I needed.

But I needed to talk to her, even if all had been relatively quiet lately. I couldn't take the chance she'd mess with Tabitha somehow and upset her while she was pregnant.

I motioned to the curb and indicated she should follow me to where I parked. She nodded and I signaled and swerved to the side of the street into an available space. Knowing full well people would probably notice us talking and make assumptions.

Couldn't be helped.

As soon as I stopped the car, I climbed out. No way was I having the conversation in my vehicle. I didn't want Misty to get the wrong idea, though who would have sex in a police car? That was something even *I* wouldn't consider.

"Aww, out here? It's cold." She rubbed her arms in her puffy coat, the fur-lined collar pulled close to her face.

"Sorry, this will be brief."

She rolled her heavily lined eyes. "That's your MO."

I ignored her. "Look, I thought we were friendly once. I also thought we were both okay with how things ended. No one dumped anyone. It just petered out. That happens."

"Nice choice of words." She smirked as the cold wind blew her dark hair back off her shoulders. "You wandered off, but you wanted me back. Did you forget that?"

I stared at her blankly. "What?"

"At Christmas, you swaggered into the Spinning Wheel and bought me a drink. Remember that? Said you hoped I had a nice holiday. Waggled your brows at me. Then I called you the next day, and you never called me back."

Frowning, I scraped a hand down the back of my neck. I hadn't waggled my damn brows. Had I? But I'd had a couple of beers that night and had a couple days off to look forward to, so maybe I had.

"It was Christmas, I was with my family." Then I'd simply forgotten it as if it had never happened. *Shit.* "I bought you the drink to be friendly. Neighborly," I stressed. "Not because I was looking to hook up with you. I'd heard you'd had a hard time."

Her face crumpled, and fat tears streaked down her cheeks. "So, you did know my grandma died. You never called. Never sent flowers or a card. She raised me, Brady."

Was I supposed to do all that? Fuck it, we'd barely been friends. Yet I'd slept with her as if it mattered not at all. I'd just been in it for a fun night and hadn't considered she might not be on the same page.

Or that maybe she just needed a friend.

My breath puffed out in the cold air. "I'm sorry. I was a thoughtless jerk." I took a step forward and she held out a hand, waving me back. "I screwed up. That's on me. But you can't go around damaging property. It's not right."

"Oh, give me a break. It was just a stupid cake. She could've fixed it. Just re-frosted the thing or whatever. I hear all over the place how talented she is. How pretty and sweet and perfect. What does she have I don't have? Tell me that."

"It's not about that. Tabitha's not the reason we fizzled out. It just didn't happen for us. Sometimes it doesn't. You're a great girl, Misty. You'll find someone for you much better than me." My mind spun, her words finally landing. "What cake?"

She took an evasive step away from the car. "Nothing. Never mind. I misunderstood."

I snatched her arm, holding her firmly when she would've pulled away. "What cake? Don't make me bring you in to the station. I don't want to have to do that, but I will if you refuse to answer me."

She wouldn't make eye contact with me. "She didn't tell you. Keeping secrets already, huh? Or else she knew you'd do your machismo thing and it didn't warrant that. It was just a stupid message. I told her to fuck herself, okay? But guess she has you to do that for her."

The edges of my vision hazed with my anger. At her, at Tabitha for not telling me. That explained why she'd called the station last weekend at the end of my shift. I'd forgotten all about the call she'd put in to the station in the baby madness.

This was my freaking job. All I wanted to do was keep her safe.

Keep her safe when you're the one who created these situations for her in the first place. With Misty and with the baby.

"This is your last warning. Stay away from Tabitha. Stay away from Sugar Rush. I'm truly sorry for what you've been through. I made mistakes. But I didn't mean to hurt you."

"You know, I honestly believe you mean that." Her voice held no inflection whatsoever. "You're just a player, born and bred. You can't change."

Her words struck me with as much force as the sleet now slanting down from the sky. I'd hear those over and over in my head too.

With a muttered curse, she turned and headed for the sidewalk, striding off into the cold night with her small shoulders hunched.

I'd done that too. She'd made some bad choices, but my behavior had caused a woman who was dealing with some difficult changes in her life react in a probably not too surprising way.

You hurt someone, they lash out.

I climbed back in my car and slammed the door before driving down the street to our apartment building. For the first time since I'd started this thing with Tabitha, I didn't go to her place first before heading to mine to see if she was ready for Pancake.

For once, I needed her to come to me.

TWENTY

I POKED AT THE MICROWAVE MEAL I'D NUKED AFTER I GOT HOME FROM work. I'd found a pretty healthy brand for the nights I didn't want to throw something together.

The broccoli was limp, the mashed potatoes tasted watery, and the chicken could've been rubber. I ate it anyway because my stomach lining was turning itself inside out. I'd always had a more than healthy appetite, but this baby thing was taking it to the next level. I fully expected my doctor to put me on a diet tomorrow. I couldn't stop eating.

Except this crap.

Halfway through, I gave up and dumped it into the garbage and settled for a cup of hot tea. I wasn't nauseated tonight, thank God. I hadn't been all day. I'd mostly been relieved until I'd started worrying that maybe that wasn't a good sign for it to just stop. I'd been sick for most of the week, off and on. I'd finally made up my mind to trust Lu enough with my secret to see if she knew of any herbal preggo helpers for such things. Not only was she a witch, she was into everything natural and safe, especially when it came to her pregnancy.

Her baby shower was this Saturday. Had I even RSVP'd? I couldn't remember. Preggo brain was kicking my behind hard.

I smiled despite myself. *Yes, I'm blaming the pregnancy for everything, Brady. So what?*

Then the smile faded as I glanced at the kitchen clock. It was past nine. Brady should've been off work hours ago.

Where was he? He never didn't show. Never didn't call.

I swallowed the knot in my throat as I hurried to unearth my phone from my purse. Maybe he'd texted and somehow I hadn't heard it. I never silenced his calls or texts, even when I was at work or asleep.

Because he's the center of your life already. No matter how foolish you feel.

No texts.

Feeling silly, I even checked my email. Of course there was nothing.

What if he was hurt? If something had happened at work or—

I frowned at the sound of sleet against the windows. Ugh, not again. Maybe he was stuck dealing with traffic issues. Or he could've been in an accident, lying hurt in some gutter where no one knew.

My temples started pounding. He was most likely fine. It wasn't as if we had a firm time to do the puppy handoff. We kept things easy. Loose.

Just like our relationship, not including the surprise baby on top.

I cupped my stomach and took a few deep breaths. There. See, I was relaxed.

Or could be he'd simply forgotten. Maybe I'd slipped his mind.

Stop it. He said he wanted us to date, remember? And he doesn't ever forget his responsibilities. He's a very conscientious dog dad.

I threw back my shoulders and took another deep breath before grabbing my phone off the counter. I wasn't going to focus on likely needless worry. I had things to accomplish.

I texted Lu.

Tabitha: Hi Lu. I'm coming to your baby shower. I'm so excited to come. I hope I told you?

Crap, I needed gifts. By Saturday. I should go to the mall. It wasn't closed yet.

But Brady would be coming—probably—and I didn't feel like driving all the way to Syracuse in this weather. I could go tomorrow after my doctor's appointment. I'd taken the afternoon off—gah!—and I needed an outfit for our date anyway. Unless I dug out the sweater dress I'd wanted to wear for Valentine's Day. Assuming I could find it. My closet needed an excavation.

And I officially wasn't thinking about any of that right now.

Luna: hey babe! No, you didn't RSVP, which I thought was super weird. U R always on top of everything.

I sighed. Pre-baby, sure.

Tabitha: I'm so sorry. I hope it doesn't mess up your counts or anything. I want to come! Just my life is a bit chaotic & I'm forgetting stuff right & left.

Luna: Oh, I just bet. How's it going with your hottie cop?

Tabitha: He knocked me up.

So much for easing her in. I shook my head and kept typing.

Tabitha: Sorry, I was going to say that in a smoother way. But yeah. Baby. In me. Oh, by the way, how's your baby? Still inside? Didn't drop out early?

Luna sent over a bunch of shocked faces and laughing faces emojis.

Luna: OMG, congrats! Are you happy? I'm sure freaked out too. I so was. I still am. My baby is great. Super huge. I feel like a whale. But TG, still cooking. Not long now tho.

I stared down at her text. God, I *was* happy. I really was. This baby was already so important to me. So vital and loved. I was even pretty sure Brady was on his way to loving him or her too. Like he was concerned we were okay, me and baby.

So, where was the jerk? He better not be hurt or in trouble. I'd yell at him for scaring me then smother him with kisses.

Tabitha: I'm very happy, TY. Scared witless. Sure I'll never manage it all. Afraid out of my mind to squeeze out a baby out of that very tiny place. You know, the usual.

Luna: I wanted natural childbirth but changing my mind as it gets closer. Pain sucks. At least I'll go thru it before you so you can feel more comfortable.

Tabitha: I don't think anything will make me comfy except lots & lots of drugs.

Lu: I hear u, sister.

Tabitha: Hey, I've had a lot of nausea. Do you have any herbal remedies or teas that help?

Lu: I sure do. But you need to hit up Kinleigh. She's selling something new in the shop that came from Asher. You know, the podcast dude? He turned her on to this ginger candy recipe from his grandfather & they're the best stomach settler ever. I'm low on my supply too.

Tabitha: Bless you. Thank you. I'll talk to Kin and August while I'm at it. I'll need a crib.

Kinleigh ran this super cool vintage shop in town that was expanding into all kinds of new products, including carrying her husband August's handmade furniture. August was Luna's husband Caleb's older brother and he was incredibly talented. He had a special line just for babies and children too. He even did made-to-order custom pieces.

I swallowed hard. I needed to outfit a nursery. And where would I put this baby furniture? I lived in a small apartment. I supposed I could make some room in my bedroom if I got rid of my bookcase. It wasn't as if I had time to read anymore anyway.

From there, we were off chatting about nurseries and baby clothes and medicinal elixirs from Lu's favorite witchy shop that helped with fatigue and nausea.

Luna: And there's even one that boosts sex drive. *winky face*

Tabitha: I'm good there. I'm a horny cow already.

Luna: Me too. Well, I used to be. Now I'm more likely to threaten Caleb with death if he pulls down his pants. But during the second trimester, I couldn't get enough.

I just sent through a couple of smiley faces because thinking of sex right now made me sad. I hated feeling so distant from Brady. It wasn't even that he hadn't called or texted. This whole week, things between us had felt off. I didn't know how to live my life now without having him enmeshed in every part of it.

I didn't *want* to.

I'd thought we should take a little break to think. We both needed to. But all I'd come up with was that my life had changed a lot recently and I was changing too. I didn't want to go back to the old Tabitha with her old life. I couldn't.

Tabitha: I should let you go. Thanks 4 everything. I'll see you Sat.

Luna: Sure thing. Hey, if you come by a little early, I'll hook you up w/a quickie tarot reading. One for you, one for you & your hottie plus one for the baby.

I teared up. Shocker.

Tabitha: TY. I'd love it. But don't you need to help set up 4 the shower?

Luna: Nah, my best bish has it handled. Even if anything baby related makes her nervous she'll accidentally get pregnant by osmosis. I think Ryan's even getting afraid to drive thru the Cove.

I giggled. I couldn't help it.

Tabitha: Who can blame her? This place is potent.

Luna: Esp since I'm pretty sure her dude Preston's practically ready to outfit a nursery now.

Tabitha: Aww, that's sweet.

Luna: It def helps to have a good dude. You have 1 too.

Tabitha: Yeah. I do.

I almost clarified he wasn't really mine. I wanted him to be and it felt as if we were working toward that, but nothing was certain yet. But for once, I didn't diminish what we were together.

Maybe what we had could build a real foundation. I just had to have faith.

Luna: The guy never stops helping people. I saw him a few hours ago when I was walking back from my shift at Kin's shop. He was talking to that Misty chick. I couldn't hear what he was saying, but his aura was soft blue. He's very compassionate.

I might've been moved by that if my vision hadn't gone a little fuzzy at reading Brady was with Misty around the time he was supposed to be with me. What was going on?

Maybe she's just become an easier proposition to deal with. No baby on board there.

I rubbed the heel of my hand over my chest. Either I had heartburn from my unsatisfying meal or I was jealous as heck.

Maybe something else had happened. Some kind of property damage—other than the lawn and the cake I still hadn't told him about. Could be she'd given up on taking shots at us and had decided to take another tack with him entirely.

In the back of my mind, I knew he'd never go there. But the green-eyed monster was trying to convince me not to listen to reason right now.

My spine locked. It was time for me to pay Brady a visit.

If he wasn't home, then what? I couldn't text him like some shrew and demand his whereabouts. Even if he had absconded with my puppy.

First your puppy, then your baby. He wants the kid to have his name. Maybe he has nefarious plans.

Ugh, enough. I was not going to go postal without provocation. I hoped. I didn't feel too even-tempered right now. I was hungry, tired, and worried. Not the best combination for being rational.

I quickly texted Lu.

Tabitha: I have 2 run. I'll see you Sat tho. Thanks again! Xoxo

On my way across the hall, I stopped to brush my hair and realized, shockingly, I needed to pee. I took care of that then noticed I'd dropped watery mashed potatoes on my shirt so I hurried into my bedroom to find a clean top. Of course I decided my sweats weren't cute enough if he'd been off talking to his not fully balanced ex, so I pulled on my favorite jeans, only to discover I couldn't get the zipper up without extreme calisthenics.

I finally managed to shoehorn them on although oxygen was now at a premium. I pulled on my shoes and grabbed my purse before marching over to Brady's and knocking. I was prepared to use the key he'd given me for dog emergencies if need be.

He opened the door right after the second knock and started to smile. His kissable lips twitched, starting to slide into their usual position before turning down into a frown.

"Tabitha." His voice was flat as he hooked his arm on the doorjamb above his head, seemingly impossibly tall and broad as he stared down at me. "What's up?"

I tilted my head. "Hi. My name is Tabitha. I'm assuming you're Brady, the cop who served me by saying it would feel so much better without a condom and that he couldn't impregnate me before doing exactly that?"

"So I've heard twenty times. Did you need something?"

I attempted to peer around his stupidly muscular body. "Where is my dog?" A telltale bark sounded from down the hall in his apartment along with a deeper one that was clearly Daisy. "Where have you imprisoned them?"

He snorted. "Again, with the podcast melodrama. Sorry, I don't have an attic or basement to keep them captive."

"That doesn't mean you couldn't stash them away elsewhere. Don't think you can get away with it. First, you'll ask for the baby to have your name, then you'll go on an unplanned trip to Mexico. I know how this stuff goes, pal." I nudged him in the chest, but he didn't budge out of the doorway. "Move."

"Why don't you make me, Strawberry?" As soon as the nickname fell off his lips, he pressed them together.

I frowned. "Why are you acting so weird?" I narrowed my eyes. "Is she here? Have you got her hiding down the hall with my dog?"

"She who?"

"Oh, you know who. You just didn't expect me to know about your little rendezvous."

"I had a rendezvous? Must've not been that great since I have no idea."

"You didn't talk to Misty?"

"Talking does not equal a rendezvous." He gave me what I thought of as his cool cop look. "What was *your* last contact with Misty, Ms. Monaghan?"

"Mine?"

"Yours." He crossed his arms, stretching the sleeves of his navy Henley in disturbingly sexy ways. "Not that I'm supposed to know about that. Why would I be informed? I'm just your freaking boyfriend."

"Now you're my freaking boyfriend?" I jabbed my nail in his forearm. "You should've clued me in. And I tried to tell you the other day. The baby you implanted in me and the fact I was sick as a dog took precedence."

"I did clue you in. I said I wanted to date you. Last I knew, we were going out tomorrow. Unless something has changed and you didn't see fit to tell me."

"I tell you everything."

"Oh, really?"

"Except that one little thing," I muttered. "I just didn't want you to lose it because she called me fat."

"She what?" he roared. "She told me she told you to fuck yourself."

"That was okay though?" I would've laughed if he didn't look positively murderous as he strode away from the door. He stopped at the side table beside the couch to grab his wallet and keys, and then he marched back toward me. "What are you doing?"

"Obviously, I have more to say to Misty. I'll be back soon, if you can watch the imprisoned dogs. They're in my bedroom. Probably chewing on my nightstand in protest."

"Wait. You're leaving? You can't leave. It's sleeting out. And I'm yelling at you." Although the reasons why were getting murkier by the moment.

Probably just because I was hungry at this point.

"Save it. I'll be back in a bit." He started to brush past me so I did the one thing I could guarantee would stop him in his tracks.

I grabbed his cock.

He stopped, all right. The look he aimed down at me was pure smolder. "Save that too."

"Nope. It's a one time offer." I frowned, gazing down at my fingers as they tugged at the zipper of his jeans as if they were operating independently from my brain.

"Too bad for me then." He reached down, circled his broad fingers around my wrist, and drew my hand away.

I wasn't dissuaded that easily.

I undid the top few buttons on my shirt. He probably thought I'd craftily intended not to wear a bra on purpose, but my breasts were so oversensitive right now that fabric sometimes made me want to shriek.

"Tabitha," he warned. "I'm not amused by you right now."

"Ditto." I yanked the shirttails out of my jeans and let out a gasp at the constriction around my waist. "Dear God."

"You can say that again," he muttered as I kept unbuttoning.

Except I skipped the last few shirt buttons to undo my jeans and I let out a moan—one that was not faked porn star-worthy enticement, but from sheer relief at breathing freely again.

It didn't seem to matter. His sexy dark eyes glazed before his expression shifted back to pure cool cop as if my diamond-hard pink nipples weren't on full display.

The magic must already be fading. Unless he'd noticed the red ligature marks from the denim. That probably cut down on some of the sexy factor.

"I'm eating for two, dammit," I announced for no reason in particular.

"I know that and it only makes you hotter. And you were already the most gorgeous woman on this planet." He stepped closer and stared at my belly. "Why are you suffocating my baby?"

"Because beauty is pain?"

"Well, stop it." He shoved the jeans down my legs, making a tormented sound at my blue satin panties. "Woman, you're going to kill me."

"It's not a thong."

"So?"

"Just saying." I swallowed and tried to see myself as he did. I was pretty sure my belly obscured part of my panties. The belly that was growing by the minute. "You're good for my ego."

"I'm glad. Even if you're hell on mine." He crouched to untie my sneakers as if I was a kid, easing them off my feet before he drew down my jeans the rest of the way.

I sifted my fingers through his hair. "I'm sorry. I may be acting like a shrew."

"May?"

"I'm pregnant."

His lips twitched, and this time, he didn't try to stop his smile. "I know. I'm so happy and I want to tell everyone, but I can't because maybe you're ashamed or scared or—"

"How can you think I'm ashamed? I just wanted to keep it quiet for a bit longer because a lot of pregnancies don't make it through the first trimester."

"I didn't know that. God. That's so..." He sat back on his knees and gripped my waist, staring up at me so earnestly that it would've taken a much stronger woman than me not to fall head over heels for him. "Ask me to your doctor's appointment tomorrow. Please."

"Of course you can come." I sniffled. "You really want to?"

"With my whole heart." He rested his head against my belly.

I wove my fingers through his hair. It was longer now than it had been when we'd met a month ago. "I didn't really think you were having a rendezvous. I just missed you. I was so worried. I didn't know why you didn't bring Pancake. Or text or call. Or send up a smoke signal."

"I wasn't even sure you cared."

"How can you say that?"

"Because you don't *say* anything. You didn't tell me about Misty. You probably didn't even want to tell me about the baby. You think I'm a player who won't stick around. You don't trust me."

"Brady, I'm scared out of my mind and afraid to make a mistake. Can't you try to understand that?" I pleaded.

"I'm trying, Strawberry." He pressed a kiss to my belly button. "I swear to you, I won't change my mind about this. About you and me. About our baby. I want a family with you. I love—"

"Don't. Please." Though I hated myself for it, I covered his lips with my fingers. "If you say that, I'll say it back and those words are promises. I can't say them and go back on them."

"I don't want to go back on them, can't you get that?"

"I'm trying." I cupped his scruffy jaw. "Just give me a little more time. Please."

His Adam's apple bobbed and he stared up at me for a long moment before nodding. "I'd give you anything you asked for."

"Okay. Don't go talk to Misty."

"Low blow."

"You already did, right? I'm sure you made your point clear."

He nodded. "But she hurt you. I can't let her get away with that."

"She actually didn't exactly call me fat. She called me Grimace."

"Huh?"

"The big purple character from McDonalds from years ago?"

His blank expression didn't change.

I waved it off. "Anyway, she said 'fuck you, Grimace' though the writing was kind of sloppy so I'm not even entirely certain. That's what I thought it said. But you can't blame her completely because look what sex with you did to me and I'm fairly sane." I frowned, mentally replaying my recent behavior. "I used to be anyway."

"Maybe it wasn't the sex. Maybe we just fell for each other."

No *maybe* involved. But I had to make a joke. "Your penis played a part. I'm quite certain."

Pancake let out a howl down the hall so Brady kissed my belly and rose, doing up the buttons on my shirt with quick efficiency. "Time to spring them."

"Why did you lock them up? And why are you dressing me? Usually I get naked and we get—"

"I'm not sleeping with you before our first date."

If my eyebrows had climbed any higher, I would've gotten a headache. Somehow the one I'd started to get before had vanished.

Brady magic. "Um, not to be a killjoy but…" I cupped my belly and his eyes softened.

"You're so beautiful. Even more so when you do that." His hand covered mine and it was my turn to soften. At this rate, I'd be in a pool on the floor in no time. "I want to retrace some of our steps. We missed some vital ones."

"Yeah."

"If we take them more slowly, you'll learn to trust me. I'm persistent, baby."

"Even if you got pissed at me for not telling you about the cake and put the dogs in jail?"

He laid his lips lightly on mine. "Even if. And I didn't put them 'in jail' until you showed up and I wanted to have a conversation with you without them leaping all over."

"But you didn't talk to me at first."

"I know. I was there. Do we have to do a play by play?"

"Man, you really aren't used to relationships, are you? You have so much to learn."

As did I.

He gave me a dirty look as he stepped back. "Strawberry, hotness only gets you so far."

I cupped my belly again. He had no idea how much effort it cost me to be playful and casual about something that still was so huge for me to contemplate. "Yeah, but this should get me the rest of the way."

He pretended to think it over while Daisy added her accompaniment to Pancake's whining. "At least I didn't fall for your cock grab. Low blow, by the way."

"A lady has to use what's at her disposal." My gaze dropped to his jeans. "I really don't like this no sex thing."

"Me either."

"Am I supposed to go home now?"

Halfway across the room, he strode back to me and drew me hard against him. "No. No sex doesn't mean we have to spend the night apart. I can't sleep without you any longer."

"Me either." I tipped my forehead against his chin, absorbing the rightness of his arms around me. "Plus, your bed is much more supportive."

He pinched my ass. "Because you're pregnant."

"No, because I worked ten hours today and I'm tired as hell. Jeez, stop putting words in my mouth."

"I don't like you working so much."

"You just want me to lay about and be ready for sex at a moment's notice."

"Is that an option on the table?" Before I could reply, he added, "Feel like Chinese takeout?"

"Yes. With extra duck sauce. Oh, and extra fortune cookies. And extra—"

"Extra crab rangoons. Yes, I know your order by now."

"God, you turn me on." When he started to walk away, I snagged his hand and drew him right back again. "Turns out I can't let go of you just yet."

"Even if the dogs are in jail?"

I locked my arms around him and released a long sigh as I melted into his strong chest. "I'll make it up to them with kisses later." I brushed my lips over his jaw. "Can you just hold me?"

"I'll hold you forever if you let me."

I was afraid by how much I wanted exactly that.

TWENTY-ONE

CHINESE AND AN EARLY BEDTIME MEANT SOMETHING MUCH DIFFERENT now than it had a few weeks ago, but it worked for me just the same.

Daisy was giving Brady the silent treatment because of his cruel imprisonment, so she curled up on one side of me and Pancake wrapped himself around my head on the pillow. Brady took the other side, thereby ensuring that getting up for my bi-hourly pee trips was a process.

"You okay?" Brady's sleepy voice in the darkness after my third trip made me smile.

"Yeah, just much peeing."

"Pregnancy thing?"

"So I've been told."

"It's a lot of work to have a kid."

"You're telling me. Why I wasn't ever sure I wanted any." I crawled back under the covers and snuggled with Pancake for a minute or two before Brady turned and hauled us both close. Daisy had wandered off at some point so we had more room.

"I didn't ask if you wanted the baby. I just assumed. Do you not—is this not—" He took a breath. "I don't want to do something you're not ready for."

"Are you ready?"

"I think I am," he said after a minute. "I'm scared shitless, but it feels good. Right. Just like everything has with you from the start."

I rested my head on his chest and his heartbeat thudded quickly under my cheek. "I want to have this baby with you." I tilted back my head, peering at him in the darkness. The words weren't as hard to say as I would've expected. "You make me so happy."

"You make me happy too. I'm excited about this next step, even if I don't know what it will look like yet." He reached down to cup my belly and Pancake wiggled down my body, resettling himself until his butt was in Brady's hand. We both laughed as I cuddled closer to them.

My family. Even if it was too soon. Even if I was afraid it couldn't last.

Right now, it felt wonderful.

"Tonight I told Misty to stay away from you and Sugar Rush."

"Okay. Thank you." I wasn't going to demand details or make it bigger than it was.

I was working really hard at trusting him, along with my own judgment. I made good choices when I followed my instincts.

All of them led straight to Brady McNeill.

"Apparently, Misty got some mixed signals from me at Christmas, so that's on me. I didn't always take enough care with people I dated. Or with friends and family. I take people for granted."

"We all do that. No one is perfect."

"No. But I'm going to do better. I talk shit about my dad sometimes, make jokes about his inappropriate questions for people we're dating or our friends, but he's such an honest, decent man who loves his family above all else. I want my kid to be proud of me like I am of him."

"It's 2 am. Don't make me cry." I reached down to link my fingers with his. "And no worries there. Your kid is going to be proud of you. *I'm* proud of you."

"You are?"

"Your first inclination was to help me with Pancake," I said slowly, realizing I'd already seen daddy Brady in action and somehow hadn't equated his behavior to how he'd be with a human child. But he'd loved and cared for our dog from the first. Despite being at the end of a long shift at work and though he'd barely known me, he'd jumped in with both feet. "You're just that kind of guy. Someone who helps and puts himself out for people. You're so used to doing that you don't see how women react to your natural friendliness and protectiveness. We all want a man like you."

He was quiet for a moment. "You've never not mentioned my penis in my list of qualities before."

"Oh, I'm thinking it."

When he tugged on one of my curls, I gave him a quick kiss.

"Maybe someday you'll be okay with meeting my parents."

I didn't say anything.

"Mav suggested it the other day and I basically told him hell no. Now—"

"Now…" I echoed softly, trying not to stiffen up.

Meeting the parents was so enormous. I just wasn't ready yet. I hated disappointing him, but I just couldn't go there right now. If I didn't measure up to the perfect woman they probably had in their head for their son, it would cut too deep.

"Now I want them to meet my girl. I'm proud of you too. I want to show you off to the world." He chuckled softly. "I especially want to tell everyone I knocked you up. A billboard isn't out of the question. The place that puts them on the highway runs good specials," he added as I kicked him playfully under the covers.

Probably served me right the toes I'd whacked on the coffee table the other day still ached.

"You really haven't told anyone?"

"You asked me not to."

"Not even Mav?"

"Definitely not him. He'll probably take a vow of abstinence in case pregnancy is contagious."

I giggled. "It practically is in the Cove."

"Oh, wait." He frowned. "I lied."

"About what?"

"I did tell someone."

"I knew it. Jared?"

"No. A kid at the learning center."

"Huh?"

"Yeah, while I was volunteering there, it just kind of spilled out to Connor. I'm taking him on a tour of the police station and shopping and to get a haircut this weekend. Just for something fun to do. He has a dance coming up and—what?" he demanded as I stared.

"You're such a good guy. Can't you see that? Your kid is going to be totally spoiled having you as an example."

"Are you trying to break my will about the no sex thing?"

"Is it working?"

"Oh, I'm storing up, trust me." He kissed my forehead and I had to work at not sighing like a helpless teenager with her first love. "You've already made me bend my rules about staying in our separate apartments before our date."

"This week apart was torture."

"Yeah." He smudged his thumb over my cheek. "So, I'll pick you up at 2 tomorrow?"

Of course he knew what time my doctor's appointment was, because I'd mentioned it in passing on the way back from the hospital days ago. That was just who he was.

Finally, my vision was clearing enough for me to see him for the man he truly was instead of listening to my fears and misconceptions —and foolish gossip.

"Okay. I'm glad you're coming."

"Me too." I could hear the smile in his voice as he leaned in to line up our mouths.

Pancake popped his head up between us, sticking his big black snout against mine so Brady nearly got a mouthful of puppy tongue. "Guess I'll try that move again later."

When he kissed me as he dropped me off at the bakery in the morning, we weren't interrupted. Not counting the totally unnecessary cheering from my employees.

Most notably, his sister.

It didn't help that he continued kissing me while Honey whistled on her fingers Van-style. My sister was probably giving her pointers.

I whispered between kisses, "We should tell Honey."

"Mmm-hmm. This kitchen smells like your frosting." He dipped his head to kiss my neck despite our audience. "You know what that does to me."

He wasn't kidding. He had an erection that could've poked out an eye had I been perfect BJ height like my sister.

Which made no sense. That would mean she was waist-high and she wasn't *that* short. Leave it to Van to make a catchphrase out of nonsense.

"I'll bring some home. Now go." I gave him a light shove out the back door of the bakery to the sound of catcalls. "Have a good day at work. Be safe."

"I will. See you later, Strawberry." He gave me a meaningful look before striding away into the sunshine.

I sighed and leaned against the doorjamb while my employees continued their playful harassment.

"Bye, sugarpuss! Make sure you keep that gun holstered!" Tiffany called.

"Or maybe not, because I imagine that's a sight to see," Lea added.

"Oh, she's seen it enough already, trust me, because soon she won't be able to see—" Van broke off with a loud cough as I stared her down. "How about those Lakers?"

I turned to face my employees. Mickey had an early class so she wasn't there, but I figured Honey would share our news with her.

Maybe I should've waited for Brady to tell his sister, but he hadn't said he wanted to be there. And all of a sudden, I was bursting with my news.

"So, I'm having a baby," I announced, twisting my fingers together tighter than my braided cinnamon bars.

No one said a thing.

Maybe I needed to add one of Van's dramatic touches. "Probably not twins," I added. "But you never know, since I'm a twin. And frats run in families—gah!" I gasped as all of my ladies swarmed me at once until we were in a giant laughing, talking pile of...happiness.

That was what I'd found here. Not just overwork and the beginning of financial security, but a family. I'd built the frame, but the people I'd been lucky enough to build with were the ones constructing the walls and floor and the supports that would make it grow strong.

It already was.

"I realize it's not fair to ask you to keep my secret, but we are kind of keeping it on the down-low since it's still the first trimester and if something were to happen..." I trailed off and made myself smile to keep my voice from wobbling. "It's just early."

"We won't tell anyone," Tiffany said.

"Pinky swear," Lea chimed in. "Oh, you're going to have the most beautiful baby!"

I smiled. "Just as long as he or she is healthy, we will be happy."

Honey tugged on my arm, pulling me out of the circle. Her brown eyes were wide with excitement. "Does Mav know? He's gonna flip. He's allergic to babies."

I laughed. "No. Hardly anyone knows yet. Now just you guys and some kid Brady told at the learning center."

"I'm honored I was in the early group." Honey flipped back her long dark hair and then her mouth rounded. "Wait, no parental units yet?"

"Um, no."

"Sunday dinner?"

I blew out a breath. "No."

Honey didn't badger me. Instead, she nodded understandingly. "My mom being in the FBI scares off people even though she's retired now. Mav hasn't brought a girl home since high school graduation weekend. He claims she tried to get the girl's social security number so she could run a report on her, but that's just McNeill family legend at this point. But Dad did ask if she wanted to go smoke in the backyard."

"Oh, wow. One open-minded, one not."

"Really open. He wasn't referring to cigarettes." She rolled her eyes. "Dad's an aging hippie who loves Elvis, TV psychics, and bearskin rugs. He still has his old VW Bug. He's been threatening to restore it for years but claims he doesn't have time. He sells lava lamps and other vintage items at Hip2BeSquared in downtown Turnbull. Dad has this one blacklight picture of Elvis..." She shook her head. "It's fuzzy and Mom wants to set it on fire."

"Oh."

"I think he knows if he restores the Bug, Mom will be on him to get it back on the market. So, he hides it in the garage under a tarp that says *make love, not war.*"

"Oh."

"I hope I'm not scaring you away. Please don't leave me alone with these heathens any longer." She tugged me into a hug. "I'm so happy. I'm gonna have a niece."

"No guarantees there," I said vaguely, still trying to process how a woman in the FBI with two sons in law enforcement had married a man who sold lava lamps, collected fuzzy Elvis posters, and offered tokes to high school students.

Love was mind-boggling. And these people were going to be my in-laws.

Well, not in-laws exactly, just extended family. My baby's grandparents. Brady and I weren't getting married.

"Whoa." I gripped my stomach as it rolled. "Here I thought she was on vacation. I mean, he."

"See, you know it's a girl."

I laughed and waved her off to get started with some of my normal morning tasks.

In between throwing up. Only twice though, so I considered it a win.

Van pulled me aside after my last purge, luring me into the back with a perfectly decorated orchid flower cupcake. "I did this," she announced before taking a giant lick of the frosting. "I brought you a tulip." She produced the other cupcake from behind her back and set it on my desk next to the one she'd already half demolished. "Hey, there's a good baby's name."

I laughed. "For a girl or a boy?"

"Either. Why not?"

She had a point, but I had a sneaking suspicion Brady probably wouldn't want his son to be named Tulip. Probably not his daughter either.

His dad, however, might just approve.

Van sighed. "Listen, it's been so crazy around here lately, we haven't had time to talk."

Uh-oh. Never knew what was up when my sister was feeling chatty. "Are you still obsessed with those tiny houses?"

She nodded vehemently. "I have too much stuff. I'm gonna ditch my apartment and live simply."

"Um, okay, you do that. I have way too many pots and pans to ever consider anything like that. Not that I would." I shuddered, picturing my hellhole closet. "Though maybe I could pare down some. I need to make room for the baby."

She snorted. "Brady is going to sweep you away and you're going to be blissfully happy arguing over spaghetti or tater tot casserole for dinner while the kid wails away in his Pack 'n Play and I'm never going to see you anymore." Her face crumpled and I glanced over my shoulder to see if she'd finally made good on her promise of getting a camera crew in here for her reality show idea.

"Van?"

"I'm fine. I blame you." She dashed under her eyes. "I've been a hormonal mess and you know why that is, don't you?"

"Sympathy preggo?"

"Exactly. And now I'm afraid I'm losing you instead of realizing I never could. Back in the old days, badass me would've been certain of that. Aka before you got knocked up." She yanked a tissue out of the box on my desk. They were necessary nowadays and not just for my allergies.

"Wow. No cameras?" I glanced around once more.

"No of course not. Why?"

"I thought you'd had your tear ducts surgically removed when you had your nose job."

She whacked me. "I had a deviated septum, you cow."

I had to laugh. "Okay, okay. I just haven't seen you cryhaha in so many years."

"Yeah, well, you had to get pregnant and be so happy you're glowing, now didn't you?" She shocked the hell out of me by grabbing my cheeks. "Don't screw this up. You deserve to be happy. You deserve to be in love and getting regular sex and maybe even to have a little squishmallow attached to your boob." She shrugged. "You know, if that's your thing."

"I'm still figuring out my things."

"But Brady's one of them?"

I nodded. "He is. He makes me so happy I'm scared all the time. Surely it can't be natural."

Van laughed and mopped her cheeks with her tissue. "Just enjoy it. Don't overthink. Don't overwork and drive him away. And don't make a joke about how it happens to every guy now and then. They don't find jokes about not getting it up funny. Ask me how I know." She wrinkled her heavily freckled, not surgically enhanced nose. *Ha.*

"Trust me, Brady has the endurance of an eighteen-year-old. It's kind of freaky. I would've needed more vitamins even if I wasn't pregnant."

"And now you're just showing off." She dragged me in for a tight hug. "I love you, sis. I'm so happy for you. He's so lucky to have you and if he ever forgets that, I'll complete his vasectomy the old-fashioned way."

"The doctor didn't say it wasn't completed—"

"Let's not get too technical."

"Okay." I grinned and rubbed her back. "You know you can't get rid of me, right? Sisters forever."

"Yeah." She smiled. "Anyway, I'm going to be the best aunt ever. You don't even have to name her Vanessa unless the spirit moves you."

"Okay, thanks." No way would Brady name her Vanessa when I was pretty sure he was mildly terrified of her.

Not an unusual reaction to Van.

"I'm going to go remake my perfect orchid cupcake and actually put it for sale this time." My sister grabbed her half-eaten cupcake and devoured it in two bites. "I may end up a master baker like my sis yet."

The next time I saw her, things were back to normal between us with no tears. Thank heavens.

I scarfed down a lunch of half a sandwich and some soup while standing up at my desk while she ran some figures for me for the new bigger freezer I'd been eyeing. I was still debating the purchase as I went back out behind the counter to help with the lunch rush.

Three customers in, a harried-looking Seth Hamilton strode in, clutching a sketch in one hand and his wallet in the other. He slapped both on the counter. "I need unicorn cupcakes by tomorrow. I'll pay anything."

Though Seth was a friend, I couldn't deny I heard the *ca-ching* of a cash register as I visualized my brand new stainless steel beauty. "We're already booked, I'm so sorry." I almost couldn't believe what was coming out of my mouth. "But if it would help I can refer you to—"

"No, no, please. This is for my daughter's party tomorrow. I totally messed up and didn't put the order in weeks ago when Ally told me to and now if I don't have these unicorn cupcakes for Laurie and her friends, she's going to cry her eyes out. She drew them herself, see." He slapped the surprisingly nuanced unicorn sketch on the counter, holding it down without shame with his wallet. "Honestly, charge me whatever. There is no price too high. We got some, well, not exactly bad news today, more weird news. I'm so desperate that I'll use it to try to get these for my daughter. My mom died." He dragged at the collar of his golf shirt as if he needed more air.

I covered my mouth. "Oh, Seth, I'm so sorry for you and Ally. And Oliver and Sage and the kids."

He waved it off. "We didn't have a relationship with her for years." He lowered his voice, evidently realizing there were far too many curious ears about. This was the Cove, after all. "But apparently, we have a younger brother and sister she neglected to tell us about."

212

"Oh my God, really? How…weird," I agreed when I couldn't find a better word. "Much younger?"

"No. Just a handful of years. So, we missed out on their whole lives thus far." He pinched the bridge of his nose. "That's my parents, making our lives as awkward as possible since time began. For once, it isn't my dad to blame."

"At least you can make up for lost time now."

"Yeah, we'll get to meet them while splitting the will. The will reading is going to be here because she still has family in the area though she's lived on the other side of the country for years. I don't even get why we're in her will. We haven't talked in so long. She never met my son and barely knew of my daughter."

"Oh. Ouch. Awkward," I agreed, well aware I was starting to sound like a parrot.

I was also aware that there was no possible way I could turn down a guy who just wanted to get some special cupcakes for his daughter's party. How many could there be? A dozen? I could handle that.

You have a date tonight. The most important date ever.

And a baby shower tomorrow.

And shopping before that. Maybe even with Brady's young friend at the learning center if the timing worked out right. I was all about multi-tasking, and if I could find some shower gifts while Brady shopped with the boy, that would work out well. The mall had all kinds of shops, right?

Not that he'd asked me to come. But I wanted to spend some time with him and the kid.

I blamed my overactive ovaries.

Seth exhaled heavily. "Tell me about it. Apparently, my mom made a ton of money as the owner of Homespun Hearth, a damn decor company. The woman who sold her kids." He cleared his throat at my gasp. "I'm exaggerating a little but not much. My familial past is the stuff of Jerry Springer."

I gave him a weak smile. "Well, at least you have your twin brother. Twins are something I'm well acquainted with."

"Oh, yeah, until Oliver blows his top about all this. I don't think he knows yet. I haven't gotten the phone call. Dex, my lawyer, explained it all to me. We went to college together, so I called in a favor," Seth explained, scraping his hand over the top of his closely cropped dark hair.

"Oh, hmm. That's good you have an old friend representing you."

"Yeah, though he's a divorce lawyer. I don't think he knows what he's doing, but he told me not to worry about it. I agreed not to since I can only worry on so many fronts at once."

I knew what that was like.

"Anyway, I need these cupcakes. My daughter still loves me and so does my wife, but if I don't provide these cupcakes, I'll only have my little boy to turn to. And he'll desert me for them soon enough because his mom is a far better cook. So....please?"

I juggled orders in my head and quickly ran through who was working tomorrow and what their schedules looked like. Forget my schedule. That was the most flexible one and it wasn't flexible at all.

I really wanted to have my date with Brady. I extremely wanted to have my post-date sex with Brady.

Blowing out a breath, I grabbed my order pad. "Let's talk details."

"Oh, thank you, Tab. I appreciate this more than you'll ever know. When you have kids, you'll do everything possible to make them happy, you know?"

I smiled. I was already beginning to. "Yeah. So, what time do you need them for?"

By the time Seth walked out of there, I'd decided if I worked through dinner I could handle it. I'd just be not taking the afternoon off post doctor's appointment after all.

Except I forgot that I now kind of had a significant other and that required conversation and compromise.

Especially when my post-date sex was at imminent risk.

"Absolutely not," Brady announced when he picked me up for the doctor. I'd just told him what I had cooking—including the fact that I'd have to try to recreate Laurie Hamilton's sketched unicorns on two dozen cupcakes by tomorrow.

And they were really amazing unicorns. She had a lot of artistic skill for such a young girl. I hoped I could do her drawing justice.

"Not happening," he added as if I hadn't understood the first part.

So, Brady wasn't awesome at the whole compromise thing either. I'd even brought him an eclair wrapped in my pink signature Sugar Rush tissue paper, along with a container of my special purple passion frosting that tasted like juicy grapes for us for later—which he did not know about yet and wouldn't if he kept up that attitude.

Okay, he probably still would. Because let's be real, I definitely still wanted to have sex with him even if he was being boorish. Possibly even more. Something about a man who took charge stirred me, even if I wanted to kick him with my sore toes. They still ached from the last time I'd tried to kick him.

"You're pregnant. You need time off. You can't keep running yourself ragged. Seth Hamilton can keep his big bucks and go fuck himself."

I lifted my brows. "Aren't you supposed to be a public servant? What did Seth ever do to you?"

"He tried to overwork my woman, that's what. Siri, call Maverick."

I frowned. "Why are you calling your brother?"

"Hey. You busy tonight?" he asked when Mav answered.

So much for our date.

"Yeah, I need your help. Tab has a big order going for that Hamilton fucker. No, not the one with the suits. The nicer one." He laughed, looping his wrist over the wheel as he drove. Unfairly hot. "Oliver's pretty cool too. Honestly. But whatever, Seth's rushing my girl so he's on my list. At least until we get this done. But I need you. Well, *we* need you. He has some pretty intricate ideas for these cupcakes, and you're the best artist I know." He reached over to grab my hand, the one I was currently balling up in order to better strike him with. "Other than Tab."

By the time the call ended, I didn't know if I wanted to slug him or kiss him.

"Did you just ask your brother to help design twenty-four cupcakes for me?"

"Yeah." His jaw worked. "I know I should've gotten your permission first, but you've seen his work. He's amazing. Obviously, this is a new medium for him. Even so, you heard him, he's up for the challenge. I don't know how it'll work for the frosting, but he and Honey are a good team. I can even help out."

At my laugh, he shot me a narrow-eyed look. "I can mix shit. Especially if all it requires is pressing a button."

I laughed again and took off my belt to slide closer to cover the side of his face with kisses. "Sometimes you're an overbearing jerk who needs to respect boundaries."

"So, why are you kissing me? Also, why are you unbelted? Not. Safe." He nudged me back, gently but firmly, his lips tilted into a smile.

"You always put me first. No matter what." I snapped my belt into place. "I've never had someone do that for me before."

"Well, you do feed me well." He gave me his best lascivious look. "In all ways."

"Sex was already assured. You're lucky I didn't try to mount you in the parking lot."

"Lucky? Sounds like I lost out." He reached across the console to grip my hand and this time, I laced my fingers between his and held on tight.

"Thank you. I know Mav is an amazing artist. He's about the only one I'd trust to try this. Though artistry with frosting is a bit different, but I'll be there to help. And Honey is a whiz already."

"McNeills get shit done." He grinned at me. "That includes you though I wish you'd just go to bed early and trust us to handle this. I mean, mostly trust them. I'm clueless."

My heart started banging against the walls of my chest. Had he meant he wanted me to be a McNeill too? Maybe he'd just misspoke. Or maybe I was overthinking. I didn't have time for all this right now. We were on our way to our baby's first doctor's appointment, and I had this rush job to handle, with the help of the McNeills.

"Other than Van, I've always been on my own," I said quietly. "My parents would help as they could, but they're both college professors with busy lives, and well, I didn't want to rely on them. Our family environment was…austere." It was the best word I could find for it. "They love us, but they had no clue what to do with someone wild like Van. I was the good one. The steady one. They paid for some of my college, and I figured they'd done their share. It was my turn to make things work."

"And you have. Spectacularly. Look at all you've built so young." The awe in his voice went a long way to easing the nerves brewing inside my belly.

"I want to keep building. That's all I've wanted for so long." The medical group where my doctor's office was located came into view just before Brady turned into the parking lot. "Now I have more in my life. More I want." I slid him a glance. "I do trust you. More every hour. I'm grateful I can rely on you. Today just proves how much. I wasn't going to ask for help, just do it myself, but you swept in to make things easier for me. Not saying I want you to necessarily do that again, because hello, my business, so maybe ask, you know? But thank you."

His lips twitched. "You're welcome. Would it be inappropriate to keep Honey and Mav making cupcakes while we desecrated your office? I'm sure they wouldn't mind. Pregnant moms need stress relief. And dads."

"Uh-huh." *I love you.* The words were right there. So close. But I just grinned and climbed out of the car after he pulled into a space.

He met me in front of the hood and held out his hand. "Ready?"

"Yeah." I took a deep, bolstering breath. "I finally am."

TWENTY-TWO

 **BRADY**

WE SPENT PART OF OUR DATE NIGHT UP TO OUR ELBOWS IN CUPCAKE prep along with sneaking kisses anytime Mav—who swore a lot while he worked—and Honey—who hummed annoyingly twenty-four/seven—were out of eyeshot.

Sometimes even when they weren't.

"You two are disgusting. Stop it. What will the baby think?"

Mav's head jerked up from where he was refining his sketch. He'd tried a couple so far and wasn't happy with any of them. "Baby? What?"

"Oops," Honey mumbled.

"You told her?" I asked Tab, who nodded sheepishly.

"Not just me, she told all of us." Honey ticked off names on her fingers. "Tiff, Lea, Mickey by osmosis because everyone knows the instant I know something she does too, and of course Van."

"Van already knew." I stared hard at Tab. "I thought you wanted to wait."

"I asked about Honey this morning. Not my fault you were too busy sucking on my neck to pay attention."

"How you got that baby, I'm guessing." Honey lifted her eyebrows in a picture of innocence as I turned my stare on her.

"Baby? Really?" Mav frowned. "Did the doc snip the wrong thing?"

"Funny. Sometimes it doesn't...take." I puffed out my chest. "I'd assume it has to do with virility."

Tabitha tossed a hunk of bread at me. I caught it one-handed and I was hungry, so I bit in. Damn, my girl was good. I didn't even know if she'd made this one, but she had a hand in almost everything here so probably.

"Well, damn, now there's no point in me doing it." He tossed his charcoal pencil. "If it didn't work on you, no way will it work on me. There's no possible way."

"I recommend a monastery," Honey said soberly. "Only way the unsuspecting women of the Cove will be safe."

"Um, who's talking? You're of birthing age yourself, so don't get too cocky."

"I don't live here, remember?" Honey asked sunnily. "I'm still with the 'rents in Turnbull so my sex life is safe. Though it's dead as a doornail currently."

"Good." I pointed at her. "Keep it that way."

"My house is on the town line on the other side of the lake. Half in Turnbull, half in the Cove. I'm safe. No neighbors anywhere around even except for the empty lot next door that's up for sale. Probably will be snapped up by that big fancy developer in town." Mav grabbed his pencil and went back to shading. "Okay, I think this works, if you two can stop breeding long enough to take a look."

Tab hurried over and bent over his shoulder, letting out a gasp that had me joining her. I nearly gasped myself.

And only partially to distract from one of Sage's employees from the bed and breakfast sneaking in the side door with a cart full of covered dishes. If we couldn't go on our date, the date would come to us.

"This is incredible. It's even to scale. Holy crap. I wonder if Laurie would like one of these in ice out here next winter." Before Mav could answer, Tab gave him an enthusiastic hug. "You're so amazing, thank you! She's going to be thrilled. Coming up with a design to echo hers would've taken me hours, and now I can just trace it onto—"

I cleared my throat. "Do you have to say all that while hanging onto him?"

"Yes. She smells like heaven." Purposefully, Mav turned to loop his arms around her waist. "Please continue."

I had to laugh. "Such an asshole. But it is an incredible design, man. Thanks."

"You're welcome." He motioned to Tab. "Keep fawning."

She rolled her eyes at us. "You're cut from the same cloth."

"Exactly why I believe in double bagging," Mav said seriously while Honey thunked him in the back of the head.

"See what I mean?" she said to Tab. "Smelly boys. You have to promise to give me a girl. I implore you."

"We had our first doctor's appointment today. Baby's due around November 7th."

"Butterball turkey time!"

I ignored my brother.

"The baby's the size of a poppy seed," Tab informed him, cupping her belly in that way that made every protective instinct inside me jump to the fore.

Was it wrong to be even more turned on by her when she did stuff like that? Probably. But it couldn't be helped. At this rate, I'd pop a boner at her eating the chicken breast with orange glaze—or demi-glace—I'd ordered for our dinner.

"Wow," Honey said. "Tiny."

"Yeah, it's too early to tell if there are twins yet, but the doctor said it's possible since she had such crazy symptoms so soon." Mav appeared to have some kind of coughing fit while I continued. "Or she was just running herself too hard and some of what seemed like pregnancy symptoms were a combination of exhaustion, dehydration, and poor nutrition. Or she could be just super sensitive. Some women just know almost right off. And the early response test picked up the hormones so—"

"I'm sure it's because you're so virile," Honey interrupted, making the peace sign.

I sighed. "Why wasn't I an only child?"

"Because Mom and Dad kept trying to improve upon their first attempt despite the long odds?" Mav speculated. "And thank God they did. Minus the crazy names Hon and I got saddled with."

"Watch it. I like my name, Maveroni."

Mav groaned. "I haven't heard that since I was ten."

A clatter from the back room made me jerk forward to stomp on my sister's instep. She shrieked and when Tab turned her head toward the back in confusion, I put my finger to my lips.

"Oh, spider!" Honey managed, flailing.

"What? My bakery doesn't have spiders." Tab rushed for the broom and began sweeping frantically where Honey had just been standing.

"I'll go get the...um, paper towels." I rushed down the hall to her office, letting out a relieved breath when I saw that Sage's employee had unfolded a little table and set the scene as well as possible considering it was a small back room. He'd even used a tablecloth and placed a couple of stubby candles next to our plates.

"Thanks, man, this looks great. Cloth napkins were a nice touch."

He sniffed at me as if I was hopelessly pedestrian, but I passed him a roll of bills and his attitude marginally improved as he rolled out his cart. "Enjoy."

I rubbed my hands together. "Oh, I will."

I dragged out my phone and sent my sister a text.

Brady: Send her back, would you? Minus the broom. And tell Mav to get started. I don't want her to be working all night and she will if there's a ton left to do.

Honey: Mav says he's not a baker & fuck you, he's not going to be painting unicorns in frosting while you screw.

Brady: The fifty I gave him says otherwise.

Honey: He said make it a hundred & it's a pleasure doing business with you.

222

Brady: Deal. Now send her back.

Honey: One sec. Van's here.

The Chaos Master had arrived. But at least she was a quick worker, and Tab would feel more comfortable taking some of the night off with her sister here.

Brady: Never mind. I'll come get her.

I returned to the main part of the bakery just as Van was holding court by the door. That her audience was just Honey and her sister didn't seem to slow her down. Mav was sketching away with his head lowered.

Probably hoping he could avoid detection.

"So, anyway, I told the dude that—oh, hey, Hero Pants. Did you come here to save the day again?" Van tipped her head to the side, her eyes shielded by her round purple-tinted frames. How could she see in those in the dark outside? "I heard you called in the B-Team." She nodded to Mav, who ignored her.

"That B-Team is saving my ass, sis. So, hush."

"Desperate times and all that. He is cute, at least. How's it hanging, GQ?"

He didn't appear to hear her at first then he lifted his head. "Better before when it was quieter."

Honey giggled. "Oh, he's choosing violence tonight."

Van dusted her nails on her shirt. "Let's see what you've got then."

He looped his arm over the back of his chair. "Name the time and place, Pocket Plus."

I'd already seen enough of their posturing. I stepped behind Tabitha and leaned down to nudge her hair out of the way so I could kiss the back of her neck. She immediately leaned back against me, melting into my chest in that way that never failed to make my pulse race.

"Let's go in the back."

"Brady." She laughed softly. "We can't."

"Not for that." I reached down for her hand and she tucked hers in mine so trustingly I had to swallow hard to find my voice. "We're going to have our date. Close those beautiful blues."

She glanced up at me before closing her eyes without question. And I guided her across the room and down the hall without Van even noticing, since she was currently sparring with my brother.

I couldn't tell if they hated each other or if something was brewing there. I didn't want to consider it, since Van's nether regions were vaguely reminiscent of a Venus flytrap to me.

Then again, that would probably appeal to Mav. Best I not contemplate it.

In the doorway of Tab's office, I nipped her earlobe. "Open your eyes."

She opened them and made a low noise of pleasure. "Food. Candles. Hello, fancy."

I laughed but I didn't have time to reply before she spun around and hooked her arms around my neck, showing her appreciation in a manner I'd never forget. She pressed her full breasts into my chest and sifted her fingers through my hair as our mouths collided. It was a messy, hard kiss, lacking any style whatsoever, but I couldn't breathe from wanting her so much.

Finally, I eased back. "It's been a long week, Strawberry."

"Too long." She shocked me by dropping her fingers to the buttons of my shirt. "This door actually locks. But I can smell that chicken so don't dally."

I laughed before her mouth met mine once again. The temperature between us went from hot to scorching as she finished undoing my shirt and yanked it out of my waistband then dropped to her knees to work on the button and zipper of my pants.

"Hey, wait. This date was for you—oh, fuck." She had me out of my boxers in a second and slid her cool lips over the swollen tip, drawing me in so deep my head spun. I slapped my hand against the door and fisted her wild updo with the other, trying to keep my hold gentle.

Too gentle, apparently.

She drew me out of her mouth, trailing wetness between us and over her chin. Then she took her time dragging her tongue up the side of my already throbbing length. "Oh, no, you don't."

"What?"

"You know what I like and it's not that." She reached up and cupped her hand around my fist in her hair. "Pull it like you usually do. Hard."

My knees actually trembled. I couldn't hold on when she was dirty like this—especially after the longest week of my life without her. "But that was before."

"Yeah, and that's how you got me pregnant. So, don't be tentative now." She pressed a kiss to my lower belly and my stomach quivered. "Do it right, Hot Cop. Show me you want me. I won't break."

She damn sure wouldn't. I could tell that from the hungry blue of her eyes, pulling me down so far I couldn't say no.

I fed her my cock slowly, and she took every inch as if she was built for me. Halfway, she stopped, using her hand to work the rest of my length while she sucked. I dropped my head back against the door and fought to hang on as she did her worst, knowing she wanted me to lose it. But nothing would do for me tonight other than coming deep inside her.

My hand tightened in her curls and I jerked her up my length, almost involuntarily. Her moan rippled over my shaft as my cock jerked in her mouth, on the verge of blowing. Her eyes begged me silently to finish what she'd started.

I wasn't strong enough to say no. Didn't want to.

I slipped my hand deeper in her hair and let the rhythm of my hips take over, pumping between her lips while her moans flowed over my aching flesh. She reached down to fumble her shirt down below her bra and she tugged out her breast, freeing one dark pink nipple. Seeing her touch herself so freely made my breath shorten and my skin hum. This time when I pulled her hair, it was to drag her up enough to hold her still while I let myself go into her mouth.

I was still shaking when she rose to kiss me with her swollen lips that tasted of me.

"My dirty girl."

She drew back and pressed her damp forehead to my chin. "My breast is killing me. Why did I do that?" She let out a pained laugh.

Fuck, should we not have done this?

Worried, I drew back to look at her. "You okay?"

"Yeah. Just really sensitive."

Carefully, I pulled off her shirt and bra then I bent my head to where she'd tugged so recklessly, soothing her with a soft kiss. At least I hoped it soothed her. "Be careful with these. They're the center of my world."

She laughed as I peppered her breasts with kisses. For good measure, I crouched to kiss her belly. "Nope, I lied. This is."

Her sigh poured over me as sweetly as wine. "You've given me so much, Brady. So, so much."

My mouth already had a new target as I peeled down her stretchy pants and her red panties. Red panties that were already damp. "I'm about to give you something else. Grab that hook on the door," I said, jerking my chin upward.

"I'm not sure that can withstand—"

"Do it, Tab."

She did it.

I covered her pussy with my lips, going at her like a man starving. If she was sensitive down here too, I probably should've warned her, but from the sounds she was trying to muffle against the inside of her arm, she didn't mind. Her clit was so hard against my tongue. So desperate for what I loved to give her. I lapped her while I teased her with the tip of my finger, shallowly darting in and out as she squirmed for me.

I knew what she wanted—what she needed—and my finger wasn't even close.

She arched onto her tiptoes, making the hook squeak as she pulled on it with every lick of my tongue over her soaked folds. I swapped my finger for my tongue, dipping into her while my thumb circled her clit over and over. She was so close, so wet, and the hardness of my dick was already becoming a situation again.

So, I gave her one more filthy kiss before rising to my feet and dragging her over to her desk. Instead of pushing her back to sit, I shifted her around and pushed her forward, whispering for her to lean on her hands. Then I eased off her shoes before removing her pants and panties all the way to give me room to move.

"You ready for me, Strawberry?"

She looked over her shoulder, her curls dipping over her eye. "Bring it."

I was smiling as I did as she asked. Rather than driving deep, I sank into her achingly slowly, savoring every second. This was where I belonged. With her scent surrounding me and her hair against my mouth as I shifted to kiss the back of her neck. Her pussy enveloped me and I snapped my hips back and then plunged once more, smothering my groan against her warm fragrant skin. My favorite thing was when she not only smelled like her, but like me —like *us*.

I fucking loved us.

Bending my knees to change the angle, I surged up into her far enough she curled her fingers around the edge of her desk. I wrapped my arms around her, holding her against me as I retreated and returned again and again, kissing every bit of her I could reach as I took us to the limits of our endurance. And then beyond. Skimming the edge of my teeth down her shoulder, I slid my hand between her legs, rubbing her clit while she struggled not to shatter. She was fighting her orgasm with every breath.

I pushed her over the desk and as she splayed beneath me, I reached around to grab her chin so she'd meet my gaze. Her lower lip trembled. "I don't want it to end," she whispered.

"It's never going to end." I bit her lower lip, my eyes centered on hers. "Never, Strawberry."

As if I'd given her permission, her pussy vised around me, yanking me right along with her. I swallowed her moans as I emptied myself inside her. Not just my release. All my needs, all my fears, all my love —I poured them into her because I trusted her to take them.

She accepted every bit of me, shaking even as I shook.

Without catching my breath, I reared back, pulling out of her so quickly she slumped over the desk. "Where's the fire?"

"I'm not going to crush you now."

"Oh, but it was fine before. Nice to see where I rate."

"Smart ass." I gave the back of her thigh a light tap, and she cocked her brow at me over her shoulder.

"Hope you intend to step up your ass game when we're at home."

I had to laugh. "Be careful what you wish for."

"Oh, I'm wishing. After I get cleaned up." She smacked her lips. "Now where's that chicken?"

TWENTY-THREE

Since my day had blown up so exceptionally yesterday and even into today—impromptu cupcakes that turned out really great considering the short notice, a stupendously late night with my Hot Cop, and a quickie trip to the mall this morning with a great kid who I hoped to see again—my baby shower gift had fallen into the lame category. I could get away with the cute outfit I'd found, but it didn't have the magic that Luna required.

I fussed with the small silver bag I'd gotten at the drugstore with a happy stork taking flight with a little bundle in its mouth. It had made me laugh when I found it, but now it just looked like such a half-assed present.

I hadn't made the time for a lot of friends outside the bakery, but Luna was definitely one of my favorites. She'd made me feel very welcome when I moved into the apartment building, and she'd cheerfully forced me to get a bit more social. She'd even opened my eyes to my more mystical side.

Not that I'd had time to play with my tarot deck and small collection of crystals in quite a while. Sugar Rush had exploded into even more than I'd hoped.

I gathered my present, my purse, and a light jacket then kissed the dogs before leaving. My Hot Cop had pulled a weekend shift, so Van agreed to come and take out the babies.

Soon enough, there'd be another baby in our crazy little family. My hand drifted down my still mostly flat belly. I'd always been a little soft thanks to my love of baking, and look at that, now I was baking a human.

Such a weird life.

Lu's baby shower was being held at Kinleigh's Attic. It had undergone a bit of a name change when she hooked up with August, but to everyone in town, it was still Kin's. Handily, it was practically across the street from my apartment.

Before I crossed, a bundle of balloons down the street caught my eye. There was a brightly decorated sandwich board promoting a trunk show at Every Line A Story. Maybe I could find something special there.

I took the detour down Main Street to the craft shop. Downstairs was full of books, art supplies, and a small framing section. I couldn't put my finger on the proprietress's name, but she'd been friendly when I'd seen her out in and about during the Valentine Fest.

"Tabitha! How did you ever get away from your counter?"

I sneaked a quick look at her name tag before smiling brightly. "It wasn't easy, but I took a few hours off because my friend Luna is having her baby shower today."

"Do you need something framed?"

"I wish I'd thought of that." I laughed and lifted my little bag. "I found a sweet little outfit, but I was hoping maybe I could find something at the trunk show."

She slid her arm through mine and started walking me to the stairs. "I know just the thing."

Startled, I couldn't do much else but follow her. I wasn't used to people invading my space and this week had been full of it. From the insanity of the bakery to my doctor's appointment, I'd had to learn to go with the flow.

I was trying, anyway.

Colette patted my arm. "Aren't babies sweet to buy for? I've had to up my baby game when it comes to yarn. One of the reasons why I had this trunk show. We have so many talented people in the area."

The hum of voices drifted to us halfway up the stairs. The stairs squeaked under our feet, and the sweet scent of baby powder was the first thing I noticed. As we went through the wide doorway I was instantly overwhelmed with tables around the perimeter of the room.

It had the uneven, angular ceiling of an attic space and each nook and cranny was filled with shelves and shelves of yarn. They were built-in cubbies instead of long shelves. A rainbow of colors exploded from corners, from apple boxes on tables, and from a pegboard wall with neatly lined twists of yarn. I was pretty sure there was another word for them, but I didn't know it.

I instantly wanted to go and squish all of the softness.

Colette steered me toward a long table to the left. "I saw a blanket here this morning that reminded me of a cloud. Yes, there it is." She smiled at the lady manning the iPad and card reader. "Hey, AJ, how's it going?"

"Cleaning up today."

I was surprised that she was so young. She had teal hair pulled up in braided pigtails with orange tips. Wide, clear glasses framed her big caramel brown eyes. Butterflies were stamped onto the arch of her brows like makeup and journaling had done a remix on her skin.

If Van saw her, my sister would ask for tips.

AJ held out her hand in a fist and I immediately bumped it with my knuckles. She wiggled her fingers. "Sore from getting ready for the show."

"Oh, right." My gaze dropped to the table of fluffy scarves, hats, and shawls set out in a bright colors that shouldn't work together but somehow did. At the end of the table was an apple box with a little scene set up inside. A trio of baby sweaters hung there along with a pile of the tiniest socks I'd ever seen.

"Oh..." Unable to resist, I slipped two fingers into a pair of mint socks. For my little one.

I was here for Luna, but I couldn't stop myself from picking up another pair in a beautiful oatmeal color with the matching sweater.

"It's made from cotton and a touch of baby angora. Totally safe for babies."

"Is that what makes it so soft?"

AJ pulled out a bag from under the table. She lifted out a fluffy cupcake shaped ball of yarn. "I hold it together to knit and it makes it extra squishy but easy for moms to wash."

I hugged the sweater and socks to my chest. "I'm definitely taking these."

Colette went around me. "Since you said you had an outfit, I thought of this."

I turned to see the delicately knit blanket. This one wasn't fluffy but it was crazy soft in a gray and white chevron pattern. The bottom edges were straight instead of pointed with a gorgeous intricate border in a pastel rainbow.

"If this doesn't scream Luna, I don't know what does." I pushed it over with my pile.

"More outfits for Miss Luna too?"

"What?" I glanced at Colette. "Oh, right. Always need something for the ever-growing Cove."

"Isn't that the truth." But there was a secret smile flirting at the edges of her mouth.

AJ had gift wrapping supplies as well. I let her think the sweater and booties were for the party too, but I asked for a separate bag. By the time I got downstairs, I didn't have time to drop it off at my apartment, so I tucked the adorable set into my car before crossing to Kinleigh's.

There was a closed sign on the door, but sweetly swaying pink and blue balloons had been put up with a note to take a clothespin on the way upstairs to the baby shower. Each wooden pin had a small number burned into the wood and a crystal stuck to the top.

"Only Luna." I was early enough that I had a ton to pick from. The number seven had a pink crystal which seemed like kismet to me since that might just be my due date.

I clipped it to my purse and opened the door. Lizzo's soulful voice and a decidedly disco beat lured me up the stairs with a little extra pep in my step. When I got to the top, Ryan was running around with her flowing purple dress swishing around her ankles. She was dancing to the beat as she put out carrots in a cute bunny pail.

The tablescape was full of cute woodland animals, the theme matching the invite I'd received. A beaver with chocolate and peanut butter dips with graham crackers and a duck bowl with a belly full of popcorn, celery, and broccoli garnished a meadow scene with green, red, and yellow peppers sticking up with little toothpick flags that looked like flowers.

If I wasn't careful, Ryan was going to lure my customers away.

I set my bags on the large table festooned with balloons and fringe. There were bunny bookends set up all around to keep things from falling off the table. Ryan had truly thought of everything. "It all looks amazing."

Ryan spun around. "Oh, you're early!" She rushed to me, giving me a quick spicy floral-scented hug before pushing me away with a narrowed gaze. "Or are you late?"

I flushed.

"Cove strikes again." She pulled out a chunky crystal from inside her dress and kissed it, murmuring something under her breath before tucking it back against her skin. "This town should come with a USDA warning label."

"I…" I blew out a breath. "I just found out. Did Luna tell you?"

She shook her head. "I'm not an aura girl like Lu, but there's a vibe to the pregnant women from this town. Like a different vibration I can't explain."

"Oh. Is that a thing?"

Ryan shrugged and all sorts of crystals dangled and jangled from her ears and wrists. "Maybe I'm just tuned in since the bestie is ready to pop."

"Where is she?"

Ryan pointed to a large chair set near a beautiful baby set. "Mama throne covered in daisies. Her ankles are like freaking grapefruits today." She lowered her voice. "I have a feeling she's not going to her due date, but she won't listen to me."

"I heard that." Luna's voice carried. "Get over here, Tab. Ryan is on my shit list."

Ryan rolled her eyes. "She's just pissed because I made her promise me she'd sit until the party started."

I swallowed a laugh. "I'll go sit with her. Unless you need my help."

She waved me off. "Me and Kin have it handled. August and Xavier went to get us ice for the drinks before we kick them out—girls only. We have adult and mom-to-be friendly drinks, don't worry."

I felt the flush climbing my neck again. "Um, thanks."

"Mom, I'm fine. I swear."

I turned toward Lu's voice. She indeed was on a throne of daisies. The plush pink velvet chair had daisy chains curled around the back, arms, and even the sturdy legs. She was wearing a daisy crown and had her long, almost white blond hair up in massive space buns. The daisies were even wound around them.

A loose, muslin dress with embroidered daisies at the capped arms flowed down to her calves. Her feet were bare with bright pink polish. I was pretty sure a daisy was drawn on each of her big toes. A long chain of greenish and pink crystals looped around her neck twice and rested on her fairly massive belly.

Dear God, she was so very pregnant. It seemed like the birth would be in hours, not in the supposedly few weeks she had left.

Luna pulled her mother in front of her and the older woman leaned forward until they touched foreheads. Luna cupped her mom's shoulders, probably to take the sting from her words. "Why don't you help Ryan? She is playing wonder woman over there."

"Right. Of course." The older woman had ash blond hair in a cheek sweeping bob and seemed very nervous.

Luna's face softened as she swiped her hands down her mom's arms soothingly to clutch her hands. "We're gonna have a lovely celebration for your first grandbaby. It's going to be great."

The woman gathered Luna into a hug. "I'm just so glad you let me be a part of this, sweetheart."

Lu laid her cheek on her mother's shoulder and the two rocked a little. I took a step back when I heard sniffles.

This sweet moment reminded me I would need to tell my mom about the baby soon. I didn't have a clue how she'd react. My father either.

At least I didn't have to worry about that right this second.

The woman straightened and smiled at me. "You'll look after her, won't you?"

I nodded. "Of course."

"Good." She dabbed at her eyes and shook back her hair before hurrying over to Ryan.

"My back is killing me." Luna sagged in the chair as if she'd used up all her energy to comfort her mother. She smiled up at me as she rubbed circles along the side of her belly. "This little boy is going to be a footballer, I swear."

I arched a brow at her.

"Sorry. I've been making Caleb watch *Ted Lasso*. English soccer." She laughed. "Well, rewatch it again and again because I keep falling asleep before I finish an episode."

"Oh. I remember when I used to watch television. Now I keep falling asleep too."

"It's a crazy club, right?"

"Couldn't blame the baby before," I said with a whisper. "But let's get back to the other news." I crouched next to her, my heart constricting. "A little boy?"

She nodded. "I've known the whole time, but the last ultrasound finally showed the goods."

"That long?" Brady would be a maniac if he had to wait almost eight months to find out what we were having. Heck, I would be too.

"Our baby is shy unlike his daddy." She winced as she sat up and stretched her back. "Now Caleb is strutting around like a peacock."

I laughed and blinked furiously at the sudden waterworks. "I swear, I don't know what is going on with me."

Luna laid a gentle hand on my shoulder. "You have a lot of chaos in your aura."

"Well, that tracks." I sniffled. "I fell in love with a cop, and he knocked me up in the space of a heartbeat."

I still needed to tell him how I felt. The words and the promises they stood for were important.

And so very scary.

"Sometimes it happens that way." Her bluebell eyes softened. "Ahh, there's a girl. Now you're much more blue with a tinge of pink. The baby is growing strong already." She squeezed my shoulder. "Don't worry about your little one. She's hale and hearty."

"She?" I slid onto my knees beside her. I wasn't really worried about a miscarriage, but everything had happened so fast and I was really tired of throwing up all the damn time. Especially since there was no rhyme or reason to what triggered me. So, maybe there was a teeny tiny bit of me afraid to tell people in case the universe took the baby away from me.

"A strongly bonded she. Our babies tend to be our everything, no matter if we're ready or not. She'll show you a whole new world. And Brady." She winked at me. "Talk about wrapped."

I laughed. "He's already all in. I wasn't expecting him to be so certain about everything, especially when I'm not."

"That's just fear talking. It's exhausting enough when you're thinking you are doing everything wrong when it comes to being a mom. That one seems to be especially overwhelming. I know Caleb loves me and is my partner."

"Brady's never shown me anything else." Even if maybe I hadn't reciprocated like I should've.

But everything had been so fast. I could barely catch up with my own feelings before there was another person to think about.

Luna reached into her pocket and pulled out a small tin.

I recognized the little pocket tarot deck I'd had in my wish list forever. "Oh, you don't need todo that now—"

"I don't really need the cards to know what's going on with you, but you're a logical woman. Even in the most illogical of mystical spaces."

I sighed. I struggled to understand how cards could tell the future, but Luna had told me a million times it was just paper. If you believed they could tell you things then that was the power—not the paper.

She sat up straighter and shuffled the small cards. Her ringed fingers sparkled in the sun that poured through the tall windows of Kin's shop. It was nice to see the sun. Central New York hid it more than it let her out to shine.

But it was Luna's day so I wasn't surprised the sun had made an appearance.

A single card popped out of the deck. She pulled two others, spreading them out on her very limited lap. I couldn't stop the gasp at the card in the middle.

Luna *tsked* me. "I know that Tower card is scary, but it's so very true for you. See this Nine of Pentacles? You've got everything you ever wanted with the bakery."

"How..."

Luna arched a brow at me.

"Psychic."

She laughed and her earrings danced in the wispy curls that had escaped her space buns. "I have eyes too. Sugar Rush is always busy. It's blown up in the very best way."

"Does the Tower mean it's going to fall apart?"

"No." She lifted the third card. "Three of Wands tells me it's just going to make way for a new plan. And a new beginning. It just won't be how you originally imagined."

I laced my fingers in my lap.

"I'm right, aren't I?"

"Maybe." I knew the breakneck pace I'd been keeping couldn't be sustained. Even if there wasn't a baby to think of, I deserved a life. I deserved time with my dogs—because yes, Daisy was now as much mine as Pancake was—and my sister, as well as Brady. As much as I loved our Netflix binges and late night talks, I deserved to see him in the sunshine too.

"I see that brain of yours spinning." She reached behind her to rub her back then held up the last card again. "See this boat with the sail up? Heading for someplace new. You're starting a grand adventure and that means things will change. And that's so good."

"But the Tower..."

"Well, when we did our classes, I taught you how the Major Arcana is all about big life changes. Pretty sure a baby is a big life change."

I laughed. "That's true."

The hum of voices got louder behind me. I twisted to see a trio of men hauling ice up the stairs six bags at a time. Luna sighed. I turned back to her and she was leaning on her elbow on the arm of the chair, with her head propped up.

"He doesn't look like any teacher I remember as a kid." She let out an admiring sigh..

My gaze returned to Caleb. His arms bulged beneath a white T-shirt that read, "I'm the Dad in Training" across it. "Me neither. I remember them being pasty old guys or women."

"There's a surprising number of attractive men in his school."

"Nothing wrong there." We both laughed and I straightened up. "Thanks for this. I feel much better."

"Of course."

"Can I get you something?"

"Maybe some lemon water? I think there's one of those big Pinterest lookalike jugs on one of the tables. Ryan went a little crazy on the party planning."

"It looks amazing."

Made me wonder what kind of baby shower I'd end up with. Knowing my crew, it would be pretty incredible too.

More plans to look forward to, I supposed.

A wolf whistle broke through the music. Kinleigh was weaving her way through the crowd of women who were coming up the stairs. "Stop drooling over the men, ladies. We've got a baby shower to get going."

Her husband August Beck emptied his ice bags into the huge silver tub set on the floor at the end of the wide table, then he turned around and scooped his wife up and over his shoulder.

"Put me down, you brute!"

"I'll bring her right back," he called over his shoulder.

The ten women who had showed up for the shower threw out catcalls that would make any stripper joint proud.

Ryan pointed at her guy. Preston Shaw had a big grin on his face. "Don't even think about it, PMS. There's too much baby magic in this town. You are not getting me naked in the back room."

"Would it be so bad?" His dark hair fell forward as he slid his arm around Ryan. He was a tall guy, but Ryan's height complemented his. "We do okay with a cat."

"A cat is much different, buddy." She drilled her finger into his belly. "Thanks for the ice, now scram."

He pulled her closer and dropped a kiss on her upturned mouth. As much as they quarreled, I could tell that was the usual thing between them. For lawyers—and lawyer's assistants—fighting was obviously foreplay.

It was funny to see how couples interacted. The town and surrounding areas was growing in crazy ways, not just because of the babies.

Suddenly, a woman squealed and ran across the room to Luna, who screamed in return. They hugged as if they were long lost sisters. I didn't want to interrupt the reunion, but I wanted to make sure our mama-to-be was hydrated.

I got two drinks and made my way back to Luna.

Luna was now sitting on the woman's lap as if she was Santa. The newcomer had her arms around Luna's expanded middle.

"Tab! Meet my friend Janice."

The name Janice did not fit this rainbow-hued woman. She was wearing paint-splattered overalls over a tie-dyed long sleeve shirt. Her short hair was spiky and an improbable blue.

Janice held out her hand. "We used to roadtrip before she got tied down to the teacher."

"I got tired of hunting down laundromats to have clean clothes." Luna leaned her head on her arm. "Man, remember that VW Bus? We put some miles on her."

"Too many miles. I finally had to retire her."

"No!"

Janice pouted comically. "I know. So sad. But that's okay, she became an art installation in the desert. Forever immortalized in the perpetual sun."

What was up with VWs with the people I knew? They probably had even frequented Mr. McNeill's shop Hip2BeSquared.

I handed Luna the water and one for her friend. "I'll let you guys catch up."

Luna took the cup. "Oh, thanks. I could just drink everything today." She wiggled on Janice's lap. "I can't wait until I'm comfortable again. I love this little guy." She rubbed her belly. "But I'm ready to get him out of me."

"You ready, baby?" Janice started tapping on Lu's belly as if she was a living set of bongos. But it seemed to be some secret language and they both dissolved into peals of laughter.

I laughed and left them to it. I rushed over to help Bess Wainwright, who'd made a grand entrance with a massive basket of baby things. She needed half the table.

"Thank you, dear. I couldn't stop buying." She gave me a quick squeeze. "I keep trying to convince Asher and Hannah to have another one."

"I'm pretty sure they have their hands full with two toddlers from what you've told me."

Bess waved me off, her armful of bangles tinkling before they slipped down and got lost in the sleeve of one of her wildly colored caftans. Once she'd started wearing them and getting into crystals, she'd never gone back to her "old lady wear", as she called it.

I took her hand. "I think you'll have plenty to buy for."

Bess's eyes went wide. "What?"

I held up my finger to my lips. "It's Luna's day."

So much for being circumspect.

She dragged me forward into a cloud of lavender. "How incredibly exciting!"

I patted her back. "Not so loud."

"Right. Of course," she said in a voice that wasn't even close to a whisper. She let me go and dabbed at her eyes. "The Cove always keeps me in babies, even if my grandson won't."

240

I resisted the urge to roll my eyes. Two kids was quite enough, thank you. I was sure her grandson would agree.

Kinleigh returned with a flush to her cheeks. "Okay, everyone! Luna requested no games except for the clothespin door-prize. If you didn't get your crystal clothespin, my industrious husband will bring them upstairs before he leaves."

"Can he still walk?" Came a shout from the back of the room.

"A little crooked, but he'll be fine. Mostly." Kinleigh grinned. "There's tons of booze, virgin style—"

"Are there any of those left in the Cove?" Ryan snarked.

"Watch it, Ry. Your witchy powers may not be able to combat all this baby fever." Kinleigh sassed right back.

"Never!" She pulled her and Lu's other best friend April in front of her like a shield.

"Too late," April said with a laugh, patting her own rounded belly.

The group of women laughed.

"Eat up, drink up. And if you get a little buzzy, don't worry. We have the drunk bus available—aka our array of men who are happily watching sports downstairs. Then we'll open presents once we eat. Luna is staying off her feet so you can go over to see her on her throne."

The shower sped by. I didn't have to be good at reading auras like Luna to know the energy in the room was light and happy. I recognized some people by name and others just to say hi to in passing. Luna had made a big impression on the Cove in a short time.

I floated between groups of women. Each of us drifted over to visit with Luna and fawn over her while she did her best Earth Mother impression. Kinleigh had pushed her shop's merchandise and displays back to make room for all the tables and people. She had a ton of chairs and couches from her own store and of course from August's furniture store as well. They'd blended the shops into one big combo now, which meant seating was not an issue

Luna's mother seemed a little like a fish out of water, so I kept bringing her with me as I went from chatting with Ryan, to Kinleigh, to Macy Gideon, and Vee Masterson from the café.

They'd been so gracious with helping me out when Sugar Rush was still a fledgling business right through until now. Instead of being competitive, the people of this town wanted everyone to succeed. I was happy to have a few minutes to talk with them.

It was a lovely hour of conversation, food, and community. Everything I never truly knew I wanted until I found my way to Crescent Cove. I'd originally thought it was only a thriving business I'd yearned for, but it really was *this*.

And Brady. He was now a part of every dream I had.

My hand shook as the realization unfurled in my chest. Even if the baby hadn't fast-forwarded the process, it would always be him and the way he took care of this town—and me and our furbabies along with the human one we'd made against all the odds.

I wasn't sure if the town was sprinkled in baby dust or just an abundance of second chances.

The murmur of voices lifted from happy conversation and laughter to a buzzy panic.

"Get Caleb." Kinleigh's voice rose above the chatter. She sounded calm, if a bit forceful.

"What's going on?" I asked.

Bess came over to me. "I'm pretty sure Luna's water just broke."

"Oh, God." I pulled out my phone to dial 911.

The baby dust definitely won out in this town.

TWENTY-FOUR

 **BRADY**

"Closest car available to Main Street, come in." Bonnie's sharp voice came through the radio in my cruiser. I was parked under a large oak for a touch of shade. It was a bright and sunny day in the Cove, and I'd stopped to watch the kids play pickup at the basketball courts.

I rolled my eyes. There was only one of us on today on a quiet Saturday afternoon. Also, Main Street took up most of the town.

I leaned into the window and grabbed my radio. "Brady here."

"We have a code 3..." I heard flipping papers. "11-41."

I frowned. Lights and sirens? What the hell was that last code? We didn't really use them anymore. "What's going on, Bonnie?"

"Get to Kinleigh's Attic, I've got an ambulance meeting you."

"What?" My gut lurched as I dragged the cord out to straighten up. Strawberry was there today.

"What part of code three didn't you get?"

"Right." *Relax.* It probably wasn't about her.

"Tabitha called it in so get your butt over there."

"En route." I tossed the radio back inside and waved to the boys— most of whom I coached at the learning center—then got in my car and flipped on my lights and sirens. I was at the opposite end of the town, but I used my advantage to push the speed a little more than I should have on a pedestrian-heavy day.

The ambulance was a little farther out since the town was too small for its own. I pulled into the front lot at Brewed Awakening since there was no parking left in front of Kinleigh's. The ambulance needed the space. I held my gun tight to my waist as I ran across the street. The front door was open.

I took the stairs two at a time, following the excited voices. A large crowd of women and men were circled around what seemed to be a bright pink chair.

"Just breathe, Lu."

"You breathe! I'm going to have a freaking watermelon in the middle of a crowd of people!"

I recognized Luna's voice as well as her husband's strained voice. Relief practically had me bending over to catch my own damn breath.

Not Strawberry.

"Okay, let's give everyone some room." My voice was terse, but it got the job done. The crowd of people parted. I definitely wasn't prepared for what I saw.

Caleb was behind Luna, both of them on the ground. A massive sheet was spread out under Luna. Daisy flower shrapnel was spread out on the wildly colored tie-dyed sheet.

I was pretty sure some of it was formerly a flower crown on the mom-to-be in distress. What was left of it dipped over her eye while sweaty curls framed her beet-red face.

"Dear goddess, where are the drugs!?!"

Caleb's face was pale, and he was holding his wife with pure terror.

"Ambulance is coming, Mrs. Beck."

"Mrs?" Luna looked up at me. "Are you kidding me with that?"

Training had kicked in. I crouched in front of her. "Sorry, Luna. An ambulance is coming right behind me."

Her eyes were a bit crazed. "Do they have drugs?"

That was going to be a no. Paramedics couldn't give her much in the field. "We're going to do everything we can."

I stood and searched the crowd. "Until the ambulance arrives, let's get her as comfortable as possible. Pillows and towels will help."

Kinleigh came forward with August behind her. "Got it." She dragged August along with her to disappear into the store.

"I cannot believe this is happening again."

I ignored Macy's complaint. I remembered hearing something about another birthing happening in her café. Bonnie liked to tell a lot of stories heavy on Crescent Cove lore and legend during our downtime.

Vee held Macy's hand tightly and patted it. "It's okay. At least we won't be desecrating one of your couches this time."

"Just mine," Kinleigh muttered from behind them. "You okay, Lu?" She pushed people out of the way by holding a huge cushion with arms in front of her.

August had a stack of beach towels in various colors.

Luna was sprawled out with her dress hiding all her important parts, thank God. But her legs were open and there was a lot of slow breathing in between screeches.

"Okay, let's get her comfortable as we can."

I directed Kinleigh and August as well as Caleb and Luna's mother on where to put things to support her and hopefully, we could make this last long enough to get a medical professional in here.

I kept a look out for Tabitha, but I couldn't find her in the melee. I couldn't concentrate on her right now anyway. I had to do my job.

The radio on my shoulder squawked. "Ambulance ten minutes out, Brady."

I pressed the return button. "Thanks. Over." I moved to Luna again. "How are we looking? Like diameter-wise and all that?"

"I don't know, it feels like a fucking watermelon is trying to make an appearance." She arched up off the sheet and screamed as a contraction hit her. "We are never doing this again!"

Caleb was next to her now, his hand being mangled by his wife. "You're doing amazing. I love you so much."

Lu dragged him close with her other hand. "You did this to me. I will never let you have sex with me in this town again!" Then once the contraction seemed to ease, she sobbed. "I'm sorry. I'm sorry. I didn't mean it. I want to have all of the sex. Maybe in like four years though." She pressed her sweaty forehead to his. "I love you, babe."

Not sure what to do with that whole share, I looked around a little helplessly myself.

"Make way." The rolling wheels of an office chair tracked over the hardwood floors. Bess's flowing robe?—dress?—whatever—flapped behind her as she pushed the chair. She looked like a rich yogi who'd come down off the mountain to dispense advice. "You, there. Tabitha, get over here and help."

"Me?" Tabitha's voice came from the back of the crowd.

Relief flowed through me. She was fine, even if she looked ready to faint.

"You have the steadiest hands in the whole town."

"What?" The crowd parted as Tabitha came forward, wringing her hands. "No, I really don't."

"I've seen you rock-steady while icing a cake, girl. I need your help."

She glanced at me, terror in her eyes.

I grabbed her hands. "It's okay, Strawberry. I got this." I hugged her to my side for a moment before kissing her forehead. I really didn't want to see this much of Luna, but if this baby was coming this fast, it was my job to help.

I went over to stand by Bess. "Do you know what you're doing?"

"I've taken a few midwife workshops."

"Workshops?" I wasn't sure if that meant she was going to actually be able to help, or we were in a lot of trouble. This wasn't exactly in my training guides.

Bess sat in the chair and rolled forward. "Okay, sweetheart. Let's take a look, shall we?"

"Why not? Everyone will be seeing it all soon, anyway." Lu pushed back on the cushions behind her. "Dammit. Here comes another one."

It felt like an eternity, but finally, the contraction passed. Weakly, Luna dropped back on the cushions.

"You're going to have to be my eyes, Brady."

"No. I can do it. I'll help." Tabitha came forward. She straightened her shoulders and knelt next to Bess, pushing me back a little. "She's my friend." She smiled at Luna. "Guess we'll be almost best friends by the end of it, hey?"

"Where is the ambulance?" a tall dark-haired woman shouted before she pushed through the crowd of people. "I was downstairs looking for them, but they're still not here." She laughed as she dropped down on the other side of Luna. "Girl, why you gotta be so dramatic?"

Luna leaned her way. "I wanted it to be beautiful." Tears dripped down her cheeks. "This is not beautiful."

"Oh, we'll make it beautiful, I promise." The dark-haired woman slid an arm around her. The energy around Luna seemed to even out the moment the new woman arrived. She reached across to Caleb, and they both supported Luna. "Let's see how fast this is gonna go."

Tabitha looked up at me. I gripped her shoulder comfortingly. The terror was still there, but her hands were rock-steady as she peeked under the white dress. There was some fussing with clothing and then she sat back.

"What?" I asked quietly.

She glanced at me and quickly back to Bess. "There's a head."

My jaw ached with how hard I was biting back swear words. That seemed really quick. First time moms were usually in labor for hours.

Bess rolled closer and touched Luna's knee. "Honey, were you in labor all day?"

Luna shook her head. "I don't think so. I mean, my back hurts, but it hurts all the time."

Tabitha's eyes went wide. "You were really complaining when we first got here though." She fumbled for my hand and squeezed hard. I could feel her trembling and wanted to scoop her up and bring her to safety. She didn't need to deal with this.

We'd just found out about our own baby.

It wasn't her job.

She always took on so much. But at the same time, I was completely out of my depth. Just as I was about to gently push her aside to do what needed to be done, Tabitha scooted forward and patted Luna's foot.

"We're gonna do this."

"Goddess, why are there no drugs?" Luna's head dropped back as she braced.

"It's time to push, Luna." Bess's voice was even and firm.

The screech that ripped through the room had my balls shriveling up inside of me. Logically, I knew women had been doing this for eons, but right now, I wanted to dive for cover.

I'd rather face down a gunman, ten trucks of paperwork, or an angry meth head than watch a woman in pain. Knowing the same pain would be a part of Strawberry's future turned my knees to water.

I dropped into a crouch next to Tab as she and Bess coached Luna through the contractions and the pushing.

"Where the hell is the ambulance?"

As if Bonnie could hear me, my radio squawked. "Brady, the ambulance was rerouted for a major accident. We have another one coming out, but it'll be a few."

"How much is a few?" Tab muttered as she dabbed at her sweaty temple with the back of her hand.

"I don't know?"

"We can't worry about that now." Bess pulled Tab's hair back and slapped an elastic around it in a tail. "Luna, we are going to do this. We have all the mama energy in this room we could need."

Luna dropped back against her friend's and Caleb's arms. Both were helping to hold her up. "I can't."

"You can." Caleb pressed his cheek to hers. "You are the strongest woman I know. You can do this."

Lu nodded and gathered herself.

My woman's hands never wavered as she did what needed to be done. I didn't know how long it took, just that I didn't fucking move as Tab and Bess figured out the best way to bring a life into this world.

Both Luna and Tabitha were crying as finally, a squirming, yowling, pink baby crashed his baby shower.

A flurry of towels and baby wipes cleaned away the worst of things. I didn't even know if we were doing any of it right, but somehow, we ended up with a baby.

A familiar ambulance siren and the sound of pounding boots on the stairs had us all sagging with relief.

"Wow. You guys just couldn't wait, huh?" came a jovial female voice.

"I wanted to," Luna said with a happy, exhausted smile. The baby was wrapped in a huge beach towel with unicorns and rainbows proudly protecting him. "I didn't get my drugs."

The paramedic pushed forward with a stretcher. At the other end, her partner had a triage kit. "We're really sorry about that, Miss. Let's get everyone's vitals checked, shall we?"

Tabitha sagged against me, her pretty pink dress beyond repair. I scooped her up into my arms.

"Wait!" She hooked an arm around my neck. "What's his name?"

Luna and Caleb had their heads together over the baby. "Milo," she said with a trembling laugh.

Tabitha tucked her face into my neck. "That's a good name."

I kissed her forehead. "It sure is."

Luna smiled up at us. "Thank you for helping me bring this baby into the world safely."

Tab nodded and sniffled. "You're welcome."

I swung her around and tightened my grip on her.

Kinleigh came around to meet us. "You can take her in the back." She held a simple sundress with big sunflowers all over it out to us. "Go on and get cleaned up."

Tabitha took the dress and another towel. "Thanks, Kinleigh."

For the first time in my life, I left my civic duty to others and just concentrated on the woman in my arms. She was my whole world, after all.

I strode quickly through the curtained doorway to the little bathroom. "*Shh.* Just a few more seconds."

"I can't stop shaking."

"I know. It's just the adrenaline high. You're coming down." I set her on her feet, and she swayed against me.

I ripped the front of her dress. It was beyond saving, anyway.

"Brady!"

"Just saving time." I pulled off the dress and drew her to the sink. Her teeth were chattering, and she was definitely out of it if she let me take care of her without a complaint.

She leaned against me as she washed her hands and arms. "I can't believe I did that."

"Me neither. You're my fucking hero."

She looked up. "Stop. I did what anyone would do."

"No one else stepped up. Hell, you saved me. Technically, I should've been the one to do that."

"Have you ever delivered a baby?" She was a little steadier as the warm water flowed over her hands and she wiped off her chest.

My favorite thing about her...besides that big heart of hers.

"No. But I'm the public servant, not you." I pulled her in front of me in the small space and used the towel to dry her hands, her arms, her neck, and then her chest. She gave me a knowing grin as I took a little extra time there.

Then I draped the towel in the sink and wrapped my arms around her tightly. "You were amazing."

"I was, wasn't I?" She laughed as she looked up at me, her chin resting on the buttons of my uniform shirt.

"You were."

"All I kept thinking was just one more minute and the paramedics would be there. I could do another minute. Then there was this baby right there. Unbelievable."

"And I just kept thinking how I wanted to bundle you up and run."

She looped her arms around my waist. "Can we not have our baby that way?"

"No fucking way. Hospital. All the doctors."

"All the drugs," she said with a laugh.

"Our baby sounds pretty amazing though."

She grinned. "Yeah it does. Doing this together sounds even better. I love you, Brady McNeill. I wouldn't do this again with anyone else."

"Again?" My ears buzzed. I was pretty sure she'd just admitted to loving me. Voluntarily. With no bribes or prompting.

It was a banner day for more reasons than one.

"You know, the birthing thing. Because I am never delivering another baby without a doctor's supervision. I was scared to death."

"And yet you were so damn brave." I pulled her hands from behind me up to my mouth so I could kiss her fingertips. "Rock steady the whole time."

"I was shaking inside enough for eight people."

I released her hands to cup her face. "Is it only the shock that let you say the words?" I hadn't intended to ask that damn question, but I had to know.

I knew she would love me eventually, and until that time, I'd love her enough for both of us.

"Oh, Brady." She went up on her toes and met my lips with hers. "I've been running from the words, but they were always there. I just didn't want to face them. They're so huge, but after today—there are no doubts. You were right there with me the whole time."

"I'll always be right beside you, Strawberry." I slid my hand down her glorious breasts to the slight curve of her middle. "And right here for this baby of ours."

"I know. I never doubted you. Not really. You're all I've ever wanted."

I crushed her to me, lifting her off her toes. "Say it again."

She laughed. "I love you, Brady."

I lowered my mouth to hers. "Again."

"I love you."

I whispered against her mouth, "Again."

"I love you."

I smiled against her mouth as I slid my hand down to her butt. "Do you have to put the dress on right away?"

She laughed. "Don't you have a report to file or something?"

"They can wait. Nothing is more important than you."

Her hand slid down to cup the very interested party in my jeans. "You mean nothing is as important as getting *this* inside of me."

"Well, there's that too." I smiled down at her. Funny how now it was harder for me *not* to say the words than to say them. "I love you, Strawberry."

EPILOGUE

BRADY

Three months later

"Maybe I should've brought blueberry cobbler instead."

Shaking my head with a smile, I reached over to rub Tabitha's bare knee under the hem of her pink gingham dress. She matched her summery dessert, a fact I knew she wasn't thrilled about. "Croquets with strawberry frosting stuff are special for us. They'll love them."

"Can you at least pronounce them right? Croquembouche." She tugged her dress down, trapping my hand under the fabric—a place I did not mind being.

Little did she know I'd been practicing with a French pronunciation site I'd found online. "Croquembouche," I said succinctly, lifting my chin when she stared at me. "Ye of so little faith."

"Aw, you did it. Yay." She adjusted her seatbelt so she could ease closer in the front seat of my brand new Explorer to kiss my cheek. She knew I didn't go for her unbelting even for half a minute.

Especially now that she was showing just the slightest bit. She'd bought a couple maternity outfits but she hadn't worn any yet, saying she wasn't big enough. Her gingham—a word I'd just recently learned —dress had thin straps that barely held up her bounty from above and revealed her heavily freckled shoulders, so I'd smothered her with sunscreen before we left to go to my parents' place. She thought I was fussing too much, but far as I was concerned, she was lucky I hadn't suggested a thin jacket. Couldn't be too careful with that fair skin.

"I have lots of faith in you," she continued. "It's a hard word." She shifted around on the seat, carefully holding her covered dish that contained dessert. "Dammit. Not again. I gotta pee."

"You were the one who kept chugging lemon water."

"I was nervous, okay? I cut back on coffee so lemon water seemed like a good choice. I just forgot that my bladder is so touchy now."

"We're almost there. Just another mile."

She bit her lower lip. "You didn't tell me they had a fancy house."

"It's not fancy. Just a nice house for a family."

She pointed at me. "Don't start."

I gave her my most innocent expression. "Start what, Peach Compote?"

She snorted out a laugh. "You're ridiculous. And you know exactly what. Why are you so eager to change our whole world?"

The thin edge of nerves in her voice made me draw my hand away from her leg to grip her hand. "I'm not. If you want to stay just where we are, that's fine. They have bigger apartments on the upper floor. We could put our names on the list—"

"But why do we have to move? I like my apartment. I like your apartment." She bit her lower lip. "We did so well with Pancake."

I wanted to roll my eyes, but I'd learned that never served me well. And I understood where she was coming from, truly I did. A lot was changing all at once and we were still new. Just we couldn't move all that slowly when our poppy seed-sized baby was now apple-sized.

So few people in town knew yet. Just our siblings, the employees at Sugar Rush, Luna, Ryan, Kinleigh, Bess, and Connor at the learning center.

Okay, so a lot of people knew, but no one else due to me. I hadn't even told Jared or Christian.

First, we'd been waiting for the end of the first trimester to be safe. Then we were just...waiting. I was letting her decide when. I'd been shocked—and thrilled—when she finally decided it was time for her to meet my parents. She hadn't even told her own parents about the baby yet.

We'd cross that bridge on another day.

"Baby, Pancake is a Morkie puppy who won't grow much bigger than he is right now." Which wasn't big at all. Daisy could still carry him by the scruff of his neck if she wanted to. She didn't but she could have. "A baby isn't the same."

Tabitha pressed her lips together and lifted the lid on her container. "I should've made more croquembouche."

So, that was the end of that conversation.

"We don't have to tell them today if you're not ready." I gripped the wheel as I exhaled. "It's not like we're on anyone else's timetable but our own."

"You really mean that?" Her voice was unnaturally soft.

"Yeah. I'm happy where we are. I'm glad you want to meet them. Or if not want, at least you're doing it. I know the parent thing is rough. I'm not looking forward to meeting Dr. Sheldon Monaghan and Dr. Christine Monaghan either, you know."

"You're not? I'm looking forward to meeting your parents. Honey's told some funny stories, and I'm not so nervous anymore." She frowned. "I didn't know you felt that way about mine."

Great. This was what I got for empathizing. I actually wasn't that worried, but I'd played it up so she felt less so. "I'm actually okay with it. I just was trying to make you—"

"You were lying?" Her question pitched higher at the end.

Relationships were full of landmines. But they had awesome parts too. Endless supplies of baked goods, breakfasts and dinners together laughing about stupid stuff, spending time with someone who liked mostly all the same stuff on streaming, and incredible sex.

Incredible sex that I was enjoying quite a lot of, since I was a very lucky man.

"You just wanted to make me feel better. You always do that. So, since you're cool with it, you're okay with spending the 4th with them? Picnic and fireworks."

"Wow, really?"

"Really."

"Before I answer, Van or no Van?"

She laughed. "Van. Fireworks are her favorite thing since birth. My mom claims when she was pregnant on the 4th, Van would dance and kick like a maniac when the fireworks were going off. I thought maybe that meant she didn't like them, but my mom said certain kicks feel different. She'd know, I guess." Tab rubbed the side of her very small bump. "Seeing as she had two in there and all."

We did *not* have two in there. Hallelujah. If we'd been having twins, I would've been happy about it, but I couldn't deny I was relieved we'd be doing this one baby at a time. At least until we rolled the dice and tried again.

I was probably officially reversing my vasectomy. We'd discussed it and that was where we were at in negotiations currently, pending childbirth and pain.

Unless she decided we should go for the reversal before the baby's birth, since the doctor said the sooner the better for vasectomy reversals. I was ready now, but I also wasn't the one pushing a kid out of a very tiny place.

I just got to have fun practicing.

Tab bounced up and down in her seat as my parents' tidy-looking ranch appeared with its three-car garage and flowers stretching up the actual picket fence in front. I'd seen her bathroom dance often lately. "Oh," she whispered, halting mid-bounce. "It's so lovely."

I glanced at her and sunlight slanted over her strawberry hair and I had to take a breath. I did that often these days. I didn't know how I'd gotten so lucky.

Even if she stole all the covers. I mostly didn't mind since I ran hot. Not that she cared. She was also a bed hog.

And she was the most beautiful creature I'd seen since...well, ever.

"So are you," I said over the lump in my throat.

Tab shot me a look. "Don't start."

I had to laugh at her obvious consternation. "Don't start calling you beautiful?"

"Yes. Because if you make me emotional before I have to do the things I have to do today—" She wagged a finger at me. "I have to get through this day successfully. The bar is set high. I added Madagascar vanilla to my recipe." She jabbed her pink nail into the plastic cover on her baked goods. "I came to play ball."

"They're going to love you. There is no way they can't." After parking in the drive behind my mother's Jeep, I took off my belt and turned toward her. "You're basically any parent's wet dream."

"You're just glad you met me before Van."

I frowned. "As if any twin will do?"

She shrugged. "BJ height is an important qualification. How do you feel about Presley?"

"Huh?"

"For our daughter." She cupped her hand over her belly and I went to mush. Again. Still.. *Our daughter* was my favorite phrase since we'd officially found out the sex of the baby a few days ago.

Then the name she'd suggested sank in.

"Presley? For Elvis?" I rubbed a hand over my newly clean-shaven jaw. I always shaved for dinner at my parents, especially important ones. And this was the most important one ever.

"Yeah. For your dad. Since he loves him..." She trailed off uncertainly. "It's a really pretty name too. I asked Lu to do a reading and the Sun and the Star came up. The baby likes it."

I was not wading into the realm of deciding things via colorful cards before dinner with my parents. I'd wait to argue until the subject of UFOs came up, as was tradition in our home.

Besides, Presley was a great name.

"It sounds awesome with McNeill," I said before remembering we were hyphening. But Tabitha just grinned and nodded.

"It does, doesn't it? I've been doodling it for days. I figured you could pick her middle name."

"Ann?" Wasn't that popular with chicks?

She narrowed her eyes. "You've been voted off the island." She climbed out of the vehicle before I could get out to open her door.

Now what had I done? Ann was easy to spell. Wasn't that important?

I started to ask when I stepped up behind her at the front door then decided I'd just kiss the back of her neck. Much safer.

"'Let me guess. Your second choice is Lynn?"

"Oh, do you like that one better?"

She just huffed out a breath and rang the bell.

The door swung open and my sister appeared in the doorway wearing entirely too short shorts and some kind of cropped top. I was about to look over my shoulder to make sure no dudes were driving by when Tab squealed, "Oh, you look so cute!" and launched herself into my sister's arms.

"Oh, I was cleaning. I haven't changed for dinner yet. What's your problem?" Honey demanded over Tab's shoulder as they hugged/danced/acted as if they'd been separated for years instead of mere hours.

At times, females were inexplicable to me.

"He wants to give your girl the middle name of Ann." Tab couldn't have sounded any more disgusted if she'd tried.

"Her girl? Was she there at the conception and I missed it?"

"Oh, no. No no no. Ann? Really? That does not work with the first name." Honey flashed me a matching disgusted glare.

The two of them walked off down the hall arm in arm as if I wasn't even there.

I wondered if either of them in their ultimate wisdom remembered that my parents didn't know any baby existed never mind one with the awful middle name of Ann. They'd both forgotten their indoor voices in their shock and horror.

Luckily, my brother chose that moment to roar up on his motorcycle, which both drowned out their voices and lured my parents out from their respective corners—my dad from the kitchen where I could smell his famous sauce marinating and my mom from her study. She'd likely been spending a pleasant afternoon perusing the Uniform Crime Report, an activity no one found to be an agreeable pastime unless they were slightly bent.

As my mother was.

I'd detoured to the half bath—Tab wasn't the only one who'd been hitting the lemon water—and came out to find my mom standing in the hallway waiting for me.

"Why is your girlfriend buying baby booties at Every Line A Story?" she demanded before I'd so much as said hello.

"Have you been following her?"

She jerked a shoulder. "I have a network. Now spill."

"I'm spilling nothing. It's the Cove. People have babies." It was my turn to shrug. "You need a hobby."

"I have one. Is Honey seeing anyone? I can't get a bead on her activities."

"She took the GPS off her car. Yes, she found it. Seriously, your children are all grown. All reasonably intelligent adults who make good choices."

"Mav is back betting on horses."

"So? He hasn't lost his shirt. Or pants, thank God." I rotated my neck. Tension was already building. Shocker.

"We used to be close." She sighed and shoved her hands into the big sleeves of the bright purple blouse she wore. "I don't like the distance between us lately. I knew it would change when I retired, but I don't like not talking to you."

"So, you follow my girlfriend?"

She shrugged again. "I didn't follow anyone. Just put the word out to keep an eye open. She's really beautiful."

"I keep telling her. I don't think she'll ever believe it."

"You'd make the cutest babies."

"I know." At her sharp glance, I cleared my throat. "Don't put me on the spot."

"I knew it!" She dragged me into a rib-shattering hug. "You've made my whole year, B-Man. God knows your brother is incapable of parenthood. At least without a manual and six nannies."

"Excuse me? No more than four." Mav strolled up the hall and shuddered. "What am I saying? No number of nannies. Don't curse me, Ma."

"More like don't curse the rest of us."

"There's my guys. Finally. The meatballs are about to turn into leather." My dad's hearty laugh boomed out from the other end of the hall as he ambled toward us in his Don't Kiss The Cook apron. Underneath, he wore a tank top and overalls with high-top sneakers. He also had a trimmed gray beard as if he was hoping to join The Grateful Dead.

The contrast with Mav's pressed slacks, collared shirt, and slicked back hair was stunning. No wonder Van called him GQ.

And I wasn't going to think of her in case I'd accidentally invoke her presence at this pleasant family dinner.

Then Honey appeared, now changed into a much more family-appropriate top and jeans. "Um, Brady, can I see you for a second?"

I frowned and stepped away to join my sister at the end of the hall. "What's up?"

"You apparently didn't realize you'd lost your woman, but she's wrecking the master bathroom as we speak."

"Wrecking?"

She mimed throwing up and I turned to take the stairs two at a time. "She stopped doing that."

"Apparently, your badly named child wasn't done," she said in a stage whisper behind me.

"Oh, God, is she sick?" my mom asked from behind us, also now crowding up the stairs. "Let me help. I had three."

I stopped on the landing and turned to pin her in place with a glare. "She hasn't even met you yet. Would you like to meet your in-laws for the first time on your knees?"

"Happens more often than you'd think," Mav muttered from somewhere behind my mom and Honey.

Somehow no one questioned me saying in-laws. Not even me. It was a foregone conclusion in my head we were getting married. It was just a matter of time.

And logistics. And possibly bribery.

"He does have a point, Mom." Honey turned around and nudged

Mom back down the stairs. "Let the poor girl relax, and let's make her some tea."

"Oh, good idea, I have some nice ginger tea from when I had that flu last winter."

They disappeared into the kitchen with Mav trailing behind. Leaving my father staring up at me.

"Baby?"

At this point, what was the harm? I nodded. "But we wanted to tell you together."

He nodded and pretended to zip his lips before flashing me the thumbs up sign and heading back down the hall. I hurried up the stairs and took a right to head into the master bedroom with its attached en suite bathroom.

Tabitha was staring blearily into the mirror, her face blotchy and the ends of her hair damp.

"I washed my face," she explained. "I made it in time."

"C'mere." I drew her into my arms.

"I was hoping I was done with all that, but stress and excitement and well, your child decided to make an entrance."

My eyebrows lifted. "Thankfully, she didn't really make an entrance, Luna-style, because uh, super early." I reached down to pinch Tab's behind. "That's all on mama, by the way. I'm barely on time for most things."

She giggled softly and pressed her cool lips to my throat. "This is all going to hell, isn't it?"

"Think of how we started. Did you honestly expect some tidy event?"

"Good point. No one can say I'm not hopelessly optimistic." She looked up at me. "I had a plan how I was going to do this. It was not after tossing my cookies in your parents' bathroom."

"Are you okay? You're getting red."

"Panic flush." She waved it off. "I'll be fine. Mind if I skip getting on my knees right now though? I want to be semi-traditional, but they hurt from your daughter's displeasure."

I would've liked to say I didn't get hard at the mere suggestion she wanted to defile my parents' bathroom. I was no longer a teen. I'd had plenty of blowjobs. I didn't expect a woman who'd just been ill to do such a thing while my parents were just downstairs.

Then again, what eager male said no to an offer of that nature from a gorgeous woman?

Not I.

I cupped a hand in her hair. "Babe, you really don't have to do this."

"Yes, I do. Though..." She started giggling so hard she had to lean against the sink to steady herself. "Oh my God, you thought I—oh my God." She started to wheeze through her laughter. "I can't breathe."

"What's so damn funny?"

"What kind of girl do you think I am?" She stuck her tongue in her cheek. "Obviously, a filthy one."

"Kind of, yeah, part of why I love you." I cocked my head. *"Everyone* knows I love you. That billboard still may happen."

"The billboard announcing you knocked me up?"

"And the I love you like crazy billboard. Even if you got up my hopes for an ill-timed BJ. I'll recover. Probably."

"Shut up so I can ask you to marry me." She pressed something into my stomach.

I looked down at the black box clutched between her fingers. "Huh? That's my job."

"You know, I used to have the reputation of opening my mouth and inserting both feet and subsequently driving men away. But you lift your foot faster than I ever could."

"Is that supposed to be dirty? I'm getting dirty thoughts."

Shaking her head, she popped open the box. "Will you marry me, Brady McNeill? Say yes fast. Pregnant women are testy."

A wide gold band studded with small deep green stones winked up at me. "Holy shit, you're serious."

"Does anyone fake propose?"

"No, I suppose not. It's an awesome ring." I pried it out of the box and spun it around my thumb. "Not too frou frou for a dude."

"Gee, thanks. Yes or no?"

"You really want to spend your life with me?"

"Who else would I spend it with?"

She had a point. It had been obvious since day one we fit together in a way neither of us had with anyone else.

"But yes, I absolutely want to spend my life with you." Her voice softened. "I love you."

I waited for her to qualify it with a but. She didn't. Just looked up at me with damp blue eyes and her freckles winking at the corners of her smile.

I cupped her cheek and lowered my head to kiss her. "This is even better than a blowjob."

"Thanks. I think."

"Wait here," I said, pushing the ring down on my thumb more securely before running back downstairs.

"Brady, what the hell?" she called.

"Be right back!"

I thundered down the steps and joined my family in the kitchen. "Mom, I need grandma's ring."

She popped up from the table as if she'd been ready for this moment. Knowing her, she had somehow. "I know just where it is."

I followed her to her study, and she drew down the top on her big rolltop desk to fumble in one of the slots. She withdrew a small deep red box, lifted the top to check it, and then handed it over. "It's yours."

I took a deep breath and gripped her hand around the box for an extra few seconds. "Thanks. She's the one for me."

"Handy, since you're starting a family with her."

"I guess it is." I grinned and shoved the box in my pocket before holding up my thumb. "She got me one too."

"Why the hell's it on your thumb? Didn't we teach you anything?"

"Oh, yeah, I just kind of grabbed it."

"Let her put it on you right."

"I will." I gave her a quick hug. "We always find our way. Even if we stumble around in the dark a bit first." Literally, thinking back to our first night together.

"Go on, get back to her. Did you at least say yes before you disappeared?"

"Uh…"

She gave me a light shove, laughing openly. I was destined for the women in my life to find enjoyment at my expense. I supposed I deserved it.

I rushed back upstairs and met Tabitha in the hall. She lifted her brows and crossed her arms. "If you don't want to get married, just say so."

"Nope, no can do. I so want to get married." I grinned and dropped down on one knee. "Will you marry me, Tabitha Eliza Monaghan McNeill-to-be?"

She sniffled. "Cocky, aren't you? As if you know there's no way I can say no?"

"Well, you already proposed, so I kind of know your intentions there. And look at this beauty." I pulled out the ring box and flipped it open. The vintage-style ring with its square ruby offset by channel-set diamonds glittered from the bed of deep blue. "It was my grandmother's." I fought to speak over the rock in my throat. "The fire of it reminds me of you. I hope the baby has your hair. Your eyes. Your everything."

"Sweet talker. One reason among many why I'm not letting you go." She let out a shaky laugh. "Yes, I'll marry you. Even if you didn't answer me and don't even know what finger to put the damn ring on."

"I know where it goes. You just have to put it there." Affronted, I shook my head. "Some things are tradition."

She held out her hand and I slipped the ring on, shoving a bit harder than I intended to get it to slide down. "I should've gotten it sized."

She only laughed harder. "I know a jeweler. Until then, I'll wear it around my throat. Assuming I can get it off."

"Oops?"

With a grin, she slid the ring she'd given me off my thumb and put it on the right finger. "One out of two ain't bad."

"We'll get it sized tomorrow." Since I was still on my knee, I wrapped my arms around her waist and kissed her belly. "You hear that, little girl? Your mama is going to marry me. I didn't even have to tie her up to get her to say yes. Although that has some interesting—"

"*Shh.*" Laughing, she ruffled my hair before taking a deep breath. "Now I get to meet your parents with a belly full of baby and your ring on my finger. No pressure!"

"Nope." I kissed her stomach again. "None at all. I love you, and they're going to adore you. I totally married up." I rose and looped my arm around her shoulders. "So, hey, about that staying in our apartments thing. You were just messing with me, right? We aren't going to be married and live across from the hall from each other."

"Probably not." She leaned up on her tiptoes and kissed my jaw. "I do love to mess with you though."

"I've noticed." I pulled her in front of me and kissed the back of her neck, inhaling her bakery-fresh scent as if it was oxygen. Then I patted her behind to urge her down the stairs.

My parents and my siblings were waiting for us at the bottom.

"We're engaged," I announced when Tab stopped still and I was pretty sure ceased to breathe. I grabbed her hand and lifted it high like a prizefighter who'd just won the biggest bout of his life.

I absolutely had. My trophy was my fiancée and our baby and a life of chaos and love.

Maybe Valentine's Day wasn't such a racket after all. It had led to *this.*

"And having a baby." Tabitha cleared her throat. "Sorry I didn't meet you sooner, Mr. and Mrs. McNeill. Brady wanted to, I was just—"

"Scared off by blacklight Elvis," Honey put in, climbing the bottom few steps to give Tab a giant hug. "Now I get a sister for real."

Tab grinned and hugged her back without a single tear in sight. Thank God. Her tears always wreaked havoc with me, even happy ones.

My sister turned to me for a hug as Mav climbed the steps to haul Tab in close.

"There are way too many people on this staircase," Honey

complained, backing up so that my mom could take her place as Mav beat a quick sideways retreat down the stairs.

"So, when's it going to be your turn, son?" my dad asked Mav, who was in the process of trying to slink down the hall, undetected.

"Sorry to disappoint you, Dad. Some of us do better single file."

"And some of us don't." I gripped Tab's hand and squeezed tight.

"What woman would put up with him?" Honey jerked a thumb over her shoulder at Mav.

"A very special one."

"You can say that again," Honey muttered.

Ignoring them, my mom pulled Tab in for a gentle hug, saying in a stage whisper, "You have fulfilled my fondest wish."

"A grandchild?"

"Second fondest wish," my mom amended. "I now will have a real honest to goodness pastry chef in the family and won't have to eat any more of your father's Christmas cookies."

"Oh, hey, now I'm getting better. Ever since I took that online cooking class, my skills have grown." My father decided to try to wedge himself up the staircase too, grunting and groaning to switch places with my mother so he could also hug Tab. "Welcome to the family, Tabitha. I peeked at your dessert, and those croquembouche look to die for. Do you take requests?"

"I sure do."

"After she takes a nap." I put my hand at the small of her back. "She always takes a nap at 4:15."

Especially now that she was actually taking days off from work now and then. Sometimes even two days a week. She'd even mentioned maybe closing the bakery on Sundays for the summer.

We'd see about that one, but she was definitely making progress on that whole work-life balance thing. And so was I.

"I usually manage to stay awake when I'm at someone's house, but you know, he's a master hoverer." Tab rolled her eyes, her hand drifting to her belly out of habit.

"We're naming the baby Presley."

My dad's smile turned misty. "Son, you do me proud."

"It was Tab's idea." I stroked a hand down her hair. "Right, Strawberry?"

"Presley Ann," she confirmed, her lips twitching.

"Oh, I love that name," my father said with a great big belly laugh.

Tab's eyes widened as I cough-laughed into my hand.

"Now it's official."

"You're lucky I love you."

I grinned and tugged her into my side, taking advantage of the staircase's tight quarters. "You bet your fine behind I am."

We appreciate our readers so much!
If you loved the book please let your friends know. If you're extra awesome, we'd love a review on your favorite book site.

WANT TO KEEP UP TO DATE WITH US?

Please visit our website, tarynquinn.com, for details!

Next up is Maverick & Vanessa's story!
Maverick doesn't only carry a gun and handcuffs, he also knows his way around a blowtorch. But Vanessa isn't about to get naked with her brand new brother-in-law...until she accidentally loses her panties—and her heart—at Lookout Point.

Now...turn the page for a special sneak peek of COP DADDY NEXT DOOR now!

 *Maverick*

COP DADDY NEXT DOOR

LATE SUMMER MORNINGS WERE MEANT FOR LAZY, LEISURELY DOG WALKS. At least until my dog dropped the biggest specimen I'd seen since I'd changed her dog food.

She was tiny. What she'd left behind decidedly was not.

"Okay, kid, we're going back to the old food once we use up the last of the new. Got it?" I bent to pick up what she'd left behind, though she'd dropped it on the edge of my own lawn. But it was odiferous enough that there was no way I was leaving it behind.

Francie ignored me and kept sniffing her way down the street, as far as her retractable leash would take her. Which wasn't far. She was too small to be given any sort of free rein since most normal-sized dogs could trample her.

With a sigh, I tied off the poop sack and tossed it in the handy receptacle provided nearby by the town then narrowed my eyes at the adjoining property. It had been for sale for six months.

Long enough that I'd gone back and forth about buying it about a dozen times.

Could I afford another prime property? No, I could not. Buying the first one had stretched me almost to the breaking point. I was a humble public servant, the newest cop on the Crescent Cove Police Department.

Homes here were, by and large, out of reach for people at my pay scale. Luckily, I'd always been a saver—okay, just for the last four years when I'd decided I couldn't toss away money on an apartment forever. There was no way in Hades I'd ever move home again, even if my little sister begged me to get the "heat" off her.

I didn't mind having a simple lifestyle so I could live in the location I loved. Plus, I was duty bound to reside in town, so I made do. But making do was a far cry from snapping up a second property so that I had enough lawn to warrant that fancy ass riding lawn mower that twenty-year-old Mav would've scoffed at.

Hey, a man's tastes changed as he got a little older. Some, anyway.

When it came to one particular taste...

I licked my lips, taking in the view. A curvy redhead sauntered down the narrow dock attached to my modest boat launch, conveniently located just across the street from my property. The grassy knoll in front of it was perfect for a summer picnic by the water, if I was a picnicking sort of guy.

I was not.

But that sexy redhead in a thin white eyelet blouse—having a sister obsessed with clothes had filled my head with nonsense—and obscenely short jean shorts made me reconsider.

She was wandering barefoot on my property, but I wasn't about to arrest her for trespassing. Not with those curls drifting on the wind and that cute heart-shaped backside swaying provocatively. She plopped down on the edge to dip her feet, which was basically a joke because she was short as hell and probably couldn't *reach* the water.

Compact. Built for—

Oh *hell* no.

"What are you doing here?" I demanded, pulling on Francie's leash a bit too hard. She yelped and I cursed under my breath. "Sorry, baby, Daddy didn't mean to—"

I shut my eyes and prayed the trespasser would be gone when I opened them, heart-shaped ass be damned.

"Daddy?" She let out a loud laugh that proved my eyes had not deceived me. I should've recognized the sex hair. It wasn't as if I hadn't noticed it before.

How a woman could have sex hair and the spirit of a demon seemed to be one of life's cruelest mysteries.

I pulled myself up to my full height—a full foot over hers, I might add—and exhaled slowly as I tugged on Francie's leash. She trotted closer without complaint, the tiny pink bow in her brown fur tilting precariously.

Oh, shit, the bow. I had to ditch it. It wasn't as if I was a bow man. She'd been wearing one when I found her, so I'd wanted her to have something familiar even if her old owners were assholes who'd left her behind when they moved away.

I'd have to slip Francie's bow in my pocket before Vanessa saw it and crowed about my dog's stylistic choices at every family dinner until the end of time.

"May I help you?" Discreetly, I nudged my Yorkie behind my leg. I'd have to swing her up and pluck off the bow in one smooth, synchronized movement.

My palms sweating from the unnaturally hot September day should help. *Not.* And no, I was not sweating because my sister-in-law's nipples were outlined in frigging white eyelet.

Fuck me.

She cocked her head. "Did I call for you without realizing it? GQ, can you help me dip my toes?"

I ignored her, as I'd done for most of the last seven months my older brother had been dating—and now engaged to—her twin sister. Sometimes I poked fun at her. Sometimes I rolled my eyes at her.

But ignoring her was usually best for my sanity.

It wasn't fair that she was just as annoying as she was hot. Though no one said I had to talk to her to have sex with her…

Nope. That was officially off-limits. Family boundaries and all. But fantasies didn't hurt anyone. It was better than getting irritated at her, considering that was exactly the response she wanted.

Even her calling me GQ was designed to piss me off. Sure, I tended to dress up rather than down most of the time I was off-duty. But I enjoyed getting my hands dirty. I was a cop, for Pete's sake. I had a dog—something I had not planned. And I worked with wood and ice and fire and enjoyed it immensely. I wasn't some model type who strutted around sucking in my abs.

But silence was golden when dealing with Vanessa Monaghan's smart mouth.

"Not sure if you're aware, but this is my dock."

She managed to splash her feet. "Oh, yeah?"

"Yeah. So, if you need something, let me know."

She shifted to sit cross-legged facing me, her hair blowing around her shoulders from the breeze. "I was told this dock was a shared access space."

"Shared between residents," I said carefully.

She'd found a new focus, however.

"Aw, well, look at you, sweetheart. Come here." She held out a hand and my disobedient dog ignored my requests to stay put and trotted right over to her, rubbing her face into her palm with adoration. "I heard you had a dog." Her lips twitched. "Didn't know it was a cockapoo."

"Francie's a Yorkie." I angled my chin. "Who told you I had a dog?"

"Little birdie."

"Named Tabitha?"

Shrugging, Vanessa let out a delighted laugh as Francie tugged me forward and scampered into her lap. She circled a couple times to get the right spot then plopped down and laid her head on Vanessa's bare thigh just beneath the frayed hem of her jean shorts. "She's so sweet. Sure she's your dog?"

"Last I checked. You don't have any pets."

"No."

"Why not?"

"I'm not big on putting down roots. Hard to fly if you're always tethered to the ground."

With a frown, I gave up trying to urge my dog to return to me. She obviously had found a place to rest she liked better.

I also would not mind being stationed in Vanessa's lap. My mouth, at least, if not the rest of me.

"Yeah, well, you seem pretty stationary to me."

"I am now. But you never know when the open road will call." She gestured wildly. "Sometimes you just gotta split to check out some new surroundings. See new people, think new thoughts." She grinned. "Lay your head in new beds."

I clenched my jaw. "Didn't you promise your sister to be her birthing coach?"

"That's not for six weeks and you know your brother won't settle for being the backup."

I snorted. "Don't be so sure. He fainted when Tabitha cut herself in the kitchen."

"And he's a cop?"

"We all have flaws, Pocket Plus." I tugged on the leash and Francie finally dragged herself away from her new love with a look of longing that did not fit an acquaintance of less than five minutes.

Though with all the family shit going down over the next few months—the Jack and Jill wedding shower so "the guys got to be included", the impending birth of my first niece, the wedding shindig between our siblings, then assorted joint family dinners and holidays —Francie would have plenty of time to get to know my new sister-in-law.

As would I.

I was tempted to make the sign of the cross, and I was not even slightly religious.

"Your brother's a good guy," she mused, brushing dog hair off her shorts.

"Must you sound so shocked?"

"I must. Your kind doesn't have the best track record with unplanned pregnancies, gotta say. Usually, there's some variation of "it ain't mine," or "how could it happen, I wore a rubber," or even "I'm not ready," as if women are born ready." She kept on brushing off her lap as if golden-brown hair clung to every inch of her.

I frowned as the silence extended. She cleared her throat and looked up with a weighty enough glance to throttle me. "Anyway, I was there. Brady didn't do that. He stood up from the first. And kept right on standing up."

My voice deserted me. I wasn't even sure why. Just words unspoken passed between us in that moment while the birds chirped merrily in the trees and the hot sun scorched the back of my neck, freshly exposed after my haircut that morning.

And none of that mattered at all, except in this moment, everything seemed to. I couldn't quite catch my breath.

"My brother's one of the good ones," I said when my lungs finally figured out how to work again.

"What about you?" Slowly, she rose, still brushing off her shorts although there was no way Francie could've lost that much hair from her tiny body.

"What about me what?"

"Are you good?"

Now my breath caught for an altogether different reason. I hadn't imagined that flirty pause before she finished her question. But I was used to paying attention to tone and body language when questioning a suspect or trying to determine guilt. She didn't want me to get too close or to pick up more clues than she was willing to give.

"What I am is smart."

A cocked brow was her only response.

"Why are you on my dock?" I asked as Francie parked her furry behind on my shoe.

"You're like a dog with a bone." I didn't miss how her gaze dropped below my waist and lingered for a second before she grinned. "But I like a man who's persistent. Remember what I said about joint access?"

"Huh?"

"Says he's smart, though he can't recall basic details. *Tsk, tsk.* Good thing you're cute, GQ." She flicked her fingers through the ends of her hair and did a little pirouette complete with heel kick. "Haven't you wondered who would move in next door?"

My stomach twisted itself around the bacon and egg sandwich I'd had for a late lunch at The Rusty Spoon. After taking my mom to the dentist, I'd stopped off on Main Street for lunch that didn't come out of a box or a can.

The life of a single dude wasn't always roses, but the joy of limited female chatter could not be overstated. Even now, I was starting to get the itch from too much talking.

I had to admit she was easy on the eyes. Easy on the tightness in my groin too, which served her right if she'd seen anything she shouldn't have—since she'd so obviously checked me out.

But hotness was one thing. *Next door* was quite another.

"I've actually thought of buying the land myself," I said quickly, hoping the possibility Van had sneaked into the neighborhood wasn't a done deal.

I could call my real estate agent and tell her I wanted the property, draw up the papers, and see if I could secure a mortgage. Vanessa only worked at her sister's bakery on a sporadic basis. Some days she worked twelve hours, some days three. It wasn't as if her funding situation could be better than mine.

It couldn't be too late.

"Too late," she said cheerfully, patting my chest as she walked past me into the street without checking for passing cars.

I had a feeling that was how Vanessa Monaghan lived her entire life.

"See that cute little vehicle over there?" She pointed across the street. An ancient hunk of metal was parked on the rundown path that bisected the property. Normally, the only thing on that path were weeds working their way up through the cracks in the narrow strip of blacktop.

Now a rusty mint-green school bus sat in the space with a makeshift awning open on the side. A single green-striped lawn chair circa 1981 was stationed beneath it next to a cooler of the same decade. I was pretty sure I had a stack of drawings in my mom's memories trunk with the same Igloo pattern embossed on it.

Francie tugged on the leash, dragging me out of my shocked stupor. When people pointed, she thought that meant fetch. And while I wished my dog could cart that eyesore off the property, that would be an impossible feat.

"I can pay you instead," I said in a fervent undertone, ready to offer her just about anything so I didn't have to look out my window and see that thing every day.

I didn't appreciate being called GQ, fine, but I did have *some* standards for how things looked. Especially since I'd busted my hump to even get in this neighborhood in the first place.

Not to mention our neighbors would not look kindly upon her if she didn't get that out of here. Property values would plummet. She would likely be driven out of the neighborhood, something I couldn't let happen because we soon would be family by marriage.

As an officer of the law, I was duty-bound to handle this problem before it became one.

Bad enough I had to listen to Christian, my fellow cop, rant and rave about her inappropriate parking fetish. Never mind her inability to parallel park that behemoth and the van she'd driven before it without leaving two wheels on the curb.

This was just taking it to the next level.

"Pay me?" She bent to stroke Francie's wiggling ears before straightening and crossing her arms. "Whatever for?"

"I really want that land. And the property doesn't even have a house yet. So, you'd have to build, and clearly, you prefer to keep rolling on. So, you know, don't quell your impulses."

"Oh, honey, I never quell. I'm basically *unquell*-able."

Her lips were twitching with barely suppressed laughter. At me, I was quite certain.

"Tell me what you want. No limitations. I'll buy you out. I'll offer you anything you want. I should've bought the damn land. Just dragged my feet too long. I'm staying put. Probably fucking forever." I tugged Francie toward me again as she went up on her hind legs to dance in front of Vanessa.

True love must never part, I supposed.

My new neighbor put her hands on her hips, her lower lip jutting out in the faintest pout. I went stone hard in an instant.

Yet another reason she could not live mere inches from my bed. That was a recipe for disaster. For all I knew, she'd wander over barefoot and braless to borrow sugar and the use of my dick when she ran out of batteries for her vibrator.

I was weak. I'd say yes. And I'd probably live to regret it for years, if not generations. She was the sort of woman who would carve her name into my leather seats ala Carrie Underwood if she thought I'd messed up.

I had an impressionable dog to think about. I couldn't screw Van indiscriminately without considering the implications. My brother had parented a dog with Tabitha before they were committed to each other and look what happened.

Now they were having an actual human child.

And oh, yeah, there was also my brother's impending marriage to consider. Vanessa and I hating each other would not be good for family get-togethers, and there wasn't a chance in hell we could stay on polite terms if we rolled into bed.

Or onto the kitchen counter. I wasn't choosy and I was willing to bet neither was she.

Then again, maybe I shouldn't send her packing—

No. Doing this now, whatever her terms, was protecting my family from the kind of drama probably worthy of a future episode of *Jerry Springer.*

Brady could thank me later.

"Let me get this straight," she said slowly. "You're trying to buy me out so you don't have to live next door to me?"

I nodded. "Yes. If you think about it, you'll realize it wouldn't be a good idea."

"Why not?"

Because my salacious thoughts toward you would get me arrested in about twelve states if I actually acted on them. And I'm an honorable man.

At least I was pretty sure.

I was sweating heavily and not just because the sun was beaming straight into my brain. "Trust me, it's not wise."

"Why?"

"It's just not. Francie, stop wiggling and plant your behind this instant."

A sudden wetness soaked my sock.

I looked down, unable to believe what I was seeing.

My dog was peeing on my shoes. Not only that, she'd lifted her leg and aimed like a male dog, because she'd hung out with a bad crowd at doggie daycare last week and apparently wanted to thumb her nose at my rules.

Or her leg.

Vanessa swallowed a laugh as I stood there motionlessly in my dripping shoes. "Why?" she repeated. "Why is my living next door such a bad thing?"

"Do you really need me to spell it out?"

"Yes, I do. We haven't exactly been besties thus far, but I didn't think you'd want to take out a restraining order against me. Now your fellow cop with the stick up his ass is a different story. I'm toxic waste, according to that prick Masterson. But he probably hasn't gotten any since college—"

I stepped very close to her and used my height to loom over her so she had to crane her neck to meet my gaze. Finally, she closed her mouth.

Momentarily.

"I want to do the kind of things to you that don't fit a nice family dinner, Pocket Plus."

"Murder?"

I almost laughed. Almost. But my pants were too tight and my head hurt and she'd caused both. As usual.

I shook my head.

"Sexually?" She gasped it loudly enough both of my heads pulsed. "Why, you dirty bastard." Then she grinned. "I'm available anytime after seven."

"No." I pointed at her, and Francie jerked to high alert, ready to scrabble off after her nonexistent stick. "Not you, dog. And no, forget it. Not happening. You are not going to wander over without a bra and lure me into bed."

She peeked into her shirt. "I have a bra on. But that's easily rectified." She started to wrestle with her clothes, probably so that she could do that remove her bra under her shirt trick that all women seemed to know.

"I will arrest you for public nudity if you don't stop right now." I didn't point this time.

Her bluer than blue eyes fired with interest. "Cuffs are interesting."

"You are an actual menace."

"Valid." She tucked her tongue into her cheek. "Can you even walk right now?"

"I hate you."

"So...no."

She was studying me below the waist again. My dick didn't seem to mind, if the whole stretching and preening thing he was currently doing was any indication.

Usually, I didn't personify my cock as separate from me. But at this moment, I no longer felt in control of it—or this situation.

Definitely not this woman.

"Okay, I'm intrigued. What are you prepared to offer me beyond the price I paid for this property?" She licked her lips and held up a hand. "Not more money. I have enough of that."

"How? You work in a bakery."

"Never mind that. What else is on the table?" She tucked her thumbs in the belt loops of her shorts. "How about a free lifetime park anywhere I want pass?"

"I can't break the law for personal gain."

"Dammit. Then what else do you have?"

"I can make you an ice statue of your choosing. In the winter," I added, in case she failed to grasp that was a cold weather activity.

Or I could make her something out of wood, but I'd save that for a Hail Mary option. Wood was insanely expensive right now.

"Nah, you make them gratis for my sister. I can just steal one of hers." She smiled. "Keep going."

"I can convince Christian to toss one of your outstanding tickets.

One," I enunciated carefully, despite the fact I had no idea how I would pull that off.

Christian wouldn't let his own mother out of an overdue parking ticket, forget a woman with a stack a mile long.

"Try twenty and you're getting warmer."

"You have twenty outstanding tickets?"

"Actually, I think I'm forgetting some." Her tone was far too perky. "One of these days, I'll probably get arrested. Never been arrested. Yet."

She made it sound like a bucket list item she wanted to check off.

I rubbed my forehead. She was obviously crazy, which everyone knew meant she'd be off-the-charts hot in bed.

Hmm, maybe I was thinking about this all wrong. Maybe hair of the dog that bit me would be the quickest way to get through this sticky situation.

Buddy, you're in big trouble.

But there was one thing I knew I had in spades. An ability that had served me well since high school. I might get harder than a steel pike in seconds flat with the proper inspiration, but I knew she wouldn't take me down before I sank her battleship first.

"I'll make you a deal."

One slim red eyebrow arched as she waited.

"If I can make you come before I do, you'll sell the land to me."

She stared at me for so long I was sure she'd never go for it. Then she started to laugh, long and low. "You're afraid to have sex with me, so your idea to solve this situation is to…have sex with me?"

"I did not say sex. Coming does not require penetration."

"Thank you for the sex ed class." She shook her head. "You like pushing your luck, hmm? I called it earlier. Cute but not bright. Though you are male, so one can only ask for so much."

I gritted my teeth. "There are plenty of other equally desirable properties available in town or nearby. You'll walk away ahead any way you cut it."

"I'll walk away with the money I paid and one measly orgasm? Pal, I had two before breakfast." She propped her hands on her hips. "Do better or I'm headed back to my bus. Hey, do you keep your bedroom blinds open, by any chance?"

I sucked in a deep breath. "Two waived parking tickets, a pass for free parking on Sundays, the full price of the land plus five percent and one not at all measly orgasm for you to move far away. And take that traveling tin can with you."

She tapped a blood-red nail on her crossed arm. "Sundays already have free parking. Try again."

"If I get fired, I can't pay my mortgage."

"Okay, forget the parking pass. Two waived parking tickets and best two of three on the orgasms. Whoever gets to two first."

"Honey, I'm not even going to get to one, so you have yourself a deal." I flashed a cocky grin that stayed firmly in place until she extended her hand to shake.

I was supposed to touch her now? I hadn't fully considered that.

Fuck.

Stiffening my spine, I reached toward her and grabbed her hand for a quick shake. Then I wrapped my dog's leash around my hand and crossed the street.

That I managed not to speed-walk was a minor victory.

"When is this happening, GQ?" Her voice was thick with laughter.

I'd worry about that after I took an ice cold shower. "I'll be in touch."

Now Available

For more information go to www.tarynquinn.com

Have My Baby

Claim My Baby

Who's The Daddy

Pit Stop: Baby

Baby Daddy Wanted

Rockstar Baby

Daddy in Disguise

My Ex's Baby

Daddy Undercover

Wrong Bed Baby

Lucky Baby

Daddy on Duty

Cop Daddy Next Door

Protector Daddy

CRESCENT COVE STANDALONES & SHORTS

CEO Daddy

Fireman Daddy

Mistletoe Baby

For more information about our books visit

www.tarynquinn.com

MORE BY TARYN QUINN

OTHER SERIES

Happy Acres

Kensington Square

Afternoon Delight

Deuces Wild

Wilder Rock

Walk on the wilder side with these stories

After Dark

HOLIDAY BOOKS

Unwrapped

Holiday Sparks

Filthy Scrooge

Bad Kitty

Saving Kylie

For more information about our books visit

www.tarynquinn.com

ABOUT TARYN QUINN

USA Today bestselling author, *TARYN QUINN,* is the sexy and funny alter ego of bestselling authors Taryn Elliott & Cari Quinn. We've been writing together for years, but we have decided to pull the trigger on a combo name just for fun.

And so…Taryn Quinn was born!

Do you like ultra sexy small town romance full of shenanigans? Quirky office romances full of steam? Okay, look…we pretty much just love writing steamy stories. If you're all about that, we're your girls!

For more information about us...
tarynquinn.com
tq@tarynquinn.com

QUINN AND ELLIOTT

We also write more serious, longer, and sexier books as Cari Quinn & Taryn Elliott. Our topics include mostly rockstars, but mobsters, MMA, and a little suspense gets tossed in there too.

Rockers' Series Reading Order

Lost in Oblivion

Winchester Falls

Found in Oblivion

Hammered

Rock Revenge

Brooklyn Dawn

OTHER SERIES

Tapped Out

Love Required

Boys of Fall

If you'd like more information about us please visit

www.quinnandelliott.com